Agmunder's Ness.

By Barry Cooper

ISBN: 9781730750410

Third Edition
2019

Best wishes
Xmas 19
BC

Cover: Valgard returns to warn Agmunder: Chapter 2

Dedication

This book is dedicated to my grandfather

John (Jack) Pasquill.

He would have loved this story and it
was a pleasure fitting in all the things
he loved to tell me about the Fylde
its people and its history.

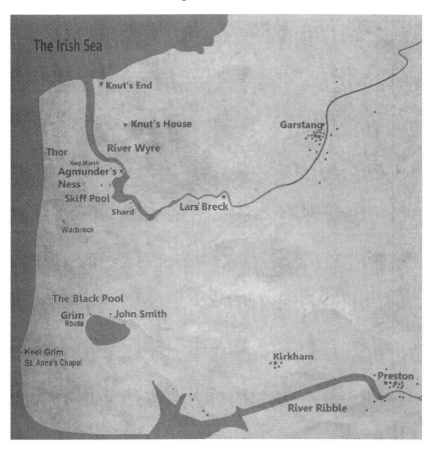

Map of the Fylde 783 A.D.

CHAPTER 1

April 781 A.D.

The day dawned, as many do on the Irish Sea, dull, wet and cold. Windblown spray collected in little pools on the canvas that provided some shelter at the front of the vessel and from time to time, encouraged by the motion of the ship and the wind, they overflowed in rivulets that ran down into the longship's decked area in the bows. The wind was strong, whipping up waves that relentlessly broke over the side of the shield wall along the gunwales. Oars missed their grip in the troughs and became impossible to move in the depth of the wave crests, as the ship approached the grey strip of flat land still three miles ahead. The sail had been dropped long before dawn as the gale increased and the men roused from their storm-broken sleep and put to the oars. Those being thrust out through simple holes below the round shields. Fifteen Norsemen on each side worked the oars against the will of the elements of air and water to bring the ship safe to its harbour. Captain Valgard, a raider of old, knew they would be safe in the lee of the headland shortly and stood steadfast in the stern watching his course and his men critically, with equal interest. From his position on the right-hand side of the longship, by the steerboard, Valgard spotted motion beneath the canvas at the front of the ship. A booted foot, and then another, came out from under the sheeting and then, suddenly, the canvas was thrown upwards and over the head of their former master and current passenger, Agmunder. The Viking stood looking at the day and the sea with disapproval.

'Good morning, Agmunder!' Valgard yelled through the constant mist of spray.

'Good? What's good about it?'

'Turn around, Sire.'

Agmunder took a firm grip of the fore-stay to steady himself and turned around. The grey strip of land was now only a mile away and looked bleak and desolate in the grey light of morning.

Valgard shouted above the wind, 'We're here!'

The spirits of the Norsemen at the oars were lifted by this news almost as much as those of Agmunder. He had waited many years for this moment.

He stood, gazing in wonder for just a few seconds, before he stooped to grab the edge of the cover that flapped in a most uncooperative manner around his wool-clad ankles. He lifted the canvas and shouted above the noise of wind and sea.

'Come out here, boy. You have to see this.'

The boy, just turned seven winters old, crawled timidly out into the blustering wind that swept the foredeck, shielding his face with his forearm. His father held his other arm, to steady him, as the deck heaved in the rough sea.

'Our new home, lad. Our new life,' said Agmunder, bending close to the boy's ear and pointing with his free hand briefly, before even he had to grab the fore-stay once again, for balance.

They watched the land approaching together. The longship finally rounded the headland, turning due south into the estuary. The wind seemed to drop with each pull of the oars and within but a few minutes they were in much calmer water, heading upstream. Agmunder estimated they might be at the natural harbour on the west bank in less than an hour. The river narrowed for the first two miles, then, just as it looked like it was getting too narrow for safe manoeuvring of the longship, a mere twenty yards wide with the oars occasionally snagging reed beds in the shallows, the river suddenly turned hard right and opened out into a wide and calm body of water. 'The Pool', as Agmunder knew it, had safe landing and good farming land immediately behind, on the ness, a headland between the river and the coast. This was the spot to which he'd vowed to return. This was where he had promised himself he would make his dwelling and his livelihood since before his son was born. Erik's name, meaning 'Ever-Ruler', was given to confirm his birthright as future Lord, only Agmunder knowing that it referred to this, new land.

This was a quiet part of the world. There were fewer than a hundred inhabitants on the whole peninsula and no-one making a home on the ness itself at all. Virtually empty land as far as Priest's Town, or 'Preston' as it was becoming more commonly called, and Kirkham in the south, holding out to remain Saxon ruled, and Garstang, several miles to the east, a small town on the frontier of the Danelaw, a Norse administrated belt of country that stretched from Lindisfarn in the north to the Wash and roughly triangular to Garstang, almost on the west coast. Agmunder had anticipated returning to this peaceful and empty area, to settle down and farm, for nearly ten years. It was ideal for farming, and for a man, one with a reputation, to get lost in and start again. Throughout the day the Viking war-band carried Agmunder's belongings in boxes, bags, barrels, rolls and bundles from the longship, up the slight incline, to the top of the low rise that overlooked both the Pool and the land to the south. This was where Agmunder had planned to make his 'stanah', His stand.

When all his belongings were safely ashore, and as darkness fell on the scene that first night, Agmunder hosted a revelry for the ship's crew and their captain, in a Viking camp. Although the war-band were set to leave on another raid to the island of fire, far to the north, at daybreak, they were determined to have a resounding farewell to their Lord and master.

Agmunder looked around the camp by the light of the cooking fires. His belongings were now piled in a huge heap that could be glimpsed by the firelight when the wind stoked the flames to white brightness. The ship's crew were busy in their cups, singing warrior songs under the slightly clearing clouds. In just a few hours, just he, his son Erik, and his woman, Svala, taken on a raid nearly eight years earlier against a disrespectful Lord of Norway, would remain, as the Vikings began pulling north on their journey, wishing they hadn't had quite so much wine. Agmunder and his little family would be the only people within a long day's walk and the work of building a temporary dwelling and supporting and protecting them would be his sole responsibility.

He wondered, fleetingly, if he was doing the right thing for his family. He knew for certain that he was doing the right thing for himself. The patchy cloud thinned a little more, as Muni, the moon, pale sister of Sunne, but recently set, rose over the fells to the east. The thirty year old, Agmunder sat with the others, near the fire, and drank to the future and into the night.

The next morning dawned brighter than the previous day, but still overcast. The wind had abated somewhat during the early hours. The cloud cover had returned, no sign of the clear patches that allowed the moon and the stars to ornament their night-time feast. Nevertheless, the war-band were optimistic about putting to sea again and sang cheerfully as they prepared to leave. The anchor-stone that held the longship to the shore was lifted into the bow and the three invaders watched as the oars propelled the vessel back towards the narrow river opening that led to the sea. Within the short time it took for the three to walk from the water's edge, back up the slight slope, to where their worldly possessions were stacked, the longship's mast was all they could see as it made its way down river. Agmunder turned to his family, standing close, watching the mast top become indistinguishable from the brambles and hawthorn bushes that lined the river to the horizon. He spread his arms wide to indicate the vastness of their possession.

'Our new home,' he said simply, and walked toward the pile of goods to begin working on their temporary shelter.

To the side of the pile were a number of long, thick beams, heavy but not taxing for a strong man to position correctly. Agmunder worked all morning to set up their first shelter, while Erik and his mother went foraging for something to eat to supplement their rations. By the time Svala and Erik returned, a little before noon, with some late nuts and a fish, a grayling, from the river, Agmunder had the frame of a dwelling erected. Two beams, twice as tall as he was, that could just be held within two hands around, were stationed at each end, meeting at the top to form a triangle, which would form the front and back of the house. He had attached three, similar thickness, but longer, beams, linking the two triangles at their apices, and along the ground between the bases, to form the sides and roof spar of the house. A prism shaped dwelling, that, for now, would be covered with canvas and provide sufficient shelter from the unpredictable spring weather.

Svala prepared their food as Erik helped his father as well as he could, to bring their bedding into the house.

They sat, to eat, on a pile of other wood that would be joined to the frame to create a lattice support for the canvas that would form the roof and walls. The meal was good, Agmunder was generous enough to admit. Grayling was a tasty fish, when fried in goose-fat.

After the meal Svala took Erik to sort through their belongings to locate the rest of her cooking effects, while Agmunder laid out the canvases and rope ties to attach them to the frames that had been laid out on top. When the canvas covered latices were ready, he shouted to Erik, for help. Erik came running, eager to help his father build their new home.

'Steady that joint, boy,' said Agmunder, pointing to the corner of a frame.

Erik, knew what to do, they had practised, a few times, in the old country before setting off. He put his foot on the corner so that when his father lifted the other end it wouldn't slip from its position. Agmunder worked his way towards Erik, walking his hands along the edge of the frame as it raised to the vertical. Agmunder held it upright as he worked his way to the other corner, at the opposite end to Erik.

'Ready?' he asked.

Erik nodded, knowing that it wouldn't be clever *not* to be ready, when his father asked.

Agmunder pushed the frame and it slowly fell onto its position on the house side, with a '*clump*' of wood on wood. Erik watched his father climb the simple ladder to secure the first side to the top of the beam triangle.

The process was repeated on the other side, with similar success. Agmunder was pleased and the house had walls.

As Agmunder climbed down from the ladder, having secured all the canvas covered frames to the beams, he shouted, 'Bring that canvas roll, now, boy.'

Erik ran over to where the roll lay in the grass. He struggled to lift it, but managed to get it in place, at the end of the house, before his father got down from the ladder.

'Well done, Erik,' said Agmunder, in a rare show of appreciation.

Soon, with Erik's willing help, the two had the house wind and watertight.

'Come,' commanded Agmunder to both his son and wife.

They both followed him to a position, about a hundred paces from the shelter. They turned round to see their first house in its setting, atop the small rise, commanding a view of the land the family intended to farm.

'Remember this moment,' said the ex-Viking warrior, 'In times to come, this will look like an animal's enclosure. From this lowly beginning, I will build us an empire.'

CHAPTER 2

Establishment

The first week was spent sorting out what went where in the house and the grounds thereabouts. Making sure everything was secure. Establishing paths to the fishing spot and towards what Agmunder stated was his first field. The plan was, as customary, to have three fields side by side and operate a rotation system. One field for the 'summer crop', one for the 'winter crop' and one left fallow on which they could graze animals and run chickens. The fields were about twelve yards wide and sixty yards long. Enough to grow food for the three of them, with twice the same again grown for trading, without the need to employ others to help come harvest.

In the second week, as they got used to living in the canvas house and as day to day tasks became familiar. Agmunder and Erik hammered in posts to outline the three fields and they spent a whole day clearing grass and large stones from the surface of the 'summer crop field'. This year, that would be the one nearest the house. The next day they cleared the 'winter crop field', the second nearest. They left the 'fallow field', the furthest, for now, largely as it was, with the exception that Svala released the three chickens, and the cockerel they had brought with them from the north-lands, onto the fallow field and threw two hands-full of precious corn, to keep them from wandering too far. The fowl immediately set to work scratching about looking for the food.

By the fifth day, the view from the house looked a little more like a farm, with the fields clearly defined in the landscape and well-worn paths crossing the ground, defining the most frequently trodden routes. Agmunder opened the box where the seeds were kept dry, in large sealed jars, and he and Erik planted barley and beans. Erik had the job of scattering the seeds over the field, while his father followed on with the harrow. A multi-rowed rake of sorts that was pulled over the ground to bury the seeds. Without a horse or an ox, Agmunder had to use a light-weight, man-powered version that required many passes to smooth the ground and seal the seeds below ground. The field, however, when they had finished, looked superb. Smooth and lightly furrowed in combed lines along the whole length. At the end of the second week, Agmunder and his son stood at the end of the path and took in the view, feeling very satisfied with their labours.

Agmunder took the afternoon, and what was left of the light, to have a good walk around the area inland of the pool. He could see the hint of an infrequently used or ancient path, leading south along the edge of the pool and decided to try the other direction. He couldn't walk directly south west because of the huge stand of hawthorns that blocked the way, and by alternate reasoning, protected the farm from approach from that direction. He walked to the north west, to gauge the landward approaches. The land was flat but boggy in places. He liked that, any attacker would have a difficult time crossing this marshy land. It stretched as far as he could see to the west and the north of where he stood. The light was fading and he decided to return to the farm and prepare for the necessary trip out tomorrow.

'I can't put it off any longer,' Agmunder announced at breakfast the next morning.

'Can't I come with you?' asked Erik.

'Someone has to protect the farm and your mother. It's a dangerous time for us. I'm sorry, Erik, but you have to stay and I will be back as soon as I can.'

They knew that soon after they arrived, Agmunder would have to make the journey to Garstang, the taxing station for the Fylde, to let the burgher know that he was farming and claimed this land. He also hoped to buy a horse and a goat, to help with work, and food. Maybe, a pig? He would have to see. He estimated that Garstang was a good three day's walk from the Pool. It wasn't going to be hard to find the town, though, as all he had to do was follow the river. If he crossed the river he could go across country and maybe save half a day, but he would be wet and the land looked boggier on the eastern side. For the sake of a few hours, he decided that a good walk was what he needed and set off after breakfast. He carried as few extra things as necessary for the journey. A summer weight cloak, for warmth, his war axe for protection and cutting wood for his fires, and a pouch of Norse silver coins to make the required purchases and payment of taxes. The payment of taxes struck an annoying chord with Agmunder. He knew he had to register his farm and to do that he had to pay a year's taxes up front, but he still hadn't lived under a tax scheme before and it seemed a bit like he was giving away something that was his to someone who hadn't earned it. And, why? So that he had the right to own something that was already his! The question of taxes took up a lot of his waking thoughts as he walked for the first day towards the town. There wasn't much else to occupy his mind save the moment he went to go through a break in the line of thorns on a distant ridge and got his cloak firmly stuck. He lost his temper slightly, as every move to unhook the garment seemed to end up with even more thorns grabbing hold. Eventually, though, through sheer perseverance and a not inconsiderable amount of violence, he tore free, leaving a small portion of the cloak as a memento of the tussle for the bush to keep. Shortly after that, mainly because of the effort it took, he decided to rest for the night as soon as the river turned east. He made plans during the night, as he sat by a fire in the open, for the next day's travel. He could see glittering lights on the horizon to the east. Garstang, his destination. The night passed without incident, save a shower of rain in the small hours, that woke him briefly. He thought how uncomfortable sleeping had been on the longship and fell asleep easily as the rain still spotted the ground.

The next morning, as he walked further toward his goal, he spotted another person, carrying a bale of sticks. It was a shock to see someone else in this deserted part of the world and Agmunder didn't know for sure how to approach the situation. Were people around here naturally inquisitive and friendly or aggressive and untrustworthy? He would have to be careful in this encounter, especially as the man was a good size. In a fight the stranger would have the upper hand in weight and strength, by the looks of him.

'Hei!' said the stranger, a Norse hello.

'Hei!' replied Agmunder, making sure the pouch containing the silver coins was hidden beneath his cloak, out of temptation's way. He thought he'd better try to strike up some sort of conversation and pass the time of day with the stranger.

'I'm on my way to Garstang. Taxes! Is it much further?' he asked.

The stranger put down the huge bundle of hazel twigs he was carrying and straightened up, puffing out his cheeks and pushing his hands into the small of his back.

'Another day from here, friend,' he said. 'Just follow the river.'

'Thank you. I thought it might be two.'

'It's been a dry spring, in the main, and the ground is firm. One more day will see you in town. My name is Lars, Lars Larsson. I am known in Garstang as *Lars the Dane,* though my family are from Zealand. I have a smallholding nearby, through that break in the thorns,' said the man, hefting the bale of sticks once more onto his shoulders with a smile.

'Feel free to call by on your way home.'

'Thank you, again, Lars Larsson. I am Agmunder, son of Asmunde,' he said and carried on his journey, happier in the knowledge that he would be away from home two days fewer than he thought, possibly three, if the trip back was equally firm under foot. He also wondered if everyone was so friendly in Britain.

The afternoon was dry, bright and warm for the time of year, despite the slight overcast, and Agmunder was thankful for it. He followed the river north-east and was glad that the clouds were thinning. He walked for the rest of the day without seeing another soul. By nightfall he had made camp and built a fire to cook on. The clouds, that had been his constant companions since coming to

Britain, had withdrawn their censorship of the sky. As the sky darkened, around midnight, Agmunder watched Jupiter, Thor's planet, drop low toward the sea, preparing to set as he ate, then settled down for the night.

About an hour after he had rested his head, he heard the sound of something moving in the bushes nearby and was instantly wide awake. Without moving he listened carefully for anything else. The wind was low, and his hearing was acute. Senses sharpened in the dark, he heard the sound of creeping feet. Another stranger? Could it be Lars Larsson, having tracked him? The sounds of gentle rustling crept nearer, tell-tale twigs and leaves crushing under foot. Now faint sounds of breathing. Agmunder's right hand was on his axe. It had been since he lay down to rest, in the warrior tradition. The sound of something heavy, disturbing the foliage, got nearer and more distinct. When it was almost upon him, Agmunder quickly grabbed a stick from the fire that still glowed bright on the end and waved it high, as he sprung to his feet with the axe also raised. A Viking ploy, to make him seem much taller than he was. The air rushing past the glowing ember brought it to life and the twig burst into flame just as it reached the highest point above his head. Light shone around and there, less than two yards from him, standing head on, was the largest boar he had ever seen. Easily above his waist at the shoulder. The next few seconds could determine one of their fates. Agmunder knew how dangerous a wild boar could be when startled and didn't give it time to make any judgements. He hopped to his left as he brought the axe down towards the animals head, meaning to bury the weapon in the boar's neck. The boar, startled by the sudden fire, wheeled away from the blow and took off into the bushes with a loud, indignant squeal.

'And stay away!' shouted Agmunder, at the quivering bushes, grey silhouettes against the black sky, beyond the furthest reach of the torch light.

Suddenly, there was a commotion and three smaller boars ran through the open area in which he camped, squealing and snorting as they careered into the bushes after the larger male.

Agmunder chuckled to himself as he sat back down and regarded the sky. The W of Cassiopeia hung in the pre-dawn sky in the direction he was taking and the first lights of activity could be seen in the town on the horizon. '*The bakery,*' thought Agmunder as he started to gather his things together and prepared to make some breakfast, eggs from the chickens, before he set off on the last leg of the walk to Garstang.

By the time he'd finished eating and had packed away, the sun was threatening the horizon with its presence and he set off towards the town. The bank of the river was damp with the morning dew and a slight mist rose from the water in the early morning air. Agmunder's untanned, animal skin boots became heavy with the water from the grass as he made his way along what was now becoming a well trodden path leading into the distance. He could see smoke rising in several small columns to his left and right, the houses themselves hidden in the trees. He entered the edge of town before the last of the mist had been burnt off by the rising orb of Sunne, the goddess of the daylight, rising today, in a cloudless sky.

The Viking walked fearlessly into the town of Garstang. The people eyed him suspiciously, but he was not berated as he thought he might be. The people went about their business as usual and Agmunder made his way to what was obviously the high street. There was a young man setting up a stall on the green to one side. Agmunder approached, showing his empty hands in greeting. In quiet conversation he discovered that the municipal building was just the next one along. He thanked the man and made for the door of the long, thatched, stone walled building that stood end-on to the street. Within the cool shade of this council building he found several tables. Each represented a different department, each presided over by a man with a stool and a clay tablet on which he recorded the doings of the day.

'I wish to register my house and farm,' Agmunder said to the official behind the first table he came to.

'There,' was the simple reply. Luckily it was accompanied by a slightly shaking

15

finger, pointing across the hall to the largest table in the building.

Behind this table sat three men and each had his tablet and stylus. Learned men to have mastered the runes.

'I wish to...'

'Where?' said the first man, a weasel-faced clean shaven, middle aged, shrimp of a man, in clothes that didn't fit too well despite their obvious quality.

'On the ness, where the river widens into the Pool,' said Agmunder, determined not to get riled by the rudeness of the man.

'How much land?' asked the second, as weasel-face consulted a list of sorts.

'I have three fields. Fifteen paces by sixty, each, and a dwelling place.'

'Crops?' asked the third, as the second duly started consulting *his* lists.

'Summer, Beans and Barley. Winter...'

'We don't need winter yet. You'll have to come back at the autumnal equinox,' said the third, consulting *his* list.

The first official looked up, distracted from his calculations by the proximity of the Viking, 'Wait over there,' he said with a dismissive wave of his hand toward a bench. It was set against the wall under a small opening high up, in which sat a pigeon.

Agmunder sat. He waited. As he waited the three men consulted with each-other frequently and occasionally looked over to where he sat. Agmunder watched a patch of sunlight make its way half way down the opposite wall and start to cross the floor before he was called to the table again.

'Name?' said the first man.

'Agmunder, son of Asmunde.'

'Amounder?'

'Agmunder, the *'g'* is like a slight cough, difficult in Saxon, I believe.'

All three of the men started scribbling on their tablets. They consulted on how they were going to spell his name and, once agreed, each continued scribbling... *Amounder.*

'Dependants?'

'I have a wife and a son. Svala and Erik.'

The three men sat back, as if they were preparing to unveil the 'big event' of the morning. The first man cleared his throat.

'Amuonder, son of Asmunde. The council of Garstang, town of the Danelaw, recognises your farm, and you, as the head of the estate. Your registration fee is an ounce of gold or four ounces of silver. Your annual tax is half of one ounce of silver.'

'Or an equivalent value of other metals or gems,' said official number two.

The sum was brought forth from Agmunder's money-bag, and all was paid in silver coin. When it had been weighed, Agmunder was handed a token as a receipt.

'Go to that table for your deed,' said the third man, pointing across the way.

Agmunder was amused that they seemed to take it in turns to speak. Walking slowly to the table indicated he stopped a little distance from the man busy behind it. He was about to speak when a voice just behind him said, addressing the man behind the table, 'This is Amounder, son of Asmunde. He has three fields on the ness, by the river pool.'

On hearing this information and without looking up from his desk, the man set to work writing with a quill on a piece of fine, pigskin parchment that had been trimmed into a square about a foot on each side.

After a few minutes the document was complete and the man took up a small hammer and a metal die. He held the die perpendicular to the page just over the 'A' of Agmunder's name and *bang*, he struck an impression into the parchment. He handed Agmunder the document and set his tools down, smiling, their eyes finally meeting.

'Congratulations. You have extended the Danelaw's reach to the sea!', he handed Agmunder the document, 'See you at the equinox,' he said.

Agmunder thanked him without acknowledgement and turned to thank the other man, but he was already dealing with someone else at the table of three. He shrugged, looked at the document in his grip and left the building, glad to get into the sunshine again after being cooped up in the shade for what seemed like half the day.

'I need a horse,' he called to the man on the stall he'd spoken to earlier.

'Down there. Blacksmith,' the young man answered, pointing to an alley.

Agmunder entered the alley and walked along. There were several pens with sheep and goats in them on the left. On the right, one yard had a cage with two small dogs in it and chickens running about freely. Agmunder wondered about what set of circumstances would have that arrangement preferable to the chickens being in the cage and the dogs outside. He continued to walk along the alley studying the uses of the other buildings as he went. There was what looked like a stable, but it turned out to be a small barn, half full of old straw that had seen a bitter winter, by the look of it. There was an empty pigsty. A fish drying rack in one yard that somehow managed to out-stink all the other yards, and last but one, another dog, asleep on a blanket on the ground of the building on the corner.

At the very end of the alley was a blacksmith's forge with smoke coming out of the chimney and also out of the open sides of the building.

'I'm looking to buy a horse,' said Agmunder to the blacksmith's boy, who was struggling to lift a full bucket of iron pieces.

The boy ran inside the smithy. Shortly after the sound of hammering stopped, a large, bald man with a black face and a huge leather apron, scorched and nicked, a testament to its service, came out of the side door holding a hammer that Thor himself would be proud to wield.

'The boy tells me you need a horse,' he said in a gravelly voice, wiping a hand over his brow and setting the hammer on a bench.

'Yes, for riding to town, a bit of harrowing on the farm, maybe even to pull a cart in the future. That sort of thing,' said Agmunder.

The blacksmith rubbed his chin and looked up toward his non-existent eyebrows, victims of too many close calls with the bellows and the coals.

The only chance of a horse around here at the moment is the small farm that

Lars the Dane has on the river. It's not more...'

'I know the place,' said Agmunder.

'Well, in that case, I'll be back to my nails,' said the blacksmith.

'Thanks,' said Agmunder, to the man's back.

'Get the iron, boy!' shouted the blacksmith from inside the forge.

Glad of the information, Agmunder set off back up the alley to talk to someone about one of the goats. By the time he was thinking of finding an inn to get a drink and a bite, he had acquired a young nanny goat, which he would pick up later, a winter cloak that was being sold cheap because of the time of year, which he snapped up, and a comb made of bone, bleached white under a hotter sun than found in Britain, for Svala.

He followed the directions asked of a monk, and quickly found the inn. There was a battered old Viking shield over the door and he assumed, naturally, that the inn was known as 'the Shield' or something similar. After a short conversation with the bartender, it transpired that the inn was, in fact, known as 'The Dogtooth Arms'. The shield had apparently once been the possession of a warrior called, Ikweld Dogtooth. The landlord was proud that he had the shield, he claimed it was two hundred years old. Agmunder doubted that it was that old, nevertheless, he was pleased that the people were friendly enough to a Viking and willing to make small talk with a stranger.

The snack of chicken and barley pie and a tough bread crust was washed down with ale. The chicken pie was passable and the ale was good, although rather pricey by virtue of him not having any small change. Something he thought he'd better remedy. He asked the landlord for silver pennies to the value of two of his rather weighty Norse silver coins. He received, by weight, sixteen pennies. A shilling and fourpence. Rather a lot. He was indeed lucky that the landlord had had a good week and hadn't put the cash away yet. Agmunder decided to make a start back to the Pool that evening. The weather looked fine and he knew that the track was good for the first three miles at least. He called in at the yard where the goat was tied up waiting. She looked frustrated at not being able to reach the ground, taking her anger out on the rope, which was nearly chewed through already.

'Three pence,' said the seller as Agmunder got his purse out. A reasonable sum for a young goat.

The goat seemed willing enough to walk on a lead and didn't stop too often to graze on the grass they passed. Long before the sun set over the silver thread of the sea, Agmunder had reached the area that Lars had his smallholding. He could see the devil's thorn bushes just half a mile ahead, so he knew it was close. He called Lars' name as he walked, waist high in grasses that baffled the goat. He had just about decided that he'd gone too far along the track and was considering making camp for the night, when there was a shout from just a hundred or so feet away. There was the impressive figure of Lars Larsson, waving from the tree-line.

'Agmunder, you're back so soon!' said Lars, holding out a hand to shake as they met, a little way off the main track.

'I was told that you might have a horse that I might buy from you.'

'Indeed. In fact, I have a choice of two. Would you like some refreshment? I have ale and cheese in the house.'

'Thank you. That would be appreciated, the walk was not easy with a goat in tow,' said Agmunder to the smiling Lars.

'Then, follow me,' said Larsson.

They made their way a little distance into the woods that lined the river at this point and came to a clearing where Lars had his house. He'd apparently done rather well for himself in whatever it was he did, besides horse trading. The house was made of large beams framing the corners and such a reed roof would not have been out of place on the council building in Garstang! The walls were plaster on wicker lattice and had been whitewashed. The view from the house was of the river and the land fell down a few feet from the back entrance to the riverside, where three small boats were pulled up on the riverbank.

'Your house would attract attention from boats on the river,' observed Agmunder.

'Indeed, if anyone ever came by. There is a very narrow, but deep, area of rapids just around that bend, towards the ness. Boats larger than these skiffs cannot get through,' he said indicating the small craft on the bank.

They sat for a while outside by the river, drinking ale and eating cheese while the sun set.

'You can have my hospitality if you like, just for tonight, I'm sure you want to get that fine goat back home,' he said with a grin.

'Thank you, Lars,' he said, then seemed to remember why he'd come, 'You say you have two horses?'

Lars took Agmunder, by the light of a lantern, to see the horses. There were indeed two animals in the barn. A large healthy looking chestnut and a smaller grey. Lars made it clear that Agmunder would have to see them in the daylight before he would accept a bid and the two returned to the house by the feeble light of the lantern.

Inside Lars' house was clean and tidy by Viking standards, the thresh was dry and looked new and the candles were the best kind, not the smoky animal fat ones, but beeswax. There was an old dog lying by the fireplace, though the fire wasn't lit. Lars indicated a seat for Agmunder and used the lantern to light the tinder in the fireplace to warm the room in the cooling May evening. He patted the dog gently and looked up to the Viking visitor.

'Not long now, for my old friend,' he said with the glint of moisture in his eyes.

'How many summers?'

'I've had him since a puppy. The dog has stayed by my side for fully fifteen summers since. I got him when I came to this peaceful land away from the Welsh border.' Lars shifted his feet, 'I used to fight for King Offa,' he offered as an explanation of his being in Wales.

Lars sat down on a stool, warming his hands by the fire, his eyes never straying far from his dog.

'I bought him from a man in Garstang,' a nod to the sleeping dog, 'It was one of the first things I did when I arrived. Looking for a blacksmith I went up this alley. I felt so sorry for him sitting whimpering in a cage in the yard.'

'I was there earlier today, Lars. There were a couple of puppies in a cage,' he thought a few seconds, 'I didn't buy one.'

'Vikings have harder hearts than the Saxons,' said Lars. 'My father was from Zealand, but settled here when I was young, I grew up with Saxon influences.'

'You seem to have done well for yourself.'

'Yes,' was all he said in answer.

The dog whimpered in his sleep and an outstretched paw trembled a little. The dog's breathing became laboured for a minute, while Lars knelt by the animal's side and stroked his head. One eye opened slightly and rolled to reveal the white, then closed again. There was another slight whimper and the old dog's heaving chest was still. The paw slowly drooped to the floor. The only sound was that of the big Dane, sniffing.

'Sorry,' he said.

The next morning, at dawn, Agmunder woke to find that Lars was not in the house. From the door he looked about the land surrounding the property but couldn't see the owner. He went outside and went down to the riverside to look over the little boats in the full light of morning. They were well made and even had painted decorations, unusual in a small craft. He was tempted to take one out on the water, but decided that those rapids didn't sound like the sort of thing a big man in a small skiff should be attempting to take on. He decided instead to go and take another look at the horses. As he made his way over the yard toward the stable, Lars came down the path, spade in hand.

'I might go up to Garstang later and liberate one of those dogs from the cage,' he said.

'I expect it gets pretty lonely out here on your own.'

'You are the first person I've seen pass by this year,' said Lars, by way of confirmation.

They walked over to the stable and Agmunder looked over the horses in the daylight. Lars was generous indeed to ask Agmunder to wait. The chestnut horse had looked by far the better animal on the previous evening but now it was obvious that the smaller grey was the more suitable of the two, for his needs. The deal was done at a price of two of Agmunder's Norse silver coins and the few possessions he loaded onto its withers, leaving room for him to ride behind with the bemused goat in tow. The men said their goodbyes. Lars gave Agmunder some of his cheese, having learned that Svala didn't have any yet. Agmunder mounted up and the horse walked along the track. As he got a few hundred feet away from Lars' house he looked back and saw Lars, already mounted on the chestnut, heading off to town. He presumed he was riding to get one of the dogs for company.

After an uneventful and quick ride, despite a half mile detour to skirt around the hawthorn bushes, Agmunder had the pleasure of seeing his little house on the horizon. Stark on the little rise against the light grey sky of the horizon, he could see the smoke from Svala's cooking fire.

There was as huge a welcome as two people could muster when he rode up the trail that led past the fields to the front of the house. Erik and Svala were pleased that he'd made it back so soon and with such a good looking horse. The goat was tied to a post in the fallow field with the horse stationed at the other end on a longer tether. Both seemed happy and ate of the grass almost immediately. Agmunder wasn't an experienced farmer but he knew that if animals aren't happy, they don't eat. The goat, judging by the way she was munching the lush marsh-grass, was very happy indeed.

'Milk in the morning,' said Svala to Erik. 'That will be one of your jobs.'

Erik seemed pleased. She had thought that he would think it was 'woman's work' and below his masculine status. Svala was pleased that he didn't make a fuss, or even complain that he didn't know how. She felt proud how she had brought him up to know that he wouldn't be asked to do anything that wasn't important or that he wouldn't be shown how to do. However, once he'd been shown he would be in trouble if he messed up. Luckily, Erik was a clever boy and always remembered how to do things he was shown.

Agmunder put away the winter cloak, after showing it to Svala. They wouldn't need that until October, or even November, in this mild climate, he hoped. The comb he saved for when Erik had gone to bed. He and his wife sat in their house on the end of the bed pallet and, by the light of a smoky goose-fat candle, he gave her the gift. Svala looked at it for a few seconds before smiling.

'I hope you had to buy this because your coins were too high value for the merchant,' she said, her eyes sparkling in the candle light.

'I bought it because I know how much you gave up to come here with me.'

'It's lovely,' she said, running the smooth white teeth through her slightly knotted hair.

The next week passed with work on the house to be done and, of course, in the fields. Erik helped remove the biggest stones from the fallow field. They had to protect the horse's hooves. Next to the house, the horse was their most expensive possession and they didn't plan on letting any harm come to it. It was a nice day and just as they were thinking of finding out what Svala had cooked for their evening meal, Erik pointed to the far end of the Pool.

'Look, Father, a boat.'

Agmunder looked where his son was pointing. It *was* a boat. A very small one but definitely a boat of some sort. They watched as it neared their position. It was heading directly towards their landing space. Then there was a strange intermittent sound. A bit like a young... a young, dog! It *was* a dog! Lars! Agmunder told Erik about Lars' old dog as they waited. Erik was sad about the old dog but brightened considerably when the puppy jumped out of the boat and ran to him wagging its tail and making its funny yapping noise that would turn, in time, into a bark. They went off to play along the track to the winter crop field, cleared but as yet, unsown.

Agmunder grasped Lars' arm in greeting as he stepped ashore. They had big grins on their faces and Agmunder invited him to stay for as long as he wanted. Introductions were made and they all were very much at ease.

'I'll walk back in the morning, Agmunder,' said their guest.

'What about the boat?'

'The Celts inhabited this area for a while, early in this century. They never made a permanent township, but they had a fleet of skiffs that they used to use for fishing and for trading with various towns. Lancaster, Priest's Town, Garstang, Glasson and Lancaster even, all were traded with fish from the Wyre. They used to call this harbour Skiff Pool, and now, you, my friend, have a skiff to keep in Skiff Pool. So, in the morning I will return to my house, and to my young dog who is spending his first night alone in the house.'

'You have two dogs now?'

The Dane scooped up the little pup with his right hand and addressed Erik.

'*I*, have *one* dog. *This* dog, is yours.'

Erik was very pleased, he'd already grown very attached to the puppy in the few minutes that Lars had been on the shores of Skiff Pool. With a *whoop*, Erik ran from the building into the fields with the young dog giving chase and occasionally uttering its excuse for a bark.

'Look at its feet,' said Lars.

Agmunder did as he had been bidden. The dog, come to look at it, had great big feet on the end of its skinny little legs.

Lars nodded, 'Big paws, big dog! Living out here all alone there will be times when you need another layer of protection. Your Viking friends use Skiff Pool as a harbour from time to time, and even they will think twice about giving you any trouble if you have a big dog.'

'I know that well. Thank you again, Lars,' said Agmunder.

The night was spent sitting around the fire, with Lars telling the family everything he could think of that might be of use to them. He told them about the other families of the *Fylde*, a Dane's word for the lowland plain that they found themselves on. Bordered on three sides by the sea and the fells rising up from boggy, unnavigable swampland at the base in the east, the Fylde was protected on all sides. He told them the dates they needed to go to pay their taxes and the best markets for their crops. He warned them away from the blacksmith Agmunder had spoken to the week before, and told them of another by the Black Pool, called John Smith. The Black Pool was a small lake, due south, in the south of the Fylde. Erik's eyes went wide when Lars told him that the Black Pool was the very lake that Sir Bedevere threw Excalibur into, in the Arthurian legend.

'Can we go Father? Next time we need the blacksmith?' asked Erik eagerly.

'We will have to see,' said Agmunder.

'Fjord will protect mother, while we're away.'

'That's a good name for your dog, Erik,' said Lars.

'It's a strange name for any animal,' said Svala, in a rare speaking moment. After all, they had company.

'Yes,' explained Lars, 'Your big dog there,' pointing at the tiny puppy, 'Will be like an impenetrable wall of rock, between the ease of the sea and the taking of the land for any that seek to come ashore here. A good name, Erik.'

'What will we feed him?' asked Erik.

'If you set a few more rabbit traps he can have meat,' said Agmunder.

'And some eggs,' said Lars, 'You have enough chickens, I see.'

They talked until long after Erik and Svala had fallen asleep. Erik with Fjord laying across his arm on the pallet and Svala curled up next to him. The men finally settled down to sleep when the ale was finished and Sunne was thinking of broaching the horizon.

They all slept in quite late, the sun had been up for two hours before anyone stirred.

Breakfast was eggs, from the chickens, milk from the goat, Svala showing Erik how to milk her this once, and bread and cheese. Lars raised a laugh when he said the cheese was the best he'd tasted. Breakfast was a banquet, in honour of their generous guest, Lars the Dane.

Lars left shortly afterwards and could be seen for many minutes, heading first west, then south around the Pool, before he finally turned south east and went over a rise and through a break, in the hawthorn bushes that darkened the horizon on the shore the Skiff Pool. Agmunder thought to himself, remembering the trouble he had with his cloak in the hawthorns, *'If anyone builds a settlement there they will have to call it Thorn Town!'*

Lars had no sooner vanished beyond the slight rise, than Erik gave a shout. Agmunder turned to see what the fuss was all about. There, entering the Pool was a longship. He looked closer, it was Valgard's longship, moving under sail in the light north westerly breeze. The Vikings on board were waving above the shield wall then quickly ran out six oars for control as they approached the shore. As the oars took the weight of the ship the sail was furled and it made a beautiful sight to Agmunder as it nosed into the shore. He went down to the water's edge to find out the reason for their visit.

'Agmunder, I have news. Important to your farm and family,' Valgard shouted while moving down the length of the longboat.

'What news, Valgard?'

The captain jumped into the shallows and walked ashore, the animal fat smeared on his boots repelling much of the water. They walked up to the house and found somewhere to sit while the crew came ashore and set up a camp, as they prepared to eat.

'There is a dangerous man in this area. We followed him from the Irish coast. One of my crew is from Iceland, Hagan. He recognised the boat as belonging to Knut Husasson. They came aground on the north shore, but not on the ness, they were on the eastern side of the estuary. We don't know what they did after they landed. If they went to Lancaster to try to ingratiate themselves with the Lord, then that area has a problem, and you might be alright. But, if he

came south to start his activities close by, then you may have a big problem. He's a thief, a cheat, violent without reason, and there are rumours that he's a murderer too. I bring you this news, good friend, so you will be forewarned.'
'I will keep any eye out for strangers and be wary. Thank you, good friend.'
The evening passed well, with much revelry and jokes by the firelight. Agmunder felt a strange nostalgia for the old days but it was tinged with the feeling that the Viking crew were an interruption to his important work. Valgard said that the Vikings would leave at dawn, their current voyage had been on hold for too long already. They would not disrupt his peace or farming any longer than they needed to. Agmunder was strangely grateful that they were leaving soon.

The next day, shortly after dawn on a beautifully sunny morning, as Agmunder and Svala waved the longship out of the Pool, Erik came running in from outside very excited because there were shoots visible in the summer crop field. The seed had germinated and the crop was on the way. They were real farmers! The three of them and Fjord went to have a look. The shoots of the barley were just showing above the soil. Agmunder was pleased that Erik had noticed such a tiny thing. It showed that he was keen, as well as observant. There was no sign of the beans yet and Agmunder's thoughts went to the construction of the frames on which they would grow. Something else they had to get on with, even before the beans showed above the soil. That afternoon Agmunder was thankful that Lars had brought the skiff. To make the frame, up which the beans would grow, they needed to cut bulrush reeds and the best reeds were out of reach of the shore. The boat would be ideal for getting to the best reeds. Erik was persuaded to leave Fjord on shore while he and Agmunder took a sharp knife to the reed beds. By evening, and five trips out in the boat, they had what Agmunder hoped would be enough. There was a large pile of neatly stacked reeds, drying in the sun, on the bank next to the skiff.

'Tomorrow will be another long day, Erik,' he said. 'Get something to eat and then to bed.'

Svala had made salt fish pie for their meal from their preserved food supplies and very welcome it was after their afternoon's work under the hot sun. Erik went to bed and Fjord slept on the floor by the side of his pallet, neatly curled up, his nose on the base of his tail. Agmunder saw to the horse and the goat before he returned to the house. He spoke to Svala about the work that had to be done to create a frame for the beans to grow up before he too laid down to rest.

CHAPTER 3

Knut

Toward the middle of August, Agmunder was well set in his new life as farmer. The paths to the various fields were well established and daily life, milking the goat and keeping the chickens, inspecting the crops, had become routine. The summer had been kind on this first crop and the family looked forward to starting their harvest. The beans had climbed the reed lattice nicely in the bottom half of the field, and would be ready for picking in another two weeks. But for now, their attention was firmly on the spring barley.

'Just a few more days of this sunshine and the barley will need to come in,' said Agmunder, 'We've spoken about this before, Erik. You will be an especially important part of the farm during harvest.'

They worked for another two hours, with hardly a word between them, clearing the winter crop field of the last remnants of stones, ready for planting immediately after the bean harvest.

They sat and ate their snack and gazed, as they often did, across the water to the other bank of the Skiff Pool. A thin wisp of light grey smoke rose from a point a little further downstream. It caught Agmunder's attention. Immediately his thoughts turned to the outlaw, Knut, that Valgard had warned him about. It's essential to know who your neighbours are when you live in isolation. There were no families living closer than his good friend, Lars, of that he was sure. This had to be investigated immediately. He thought things through as he watched the smoke drifting eastwards from the forested area to his north-east. It gave him two days to get the answer to his question and get back to the farm. Agmunder made little of it to his family that evening.

'Of course, I will be back to get on with the harvest, but I'd just like to find out if we have some new neighbours. That smoke didn't look like just a camp fire to me, not dark enough. I will go over there tomorrow and once I've seen who it is, and what's going on, I'll be back,' he said.

'Take Fjord with you,' insisted Svala. 'You'll be in more danger than we will.

You'll be better off if you have the dog. He's not fully grown but at least he's not the tiny thing he was two and a half months ago.'

Agmunder didn't argue, preferring to avoid any more questions by getting some sleep before the journey.

The next morning was spotting with light rain, but the sky was light enough that it didn't worry the farmer. It would stop soon and the sun would dry the damp off before the crop spoilt. Agmunder was preparing the skiff before Erik woke. The boy came down to the water's edge to help with the final preparations for the trip across the river. In the skiff were some food items, a rope, a hammer, and Fjord, looking excited, standing in the skiff that Erik had christened 'Waverider', looking across the water with his tail wagging. There was also Agmunder's war axe.

'Time to go,' Agmunder said to Erik, as he waved to Svala standing in the door of the house. He hoped this wasn't the last time they saw him or he them.

Waverider took him across the water in just a few minutes and was beached on the shore. Agmunder pulled her a little higher out of the water as Fjord busied himself with the new smells of the new territory. The Viking got his things from the boat and called Fjord. The two made their way, haltingly, through rushes and long grass for the first mile. The going was heavy despite the summer being a dry one. Agmunder was pleased that he'd made his home on the ness and not this boggier land. The ground became slightly better underfoot and a flock of starlings took flight alarming the young dog. There was a scuffle in the reeds and Fjord shot off to investigate, coming back a few minutes later with a rabbit hanging from his jaws.

'Good boy, Fjord. We'll have that for lunch, lad.'

It was late morning before Agmunder had much idea about exactly where he was headed, but as the sun broke through the clouds and the last of the sporadic raindrops stopped falling, he could see the smoke of the lunchtime cooking fire begin to stream into the sky ahead. He cut his lunch short and he and Fjord, filled with rabbit, headed off with renewed urgency. Within half an hour they were approaching the wooded area from which the smoke rose. Agmunder unslung his axe from his shoulder, he might need it to cut his way through the bushes. That would be his excuse if challenged on this unfriendly appearance. Sensing the change in his master's demeanour, Fjord came close and stopped his boisterous exploration. Agmunder smiled down at him, Lars was right, he had the makings of a very good dog. Agmunder stopped. There was a large house under construction, no sign of activity. The frame and door were in position and the materials to make the walls were strewn about the site. There was a pile of spears and axes, enough for a dozen men. It looked worrying. Looking around the site, he couldn't see anyone at all. Hopefully that meant that there were no more than a few people, maybe even just the one.

'Hei!' came a call from behind.

Agmunder spun round, rather more quickly than a calm person would have done. He was annoyed at himself for giving away his anxiety. Weeks with only their little family had cooled Fjord's excitement at meeting strangers and he let out a low growl as the man approached. The man was slightly smaller than Agmunder but strongly built. He didn't seem a threat currently and Agmunder slung his axe back on to his shoulder.

'I've seen smoke from across the water. You live on the ness, am I right?' said the stranger as he got closer, keeping an eye on Fjord.

Agmunder thought it was a strange question. The stranger wouldn't naturally assume he was from across the water. Unless he'd somehow seen him arrive in Waverider.

'I saw yours yesterday, from my farm. My name is Agmunder,' said the Viking.

'I am Knut Husasson. I got here just three days ago. I landed on the north shore. I trekked down here on the first day. I cut down all this wood to make my house, and put this up this morning,' indicating the frame in the clearing.

Agmunder could tell from his accent that he was not a local. He wondered how much of his story he would give away. How truthful would he be to a stranger? At least he'd given the name Agmunder expected.

'Landed, from where?'

'I am from a small settlement on the north of the otherwise uninhabited island of Iceland. We were forced to settle there five years ago, after our boat ran aground and broke up in a storm. There are a few houses in a village called Huisavik. Eventually we were visited by other Danes, who, like you, saw our smoke from afar. They had boats and materials. Many of us decided to go back home, some chose to stay. But I chose to try another country, and here I am!'

'What do you do?' asked Agmunder, soothing the still growling Fjord under his hand.

'I am a tanner by trade, but I have a mind to try farming in this green land.'

'You've got your work cut out then, if you've built a house in the woods. Where will you have your fields?'

'Just beyond that tree, there, is a large clearing. There's a brook at the bottom and the ground is stone free. I think I'll be alright.'

'I would wait until the spring equinox before you register at Garstang, otherwise you'll be charged taxes for the whole spring and summer with no crop to pay with,' said Agmunder, noticing Knut's eyes flicking to the pile of weapons and then back to Agmunder's axe.

'Oh, I shan't be bothering with taxes. I don't believe in giving someone else what I have earned! You're a fool if you pay someone who hasn't given you something in return. I would offer you a drink, but I expect you're keen to return to your farm.'

Agmunder noticed the other man's not-so-subtle suggestion that he should leave, and, being rather keen to get back himself, he politely agreed.

'We will be off,' he said, looking at Fjord, calm now at his feet, sniffing at a beetle inquisitively as it made its way along a leaf between his paws.

'Nice to meet you, neighbour,' said Knut, turning to return to his building.

'You too,' said Agmunder, not at all sure if it had been at all '*nice*'.

Over the next two hours he and Fjord made their way back to the river and his little boat. Agmunder wondered about how the proximity of Knut would affect his ability to leave the family and travel for a few days with his crop. There was something shifty about the man, he didn't trust him. Agmunder was someone who believed very much in gut instincts and first impressions, and what his gut was telling him about Knut was all bad.

They made the boat in good time to cross the river before twilight and both Svala and Erik were relieved to see him safe home. Over supper he told them all about his encounter with the suspicious neighbour, Knut. They asked questions and got answers, some of which surprised even Agmunder. Things he didn't realise he'd noticed at the time, but must have registered somewhere. The clothes that he wore were Saxon and he looked like a local, but he spoke Norse, and admitted to being new to the country. His house had probably been under construction for at least a week, not two days. Or there wasn't just him. Agmunder knew when he'd landed and it wasn't just a few days earlier. Either way both these simple things were pointers to the man being at best a liar and at worst goodness knows what!

'Did he have a dog?' asked Erik, merely curious.

'I didn't see or hear any animals, but come to think of it, there was a post for tying a horse and a rough kennel of sorts. That might point to someone else, because the animals weren't at the house. We know Valgard said he had a crew. Or they might just have been in the field he spoke of. I don't know. Fjord was happy, though. Didn't seem to be smelling other animals, you know how he gets anxious.'

'So there might be more men?' asked Svala, as calmly as she was able.

'Possibly,' he said. He thought for a second. 'Probably.'

They passed the evening talking about this new situation and how they might have to bear them in mind when Agmunder needed to leave the farm. He knew when he first came to the Fylde that there might be other families, but they had kept their eyes peeled for tell-tale smoke, and fires at night, and had seen nothing closer than Garstang, excepting Lars' cooking fire. It was comforting to know he was there. That made Agmunder think.

'Tomorrow, I will ride out to Lars and make sure he knows about Knut. I can tell him what I know,' he said, at length.

'The harvest?', asked Svala.

'We will start tomorrow afternoon, as planned,' answered Agmunder. 'It's half a day there and back on the horse.'

Agmunder went outside to look at the two smoke stacks rising from the forest. One from a proven friend, and one from an unproven enemy. One greatly reassuring and one slightly worrying.

The next morning Agmunder was riding out before dawn. He had had a fitful night's sleep and thought that it would be best to get on the way. Also, an early start meant that he would be back sooner to start getting the harvest in.

The thorn break, surprisingly, gave him no trouble in the morning light of dawn and he was soon on the track that was becoming more and more well travelled as the months went by. The sun wasn't very high in the sky when he arrived at Lars' homestead.

'Lars! Lars! Are you here?'

A dog started barking and the sound came rapidly closer. Suddenly the dog burst out of the foliage at speed making an awful racket. Agmunder dismounted and held his arms wide to receive the bounding dog. When he reached the last two yards the barking dog launched itself into the air and was caught by Agmunder with its tail threshing wildly in his happy reception.

'I hope you get over this style of welcome when you're fully grown, Skjolder!' he laughed, tickling the dog's tummy as it squirmed with delight in his arms.

'You'll never sneak past unwelcomed, Agmunder!' shouted Lars, appearing from the same bit of the bushes as Skjolder, that concealed his house from casual discovery.

They clasped hands as they met, 'I pray that I would never consider doing such a thing!'

Agmunder followed Lars, quickly, to his house and told him what he'd seen and what he'd done to find out what it meant for the people of the Fylde. He told him all he saw and what he thought about Knut and they agreed that the stranger wasn't good news for their part of the world. They both had crops to bring in and both knew that they also needed to find out more about the suspicious stranger and to neutralize any threat, if necessary. Settlers couldn't afford to leave threats to their peace unchallenged. The men agreed that *'trying to get along'* is often seen as a weakness by these types. Agmunder apologised for the shortness of his stay. The pair shook hands and arranged to meet immediately after harvest and market days. They set a date, nine days hence, to plan their next action. Agmunder mounted his horse and was on his way back to his farm before the sun was half way up the sky. *I'll be home for lunch, a good time to be starting the harvest*, he lied to himself, in an effort to keep his spirits up.

When he arrived home Svala had a look on her face, visible even from a distance, that was far from happy. Agmunder sped his horse home at a gallop for the last three hundred feet. He jumped off before the animal had completely stopped.

'What is it?' he said, worried, as he ran to where Svala was standing.

'He's been here. Knut,' she said, hugging the big man round the waist.

Agmunder looked about for signs of struggle.

'Nothing too bad, Agmunder,' she said, 'It was just scary with you gone and Erik on the river fishing. I was all alone. Even Fjord was with Erik.'

'Where is Erik now?'

'He's just got back, he doesn't know they landed, but he passed the boat on the Skiff Pool. He's racking out the fish. Look, here's Fjord.'

The dog came round the building sniffing furiously at the ground. He knew there had been a stranger, and like Agmunder, he wasn't happy.

'What did he do? How did he cross the river? What happened?' many questions.

'He said he had come to see the farm, see if there were any tips he could pick up. He had a boat, bigger than ours, it had a sail and oars for two. He looked around, ignored me when I asked him not to go in the house. Tried our bed! And the stew. Walked about like he owned the place,' Svala said, almost in tears.

'I've told Lars about this crook. We're agreed that as soon as the harvest is in, we'll solve this problem.'

'Till then?' she asked, obviously very upset by the visit.

'We have no choice but to bring in the harvest. We can't leave it, even a day or two. Lars has his harvest too, so we're both tied to our farms for now, and I guess Knut probably doesn't know it, or he would have more mischief planned than he did today.'

'Erik, come and talk to your Father about the boat,' Svala shouted through the flap of the house to where the boy was hanging the final fish of today's catch on a string.

Erik bounded into the house, oblivious to the tension between the two.

'What's this about the boat?' asked Agmunder, without a hello.

'It was big, Father. I said to mum that I don't think one man could have brought a boat that big to the river. I saw him land so he didn't come from the sea. It was brought to the pool by land. It was twice as long as Waverider, and it had a better sail. I tried to get close but I couldn't, it was fast. It's still beached on the other side!' he said.

They all went outside and were disappointed to see that the boat had gone. They didn't know if it had sailed down river or had been dragged into the wooded area by several men. *A missed opportunity to size up the enemy, thought Agmunder.* For *enemy* is how he now thought of Knut.

CHAPTER 4

Harvest Time

For a first harvest, it went very well. Agmunder was proud of the way his family worked together in this time of busyness. The crop was cut, threshed and bundled. The barley was put into barrels for storage in the farm for their own use, and the surplus was bagged for transportation to sell at market in Garstang. *The straw will be good for thatch or flooring thresh*, he thought. The beans looked like they would be ready in just a few days, maybe just two, so no time to take the barley before harvest began on those too. Agmunder saw to storing the barrels of barley next to the house in easy reach of the kitchen for Svala to make barley-bread. He positioned their hand millstone inside the kitchen, now that it was of some use. It wasn't big enough to make more than a day's flour at a time, but that was all they needed, and a larger mill-stone would take up so much more space and be so much harder for Svala to use. The hand wheel was ideal for their needs.

The very next day they had their own bread for breakfast with the last of Lars' delicious cheese and a boiled egg. Agmunder was so happy he nearly forgot all about Knut. By the time they had finished breakfast, any idea that the bean harvest would be taken in the next day vanished, as low clouds rolled in during the space of just an hour and heavy rain looked imminent. They were motivated to get on with it before the crop got damp and worked all morning and afternoon, without a break, to get the majority of the crop under cover. Agmunder had set up a rope between two sturdy posts and threw a long, waterproofed canvas over to make a sort of long tent, under which they stashed the cut bean plants in the dry. By the end of that evening, as it became too dark to continue, they had their first bean harvest in, if not properly stored. A hard day's work from just three people and a horse (and a dog). The rain lashed down all night and kept them awake as it hammered on the roof of their canvas dwelling. *Got to use reeds to make a better roof before winter*, thought Agmunder as he lay awake worrying about the crops, the house and Knut, in equal measure.

Dawn the next morning was dull, but not raining. They had their own bread again, which was very pleasing. Agmunder went out to survey the damage, if any, to his crop and was joined by Svala, Erik and Fjord. The first thing was to liberate the horse and goat from their tethers under the canvas with the bean crop. They were both dry and seemed happy to munch on some discarded bean stalks, especially the goat.

'There are just a few plants at this end that have gotten wet during the night,' he said after a few minute's inspection, 'and it looks as though we've got off lightly.' The rain had been kept off most of it and the barley bags were watertight under their own canvas cover.

'We've done it,' he beamed, 'We've had our first harvest and hardly lost a thing!'

The family were overjoyed and willingly set to to remove the beans from the plants ready for storage or market. Erik pulled a plant out of the tent and the three of them removed the bean pods. Then Agmunder dragged the spent plant to the fallow field and the attention of the hoofed animals, while Erik got the next plant from the tent. Just one day's activity saw the bean crop stowed away. All in all they had had a fantastic harvest. They counted themselves very lucky.

To get things moving and a profit coming in Agmunder wasted no time in taking four large bags of barley to the market in Garstang. The horse was admirable, never wavering and walking without complaint or fatigue under the heavy load. Agmunder was mildly annoyed when he reached Garstang, that despite having his farm deed, he also needed a license from the council to sell his crop in their market. This cost him another two of his silver pennies. Though the inconvenience wasn't much as they allowed him to sell his wares before he purchased the license. Even council officials know you can't leave a crop lying about for hours on a hot, August day.

Agmunder met Lars coming towards him on the track as he left town, heading back to get more bags of beans and barley for the next day. They talked about the harvest at first, but it didn't take long for the conversation to get round to their unwanted neighbour. Agmunder told his friend about the visit Svala had endured while he was at Lars' farm. Lars bristled with anger.

'You don't go in someone else's house when they're away,' he fumed, 'Not the done thing. I'll ask about in town and see if I can find anything else out about Knut.'

'I think there might be more than just him, though,' said Agmunder. 'He came over in a large boat, with a sail, that looked far too heavy for one man to launch.'

'We'll have to be careful, then.'

Lars seemed keen to end this stranger's *settlement* right there and then. Agmunder calmed him and promised to be ready in three day's time, when they both could relax the farms a few days and attend to *neighbourly business*.

This seemed to both calm and cheer Lars. Agmunder wondered if there was more to this man than he knew.

They said their goodbyes and both set off on their opposite journeys. Agmunder arrived home in time for the evening meal. After eating and before darkness made it difficult to follow his plan, he set out the bags of barley and beans for the next trip to market, making sure they were safely under cover in case of a shower.

The next morning, his belly full of home baked barley-bread and fried eggs, he set off for Garstang at first light. The horse made good going on the track despite the recent rain. The hard ground had resisted the penetration of the water into the topsoil to make the going tougher. The trip was good and the prices fair. He returned to the farm happy and worn out with a full purse and more than enough silver pennies to pay the taxes in September. Add to that the year's supply of barley and beans stored at the farm for the family's needs, and the plentiful number of rabbits and boars in the woods, and Agmunder should have been very content.

However, in his heart, he knew that he would not rest soundly until the problem of Knut was solved. He topped the rise approaching the farm to see Knut's boat on the pool, square rigged with a distinctive yellow and red striped sail billowing in the breeze as it made good speed away from Agmunder's Ness. Thankfully, for now at least, the boat was making its way toward the river and heading downstream. The worrying bit was that there were clearly three men in it.

Arriving home, Agmunder encouraged Erik to make Fjord bark and bark. He thought it would remind Knut that there were sharp teeth waiting their next visit. The men, annoyingly, just waved at them while the boat sailed out of the Skiff Pool to be hidden by the cover of the thick, hawthorn hedge. Agmunder's mind was troubled. He was happy that they had seemingly gone, but worried that they couldn't be seen even as close as they were. *They could put to shore where they are and be here in minutes, unseen by cover of the brambles and hawthorns that line the river to the north*, he thought. He dismounted, patted the horse and let him eat of the beanstalks and grass in the fallow field. The horse was grateful for the rest.

'They showed up half an hour ago and sailed up and down for a bit. They'd just turned and headed for the river when you arrived,' said Svala with an arm round Erik's shoulders.

'We will worry about those crooks when we've finished looking at this!' said Agmunder in a loud voice, producing the bulging purse of silver coins and emptying the contents onto a canvas he'd spread on the ground between them. Even Knut's proximity couldn't dampen his happy mood at securing another year's advancement of the farm.

'There's enough here to buy all we need for ourselves, and build up the house with stout beams and plaster walls,' he said, smiling.

'I can help with the house, Father,' said Erik.

'Yes, and with your mother's bread and our meat we will live well in this new land.'

Svala knew that he hadn't forgotten about Knut. She was happy about being secure and that the farm had paid off so quickly, but also she knew that great danger lay ahead for the family. Confrontations had a nasty habit of leaving one family or another bereft. She hoped it wasn't going to be hers.

Agmunder was trying to be positive, when he said to Erik, 'You see how easy it is? When you're a little older, you and your mum could run this farm alone if needed!'

'I hope that never comes to pass, husband,' said Svala, upset at the thought.

Agmunder hugged his wife, guilty of the statement he had just made. He realised that Svala, just like him, was thinking of Knut and the future.

'I've dug a pit in the corner of the house, covered with a thick board. I will divide the money into savings and spending. The spending I will keep in my purse and the saving I will stow in the secret hole. Tell no-one of its location. Don't let on we've had a good first year. If people get to know we have money they'll be sniffing round whenever I'm away,' warned Agmunder.

Svala cheered up a little at this last statement, 'We have money!' she whispered.

'I know we brought lots of Norse silver with us, enough for a decade of lowly living, but this harvest shows that we can live this life and prosper,' said Agmunder to his wife. 'Our wealth has gone up ten percent with those trips to market. I *can* build an empire!'

'Do we have to call you Emperor now?' joked Svala, getting ready to make lunch.

'No, not now. But soon, sweetheart,' said Agmunder, showing a big grin as he, with Erik's help, started to divide the money into two piles on the sheet.

There was a shouted greeting from the yard. Agmunder quickly threw the cover over the piles of money and stood. He drew his dagger and moved to the flap of the house door. He sheathed the dagger before going outside.

'Lars! Greetings, welcome, welcome. Good harvest?'

'One of the best, Agmunder. You?'

'Our very best to date!'

They both laughed as they sat on a log overlooking the Skiff Pool where Lars' skiff sat beached next to Waverider on the muddy sand, the dogs bouncing about in happy company.

'News, I have. Of Knut,' said Lars, gravely.

'He was on the Pool earlier, in his boat. There were two other men with him. They paraded up and down a bit, then sailed downstream.'

'Really? What a rascal,' Lars shifted in his position before continuing, 'I asked about in Garstang, at the market and at the inn. One of Knut's men had been in town drinking plenty in the Dogtooth Arms.'

'I know the Inn,' acknowledged Agmunder.

'Well, he got drunk and told the tale about his great master, Knut. It seems that the tale he told you about coming here was mostly lies. He *is* Knut Husasson. Knut's father was the founder of the village they were stranded in on the north coast of Iceland. They got shipwrecked, that's true enough, but it wasn't a peaceful existence. Rivalries and Knut's thirst for advancement made for a rough time. Just one day before the Danish ship arrived that saved them being forever stuck in that lonely rock, Knut killed his father, Husa, in a simple argument over responsibilities. He had followers, but not enough and when the Viking ship arrived the next day the people of Huisavik exiled Knut and his four faithful followers. They put them in a boat they hoped wouldn't make the journey and sent them to sea. Apparently, they were heading for Ireland but a persistent strong westerly blew them into this bay and they found shelter on the north coast of the Fylde, as you know.'

'So, he *is* a murderer as well as a liar and cheat!' said Agmunder, not admitting to being impressed by this feat of navigation in such a small craft.

Lars continued, 'He had some money about him and they aren't short of a few pennies, apparently. The man didn't say how they intend to make a living, but the impression the people at the inn got wasn't good.'

Agmunder rubbed his chin, 'There are five of them, then. More than two to one. Not good odds, Lars.'

'No, I agree. We need to recruit three or four men at arms, minimum. I know we can afford a small war-band to tackle this problem. We'll ask in Garstang for volunteers. They know he's a murderer, I'm sure there is enough unrest about Knut's presence to get a few worthy volunteers at a penny each.'

'Count me in. I will pay a penny a man too,' said Agmunder, gazing across the water to the smoke rising from the woods slightly to the north.

'I don't do this rashly, my friend,' said Lars, putting a hand on Agmunder's forearm.

'Neither do I, but we can't allow such a man to threaten our farms and families,' agreed the Viking-Farmer.

They spoke about Agmunder's plans for his farm and the market prices they had got in Garstang. They ate lunch when it arrived and Lars spoke with Svala and Erik about how they were enjoying the farming life. Neither Lars nor Agmunder mentioned their plan to eliminate the threat of Knut in front of his family. When it came time for Lars to leave he called his dog and Erik helped to re-float his skiff. There had been no sign of Knut's boat and Lars was soon a dot on the far river rounding the corner out of sight. Agmunder thought about the rapids that Lars had to fight his way past shortly, *Rather you than me my friend.*

CHAPTER 5

War-Band

There is seldom any rest on a farm and Agmunder's farm was no exception. After breakfast, just as Erik was looking at the field and thinking of riding the horse, his father announced, 'We're sowing the rye today, son.'

They got the rye seeds from the barrel in the reserve store and Erik set about scattering them across the winter crop field. The goat watched as it ate something it had found blowing across its patch. Agmunder led the horse to the winter field and lashed the harrow to its neck so that it could be pulled up and down the field by the horse. He loaded some small logs onto the harrow to weight it into the soil. With such a weight on it he could not have moved it an inch, but the horse could pull this slight load all day. Agmunder worried that the horse might fret about the weight and not take to pulling, but he needn't have. The horse seemed to enjoy the sensation and pulled the harrow in long straight lines, burying the seeds much quicker and better than Agmunder's man-powered efforts had done in the spring. By the late afternoon the left half of the field was sown with rye for the winter harvest. Agmunder went to his supper a pleased man.

After a wonderful meal of barley-bread, cheese, boiled eggs and the remainder of the rabbit stew that had been their lunch and supper for three days, Agmunder lay on his bed, thinking. The sowing date for the rest of the rye wasn't set in stone. He could delay by as much as a week or even two, given the unusually warm weather. That would also give them a staggered harvest in the colder weather of late March, early April. The more he thought about it, the more he liked the idea.

What that *really* meant, of course, was that he could leave sowing the second half of the winter crop until after he got back from sorting out Knut. For the first time in a week, he slept soundly.

Morning would have put paid to planting anyway, the rain came down heavily from a leaden sky. The wind rose steadily throughout the morning and by lunchtime Agmunder had to brave the squall to anchor the flaps of the house with larger rocks. He returned, wet and bedraggled, to the warmth of the family dwelling's interior room.

'When I return, I will begin to make this house a permanent dwelling, with proper walls and a roof that doesn't flap and bang in the wind,' he promised his family as the sat near the fire in the hearth.

Fjord looked outside at the rain, he hadn't seen such a downpour in his short life and looked as though he thought the whole world was coming to an end. Erik comforted him and together they watched the winter crop get its first watering. Agmunder was displeased that his plan to get on was being held back, but as the rain began to ease the Viking seaman in him could see the clouds in the west lightening, even through the rain.

'I'm going to ready the horse when the rain eases a little more. I think it will be over soon. Look, the wind is dropping.'

'Why don't we have a name for the horse, Father?'

'Would you like him to have a name?'

'We have a name for Fjord,' was the considered answer, but didn't answer the question.

Svala voiced an opinion, 'I think, because we have had such a warm and dry summer here, that we should call him Alsvior.'

'I've heard that name,' said Erik, screwing his eyes up like he was trying to remember.

'It's the name of one of the two horses that pull Sunne's chariot across the sky each day. The other horse is called Arvakr, but as a girl I always imagined I was Alsvior,' said Svala, with a slight nostalgic smile for her childhood in Norway.

'Alsvior, it is!' cheered Agmunder, glad that his departure hadn't saddened the family.

The rain eased over the next few minutes until, by the time Agmunder was mounted up and ready to head off to Lars' farm, the sun was thinking about showing its face between ever thinning clouds.

'See,' said Svala, 'Sunne is pleased with your horse!'

'I am pleased with my horse, too,' said Agmunder patting Alsvior's neck, thinking of how hard he worked with the harrow without complaint.

He added, 'If we get such good luck when we name our animals, I expect you to have a good name for the goat when I return.' And with that he kicked his heels and the horse trotted off down the path that afforded Agmunder a view of the winter field as he left the farm.

It was a strange journey to Lars' smallholding. Although it was early evening it seemed to be getting lighter as the clouds got thinner and thinner. About half a mile from the track that led to Lars, the overcast broke and a rainbow decorated the sky in front of him as he headed east. To Agmunder this represented 'the Bifrost', a bridge that connects Midgard, the earth, to Asgard, a region of the afterlife. The Bifrost could only be used by the gods and those killed in battle. It's what made the Vikings such a deadly foe: the belief that the *only* way to get to heaven and see your ancestors, was to die valiantly in battle. He regarded it warily as he rode onward, wondering if he was being shown the bridge because he was going to have use of it shortly himself, or, if it was to encourage him that Asgard was getting ready to receive Knut and his men. Either way, ill omen or not, it sat uncomfortably with him that he had to ride towards it to get to Lars. The heavenly bridge had all but gone as he arrived at what he thought of as *Lars' breck*, the break in the thick bushes that led to his friend's farmstead. He tied his horse, Alsvior, to a hitching post and shouted for attention. As usual, Lars was elsewhere but near by. A voice came out of the woods, 'Hei, hei.'

Lars emerged from the woods having finished doing whatever it was that the big Dane got up to in the woods and said, 'I didn't expect you for another three days, my friend.'

They shook hands in greeting.

'I have rye to plant. It can wait. I have a killer to run down. That, can't.'

'Well, you know you can rely on my support. My winter crop is sown already. When would you like to go?'

Agmunder could tell the Dane was sincere, he meant, *'Do you want to go right now? I'm ready.'*

'The rain will soak in over night and maybe the track will be better in the morning,' said Agmunder.

They sat, looking over the river, talking through the plan until the stars were shining brightly above the trees on the opposite bank of the Wyre. Polaris, the guardian of the seafarer hung directly over Knut's smoke. Agmunder was troubled again... What did that mean? Would it protect him or hinder his progress? They had an early start and so were both asleep long before midnight. The dog, Skjolder, kept an alert watch until the owls had stopped calling and there were no more sounds in the woods that closed off the small farm.

The morning dawned dull, but dry and Skjolder went off to do whatever he did after making enough noise that the men were awake before he left. Breakfast at Lars' farm involved fried fish and rye bread. Agmunder, chewing the tasty bread, spread with dripping, thought, *Svala's bread is as tasty as this is.*

'Let's mount up. We're not going to find any fyrdmen sitting here.' said Lars.

The *fyrd,* pronounced 'feared', were free-men who were contracted to fight for a cause in 'official' action. An action, such as a battle, sanctioned by the Lord of the county. Often fighting on behalf of the king, fyrdmen were well paid for risking their lives in civic duty. Anyone who could pay, could apply to raise the fyrd, as long as they registered their intent and grievance with the local council. Luckily, it was a quick process, often taking less than a day for a number of men-at-arms, fewer than a dozen, to be authorised and assembled.

They got the horses ready for riding and set off up the track. As they left the trees and took the path towards Garstang, Skjolder came running out of the woods behind them. Lars pulled up and said to the dog, 'No, boy. Stay. Go home.'

Agmunder was amazed that the dog somehow looked disappointed and turned to trot off back to the farm. He'd never seen a dog obey a spoken command so perfectly. There were hidden depths to Lars.

They made good time and were tying up the horses outside the Dogtooth Arms before two hours had passed. They entered and passed the time of day with the landlord of the inn, before heading off to the council building. If you wanted to raise a militia and hunt a fugitive, even a murderer, you had to have official permission. So, in a short time, Agmunder found himself in the council building staring at three familiar weathered faces.

'State your business,' said weasel face, showing no signs of recognising the memorable Viking, or the well known Dane.

Lars spoke, 'We want to raise the fyrd to rid the area of Knut Husasson, a murderer and exile from the Norse-lands. He has made threats to Agmunder's farm and family, even entering the building without permission. He has brought four of his followers and we believe that his presence in the locality will only bring trouble. We seek permission to hunt him down as a criminal, murderer, liar and braggart.'

Weasel face considered this for a few moments then answered, 'You cannot expect to be allowed to hunt down a man because you don't like the look of him. He hasn't murdered anyone in this land and he has not done anything beyond trespass as far as I can see. I do not think your application should be passed.'

The second man spoke, 'I appreciate that he has murdered,'

'His father...' said Agmunder.

'But, I... his father? Oh, er, yes. I... Well, I appreciate that he has murdered, as you say, his father. But, as my colleague has stated, you will need more than *possible* future trouble before we can allow him to be declared an official wanted man.'

The third man at the table joined in, 'It's just not enough, gentlemen. We understand your worries, believe me, but we have to follow the law, you see? He could turn out to be wronged in slander. Is there anything else that you think we should consider in this matter?'

Agmunder answered, 'He said he had absolutely no intention of paying taxes or registering his house. Apparently, what's his is his and no-one will ever have a penny of it.'

That did the trick. Within twenty minutes three men left the building with a signed document that allowed them to raise the fyrd to the strength of ten men. It stipulated that the fyrdmen had to be paid a silver penny per day of service or part thereof. It was signed by the three officials on behalf of the Lord of the county in Lancaster. The charge was '*failure to register for, or pay, due taxes on land, crops and property, and the matter of murder*'.

Agmunder, the council's official scribe, Martin Crookes, and Lars took their document to the town centre stocks where a small crowd was gathered to taunt a minor criminal that had been locked in the wooden device for some small matter. Agmunder took to the steps amid wary glances from the townspeople gathered in the square.

'We are here to raise the fyrd.'

The crowd stopped talking almost as one, this was an important announcement.

'We are hunting the criminal and murderer... and evil tax evader,' he smiled at Lars, 'Knut Husasson. His men have been drinking in Garstang and I think you all have reservations about having someone like that, with such a terrible crime hanging round his neck and his associates, living locally. He has been exiled from his own father's town by his family and the town officials. Since coming to the Fylde he has threatened families and property. He has taken what was not offered. He has entered property without being asked. He has broken promises under oath. In the past he has killed his own father.' This last raised a gasp from those gathered to listen. 'And, he had refused to pay his taxes to your council for the benefit of this law-abiding happy community.'

Lars took up the role of speaker, 'We are looking for eight men-at-arms to help us run him down. Knut has been added to the '*fugitive murderers*' list.'

Being added to this list meant that it was legal to kill him on sight and unprovoked. Lars knew that mentioning this fact would bolster the volunteer numbers. No-one wants to have to try to *capture* a dangerous man, better to finish him off and have no more to-do.

There were five men that came forwards immediately. A good result. Lars had thought they would have to repeat the offer at several locations.

'Lucky for us that that poor soul had stolen an apple!' he said to Agmunder, nodding at the wretch in the stocks, as he pressed another silver penny into the hand of a volunteer called, Matthew Pilling.

The names of the volunteers were all added on an official parchment list, by Martin, the council official presiding. They were dismissed to gather their weapons and armour and whatever else they would need to bring. They were told to report for the fyrd-muster at dawn the next day in the square. Agmunder and Lars went back to the inn to try their luck there. They only needed another three men. As they entered the place, humming with conversation, it went very quiet.

Agmunder saw a man at the table in the corner who was looking at him as if he'd killed his dog. The man got up and started across the floor towards the two.

'Vikings can get out!' he shouted.

'We're locals,' suggested Agmunder, 'We live here.'

'Wherever it is you live, Viking, you're not welcome,' said the man, stopping a safe distance from the war axe hanging from Agmunder's shoulder.

'Actually,' said Lars, 'It's about exactly that sort of thing that we've come to speak to you all.'

'Yes,' said Agmunder, 'We are raising fyrdmen to battle the murderer, thief, trespasser, *Viking* and cheat, Knut Husasson, and his men. Here's your chance to get rid of five Vikings, for good.'

'Why should we help you?' came a different voice from the back.

Lars fielded the question, 'Because we already have five of the good people of Garstang helping us, and if you don't sign up, you'll be letting them down. You don't have to do it for civic duty or pride, you can join us for the money. We are bound by the contract to pay a silver penny a day per man, but, Agmunder here, he says he will also pay a penny to get this man away from his farm and young family.'

The loud mouth sat back down as four or five men came forward at the thought of two pence a day. Lars had his choice of fyrdmen. Agmunder thought that it would be a quick process, but Lars took nearly half an hour to interview the volunteers and eventually settled on three of the men. He sent them to prepare and told them where and when the muster was. After that, they had a night to spend in Garstang, and made enquiries about a room. They had a room each at the Dogtooth Arms and slept well, knowing that they were finally going to sort out the threat of Knut.

CHAPTER 6

Military Action

When they rose, before dawn, they took special care to get securely dressed. They didn't want loose clothing when there might be some fighting going on. They met downstairs in the inn and, after paying the landlord for their stay, left to meet the men-at-arms in the square.

The day was bright and warming up already. The cloud cover dissipating to leave a blue sky and clear. They rounded the corner and saw the group of armed men by the stocks being watched wearily by the latest petty criminal to be immobilised in the wooden contraption. As the Norsemen approached, the fyrd assembled themselves into two rows of four, standing shoulder to shoulder, under the direction of a big man with a halberd, a kind of flat bladed spear with a hook.

The man said, 'Fyrd present and ready.'

'What is your name?' asked Lars.

'John of Kirkham,' said the soldier.

'Then, John, you shall be our captain. Men, this is your captain.'

'We will go presently to the house of Knut, the murderer. When there, we will bring him and his followers to justice and rid the Fylde of their menacing presence,' said Agmunder to the group.

The two leaders mounted up on their horses and led the troops out of the square to the north. A little way up the river, at the top end of the town to the north, was a bridge over the Wyre, suitable for horses, that led to a lane. The lane wasn't well travelled after the first half mile, but it was better than travelling across country and it led in the right direction, at least. It was lined with bushes and trees and, for the first two miles, the soldiers were at least partly hidden from casual view as they made their way through the sunny countryside. Before the sun was half way up the sky, they were in the vicinity of Knut's house. Agmunder held his hand up to stop the march and dismounted Alsvior.

'Lars and I will go on foot from here. Have a short break. Then we move in.'

'Have a break lads,' said Captain Kirkham, 'Be quiet. Ten minutes.'

The men sat or squatted and got out a bite to eat. One went off into the woods, presumably for the toilet. Agmunder and Lars stood at the end of the tree-line, looking across the slight dip toward the smoke issuing from the tree tops opposite and half a mile ahead.

'Let's hope that smoke means Knut is home,' said Lars.

'Someone is, and whether it's Knut or not, that will reduce their number,' answered Agmunder.

After a while, 'Get ready to stand to,' said John to the men, quietly as he stood. The men, including the man who had now returned from the woods, packed away their things and lined up behind John of Kirkham.

Agmunder addressed the men, 'Lars will take the left side approach with four men, including John. I will take the right approach with the rest. All persons at this house are criminal and are covered under the warrant.'

He didn't need to say more. The men knew that whoever was at the house was under sentence of death. The captain separated the men into two groups. Lars and Agmunder trusted that he'd done so to give equal experience and fighting power to each group, he knew these men better than either of the Norsemen.

Agmunder nodded to Lars, who smiled back. The two groups started their approaches to the house. At first they were just heading towards the smoke but after just three hundred or so yards, Agmunder could see the house through the trees. There had been a lot more work done since he was last there and it looked quite impressive with stout beams and white walls. As he got nearer, Agmunder found he could no longer see or hear Lars' group and knew he simply had to hope they would be on time at the other end of the house. As they neared the property he could see that there was no dog to raise the alarm. In the deserted yard were some building materials and a few chickens scratching about for something to eat. There was a goat, tied up by a patch of short grass, but no horse, and no people to be seen. Agmunder hoped they weren't, at this moment, terrorizing his family. Then, there was a noise from the house and he and his three soldiers halted, listening in woodland silence. Beyond the tweet of birds and the rustle of leaves in the breeze, there was the sound of conversation inside the house, getting louder. The door suddenly opened and a man came out calling over his shoulder, 'Knut will be back soon with the others, we need to...' He stopped as he turned and saw Agmunder and his men. It was immediately obvious that they weren't on a social call. His eyes went wide and darted about as he thought quickly. Given how close he was to the door the obvious thing to do was get back inside the house, but Agmunder's men had thought of that. With a professional class throw, a spear thudded into the door-frame at waist height, blocking the doorway and making a quick bolt for cover impossible. The next spear took the man down as he stood looking at the barred doorway and he didn't move again.

He hadn't shouted any warning. The men were pleased. Agmunder estimated that there could as many as two in the house. If Knut had someone with him, that could be one or two people. The soldier quietly eased the spear from the door frame just seconds before another man showed himself. He came out of the door as the soldier stood back, unseen behind the corner of the house with his spear ready. Knut's man slowed his step as he concentrated on the three men in the yard in front of him. He especially watched Agmunder, who slowly drew his dagger to keep the man's mind in front of him.

'What do *you* want?' the man spat at the Viking.

'We have come to rid the Fylde of that rascal, Knut.'

'Well, you won't find him here. He's gone to pay his respects to the Lord of Lancaster.'

Agmunder pointed at the fallen man with his dagger, 'Your friend here just told you that Knut was due back soon. Weren't you listening?'

Turning to his men, Agmunder said, 'He's another liar, lads.'

The men nodded agreement as the guard pulled out a seax, a long knife that gave the Saxons their name, ready to take on the three men he faced. He bent slightly to threaten them and threw his arm wide in a slashing motion, ready to take them all on. He still hadn't noticed the soldier, standing quietly with the spear at the ready, behind him. A quick thrust from behind, and it was all over at the house. Lars and his men came along the side of the building and into the yard.

'It looks like we missed it, lads!' said Lars.

'There is one or two with Knut. They're due back this morning,' said Agmunder.

'Shall we wait here? Surprise him at his own house?'

'Captain Kirkham, take two men and secure gold and silver and other valuable items for the council spoils,' commanded Lars, aware of their obligations under the warrant.

As they entered the house to await Knut, and rummage through his valuables, they saw the door at the other end of the building slowly closing. One of the men ran through the house to investigate this strange occurrence and saw a man running up the track and veering to the right. The soldier gave a shout and four of the party ran through the house and out into the yard in pursuit of the fugitive.

'I'll fetch the horses,' shouted Agmunder as Lars took chase with two others, up the path into the woods to the north of the house. Agmunder ran back round the house, jumped over the body of the first of Knut's dead henchmen, and pushed through the bushes in a direct line to where they had tied the animals to a tree stump. Quickly untying them both he mounted the nearest, luckily his own, Alsvior, and led the other. They made good time returning to the back of the house and took the path northward. Having to bow low on the horse to pass under several branches he was still quicker than the other men and caught them up as they were closing on Knut's fleeing accomplice.

The man was a quick runner and had evaded their best efforts for an impressive distance. He had broken into an open space and despite the risk of slowing down, dutifully waved a warning to his master, who was riding towards them with just one more man. As Agmunder rode into the opening he saw Knut reign in his horse, wheel about and gallop off north up the track. The second man jumped from his horse and prepared to fight in a delaying move. Agmunder drew up by Lars and handed him the reigns of his horse.

'See to this man. Knut is mine!'

He heeled his mount and sped off in pursuit of Knut, who was easily a quarter of a mile ahead already. He saw the horse with rider crest a slight ridge in the distance and wondered where he was headed as he continued the chase. The ground at this point was perfect for riding and without obstacles to give the horse problems as they entered the open space Knut had spoken of. It was a fast ride up county with the river Wyre to the west for a change. The problem was that Knut had exactly the same easy ride and it wasn't going to be a simple matter to catch him. Agmunder's horse wasn't a very fast animal, having been picked for stamina and strength, but Knut's horse had been ridden all morning, probably from the place Knut was headed. They were approximately equal, but Knut still had the lead. Agmunder worried that he might miss him completely, if Knut had his boat ready on the northern coast, and tried to get every ounce of speed out of Alsvior.

'Run, Alsvior. On, on!' he urged.

Soon it was obvious that Knut had managed to escape for now, and worse he knew that Agmunder was after him. He would be careful not to leave a trail and would not build a fire to eat later. Agmunder slowed his horse to a walk, keen not to miss any clue to where Knut had gone. The sun was starting to drop towards the horizon as Agmunder found the north coast. It was windswept with a muddy beach going out for miles and miles. He rode to the top of a grass tufted dune and looked east and west along the coastline and studied the sands. Nothing. He was heartened by the fact that the tide was out. That meant that he would easily see any attempt to launch a boat. He looked at the dropping sun. He had a decision to make. Head east toward the hills and the road to Lancaster, which is where Knut had supposedly been, or, assume that everything those braggarts had said was lies and head west toward the Wyre estuary into the glare of the setting sun.

'West it is, Alsvior,' he said pulling on the left reign and heeling the animal onwards.

They continued at a walk. No need to tire the animal completely. If he saw Knut he might need to gallop again. The sun was warm and the day bright, though the wind was picking up. The sea shone like silver to the horizon. Agmunder noted an island on the edge of visibility, just the top of a mountain or two showing and wondered if it was inhabited.

Such a clear day. I'll be at the river in just a few minutes, he was thinking, when there was a shout. Not the sort of shout when someone is trying to get your attention, but the involuntary one given by someone exerting themselves in extreme physical activity. Agmunder barely had time to react when the form of Knut, who had launched himself from the slope of a dune, barrelled into him and both men went sprawling to the ground. Agmunder was slightly winded, after landing on his back in long grass, and couldn't get his axe unslung before the figure of Knut was rushing at him again, this time with dagger drawn. Agmunder rolled and tried to run up the little hill to gain advantage of height, still struggling to unhook his axe's leash from his arm. Knut was very close behind as Agmunder slipped and scrambled over slippery shingle and stones to top the rise. At the very moment he expected to feel the hands of the murderer on him and feel the steel of his dagger, he heard a muffled cry, 'Agh!' He glanced back to see that Knut too had fallen on the slippery ground. Agmunder wasn't sure he had the advantage but couldn't see any option but to fight, the foe was so close, retreat wasn't a plan he could go with.

The Viking finally managed to unsling the axe and held it in both hands high above his head, the most intimidating stance and the most forceful attack. Knut stopped trying to climb the slope, seeing that Agmunder was now in a state of readiness. He got to his feet but kept his distance.

The two stood, eyeing each other, chests heaving hard with the recent exertion. Sweat running down both their brows in the warm, late summer evening.

'What is this?' asked Knut, holding his arms out in a questioning manner.

'I came to this land to farm peacefully. I won't let you threaten that peace.'

'I did you no harm.' said Knut.

'You do me harm by your presence. You offended your father in his own town and you offend this land.'

'Enough talking, Agmunder,' shouted Knut, moving closer.

Agmunder checked his stance. He wasn't going to move. He was going to make Knut come to him. He had the slight advantage of height and Knut was on the loose ground. He assessed the situation as Knut did the same. Knut's dagger was small and didn't have the reach or the weight of Agmunder's war axe. They could stand here all day, or Knut could lose the fight. And the choice, was Knut's to make.

'Look,' Knut said eventually, 'I have gold and silver aplenty. Let me buy my freedom. I will sail away and you won't have to worry.'

Agmunder appeared to think about this proposal, 'But you'll be free to return any time you wish. I can't allow my family to be threatened by your possible return. Besides, your wealth is already the property of Garstang council, by order of the warrant.'

Knut's face seemed to lose some of its colour as he realised that his life was over as he knew it, whatever happened.

Agmunder noted that as he spoke, Knut was shifting slowly to his right. Slowly putting the lowering sun directly behind him, making him a little more difficult to look at, and also more on the same level as Agmunder. Agmunder, in retaliation, took a step backwards, which was slightly higher up the hill and on the exact highest point. He noted that Knut now had to cross a little more space but had a slightly flatter run if he rushed him. He could see Knut's brain working hard, the sweat running down his cheeks from his brow. This move and counter-move seemed, to Agmunder, like that game he'd seen played in the Moorish south of Iberia, chess. Agmunder shifted his war axe into his right hand and drew his own dagger with his left. Agmunder now not only had a bigger, heavier weapon but also more attack options. He held the high ground and had the measure of his opponent's plan.

'Your only chance is to run, Knut. I've got you covered. We can't stand here all night, and when you make a move it's all over for you and then I'll go home and you will be using the Bifrost bridge. I saw it yesterday, it's waiting for *you*.'

'If I run you'll kill me anyway. At least like this I have a chance.'

Agmunder shook his head slowly, 'You don't even have that, Knut.'

He decided to use the advantage of surprise over that of height and position. He waited until Knut opened his mouth to speak, taking advantage of the shock value of interrupting, and launched himself down the hill. There was just three yards of separation. As he ran the short distance he swung the war axe low and back up making a complete circle, the blade coming down in a shining arc, just as he reached striking range. Knut, taken by surprise, somewhere in the back of his mind amazed that Agmunder would give up his place of superiority, could only try to defend against the weight and speed of the war axe as the Viking came crashing down the slope. Knut held up his arm in instinctive defence as he brought the dagger in from its position held out to the right. He lost the defensive arm to the first swing of the axe as his dagger got snagged in the back of Agmunder's heavy, woollen jacket. The blade pierced the woollen top coat had missed Agmunder's body by an inch. There was an anguished yell as Knut fell to the ground and slid slowly down the slippery shale, clutching the bleeding stump of his severed limb. Agmunder was quick to act. To a Viking, an enemy who had a lingering death could claim back some measure of pride in the afterlife. He quickly reduced the distance between him and Knut and, with a yell of 'For peace!', buried the war axe in the murderer's chest, killing him instantly. Agmunder stood over his defeated foe, his own chest still heaving from exertion, his enemy's still, bloody and broken.

'If it's peace you seek, I can help. Will you allow me to give the poor soul a Christian burial?' came a voice on the wind from not far away.

Agmunder turned around quickly to see an old man in a monk's habit.

'I am Brother Jacob, I live on this estuary in solitude and reflection. Daily, I try to live by God's example and pray for my fellow man. Allow me to bury this man and tend his grave as a charitable deed.'

'Brother Jacob,' said Agmunder, addressing the monk with respect, 'I have killed this man under warrant from Garstang. He was a liar, thief and a murderer. If you see fit to honour such a man, I say I will never understand your faith. But, if that is your wish. Please do. I have no use for this body. Save this.'

Agmunder bent and picked up Knut's severed forearm, a recognisable ring on the index finger of its hand.

'What is this man's name, that I can fashion a headstone to remember him by.'

'This was Knut Husasson, who met his end, a criminal.'

'Then this spot will be known as Knut's End.'

Agmunder regarded the monk, 'As you wish, Brother Jacob.'

The Viking mounted his horse and went in search of Knut's horse, another prize for the Garstang council.

That night Agmunder slept under the stars with a huge weight lifted from his life. He felt free and at peace once again. He knew that in the morning he had to try to find Lars and the others, and return the spoils to Garstang before he could think of going home. But, how good it felt to think of home and Svala and Erik, and even the chickens and the blessed goat. His family home, on Agmunder's Ness. The night passed peacefully and Agmunder had a dreamless sleep.

CHAPTER 7
The Return

When he awoke the next morning, shortly after dawn, he got the horses ready for the trip back to Garstang without making breakfast. He set off, heading east along the coast, looking to his right every now and then, searching for the track he had ridden up on. Eventually he saw it and turned south. Riding slowly he soon found himself in the woods that led to Knut's house. As he drew inside calling distance, he heard a welcome shout from the yard. He saw Lars' horse before he saw the man.

'Hei hei, Lars!'

'Hei, my friend, well met.'

'I got him,' said Agmunder, holding the forearm up for his friend to see.

'You have his horse,' nodded Lars.

'There's a monk up there who's going to bury him and tend his grave!'

'This world is a funny place, Agmunder. We cannot forgive him, nor can the law, but some religious types, it's what gets them through the day,' he smiled.

'This place looks deserted, Lars.'

'I sent the men back this morning with the spoils. I decided to wait for you. We can catch them up. They're walking.'

They rode for an hour and a half. Agmunder told Lars the story of the chase and the stand off. Lars told the Viking how the fight had gone with the last remaining soul of Knut's men, a Saxon bully, recruited from a village near Glasson. Both were happy that this quest had come to such a satisfactory end.

'And all with nary a man lost!' said Lars, in his colloquial manner.

As the band of ten rode and walked into the town square there was much merriment. The townspeople had appeared a little indifferent when asked to help, two days ago, but it seemed that they were truly grateful for the removal of the unsociable murderer, Knut. Even the men of the council ventured outside of their municipal building to thank the war-band and officially disband them in a small ceremony. The ceremony included the bit the soldiers had waited for since signing up. Payment. Both Lars and Agmunder paid the men a penny each for each day's service, and under the laws of the fyrd that meant from the minute they signed up. Three days at tuppence a day! Each man felt wealthy as they cheerfully accepted sixpence each.

The man with the biggest smile was the landlord of the Dogtooth Arms, who knew exactly where most of that money would end up. They presented the council with Knut's horse, his goat, three chickens, all the weapons found at the house and seventy two silver coins and five gold coins from the stash at the house. Ten percent of the gold and silver coins were allowed to be kept by Agmunder, who shared equally with Lars. They asked about delivering Knut's boat. There were some questions about type and size and it was agreed that, as a thank you, Agmunder could keep it. Lars was pleased with that decision. Finally, and a surprise to all, Agmunder was awarded the status of *Thane of the Fylde*. An honorary title, they stressed, but one that conveyed upon him a status of an honoured person for the service he had done society in ridding them of Knut.

The council men were also keen to point out that there would be no pension, no extra lands, no reduction in taxes and no monetary reward beyond the ten percent already given. The two friends were, nevertheless, over the moon that Agmunder's action had been officially recognised. He had been officially recognised for a service to society in a country that Agmunder, certainly, and Lars, suspected, regarded them as outcasts and dangerous aliens. Agmunder couldn't wait to get back to his farm to tell Svala and Erik, that, in name at least, he was now a minor noble and they had taken an important step towards the peaceful existence they came here to find.

The Thane and his friend had a meal in the inn with the celebrating ex-war - band. Then, after many goodbyes and promises not to be strangers, which

Agmunder found quite amusing, they mounted up and set off for Lars' smallholding in the woods.

The ride was easy and by now very familiar to Agmunder, who amused Lars by whistling a tune as they rode. Lars had always regarded his friend as a serious man. Perhaps he'd always had this anxiety that was lifted by the recognition of their good deed. Lars understood that Agmunder wanted to get off to see his family and Agmunder left Lars telling the story to his overjoyed dog.

After what seemed like hours, but was less then one, Agmunder could see the house, that required serious improvement if anyone was to believe he was a Thane, appear on the rise before him. He approached quietly so that he would be as close as possible before anyone knew he was there. As he reached the top of the ridge his whole farm lay before him, spread out towards the Skiff Pool. It was a sight for his sore eyes. He noticed that Knut's boat was drawn up on the beach next to Waverider, and wondered what circumstances lead to that. He didn't have to wait long to find out.

'Father!' shouted Erik, as he dropped the fish he was racking and ran as fast as his little legs would carry him, Fjord bounding behind.

'Hei,' shouted Agmunder.

'I got Knut's boat, Father. I took Waverider to where he'd left it and brought Knut's boat back over with mine in tow.'

'Oh, Waverider is *yours* now is it?' laughed Agmunder.

'Well,' said Erik, slightly surprised by the question, 'You can have Knut's boat. You won't need two, will you?'

'I see. That was a dangerous thing to do. Suppose Knut had lived?'

'Then I can't see how stealing his boat would have made anything worse than losing you, Father.'

Agmunder seemed impressed with this considered answer and changed the subject, 'We need a name for the new one. We can't keep calling it Knut's boat, it'll upset your mother.'

Erik helped to settle the horse and then with carrying his father's baggage and weapons. Svala was working in the winter crop field and came as soon as she heard them talking by the house.

'We've missed having you about the place, husband.' she said, almost shyly.

'I will have to improve this place,' said Agmunder, looking around, rubbing his chin in thought.

'Give yourself a minute to rest, good husband.'

'I can't rest, Svala. How can a *Thane of the Fylde* live in a glorified tent?'

Svala and Erik whooped in delight at the story, whilst Agmunder told it, as they ate their evening meal. They listened in rapt attention as they tucked in to some boar steaks Agmunder had brought from Garstang. He skipped the gory details of the fighting but drove home the honour that had been bestowed on their family and farm. Agmunder showed them the eleven silver and gold coins he had been awarded. They sat making plans for how the house would be strengthened and enlarged to one fitting their new status. Agmunder suggested that they hire two labourers to help and was confident that they would have no problem finding willing persons in the town now he was a celebrity. Svala was overjoyed that things had gone so well so far. To be truthful to herself she had thought that they would be outcasts for many years and that farming would return very little in the first few years. Maybe this was destiny and they were on the way up in a meteoric rise. Agmunder's Empire was taking shape, she looked around her, in *name* at least.

The next morning Agmunder took the new boat out for a sail around the Skiff Pool. The winds continued to blow well, though not too hard that he wasn't confident. He thought about trying to visit Lars but the thought of those rapids put him off yet again.

You're a Viking, Agmunder son of Asmunde, Thane of the Fylde. You shouldn't be frightened of anything! He chastised himself, as he tacked toward the north end of the pool, away from the rapids. The boat was good in the water. Stable and fast, as Erik had said. It could be handled by one person, though two would be better. Maybe he needed to look about for an employee, who could double up as builder's help, farm-hand and fisherman's friend. He would think on it. He steered the boat toward the landing ground by the farm and waved at Svala who was by the door. She waved back and went inside as Erik came down to the water's edge to help ground the vessel.

'Have you thought of a name for this boat, Father?' he asked, heaving on a rope to stop the boat floating away while Agmunder jumped ashore.

'I have, son.'

Agmunder bent his strength to the rope with Erik until she was high out of the water. 'I'm going to call her, *Signy*. A Norse name meaning *New Victory*, but also, close to the Latin word Cygnus, a swan.'

'Are we keeping her, then, Father?'

'I don't see why not.'

They set the anchor and walked up to the house together.

Agmunder travelled back to Garstang to source some heavy beams for the corners of his permanent dwelling and to ask about labourers. It turned out that it would be slightly more expensive than he thought to get help, as there was no way they were prepared to travel from Garstang to the farm and back every day. So they would need to live on site for the duration of the build. On the one hand that meant the expense of feeding and sheltering the men, but also it would be completed sooner because they could start earlier and finish later than if the labourers had to travel each day. Agmunder had his lunch and thought about it. He decided that one man would be enough, because he'd always be there, and the work would probably take no more time because of the longer working hours. He engaged a man born locally but of Norse decent by the name of Henrik Gunnerson. Henrik was strong and well built for his seventeen summers. They had a long chat in the afternoon about what Agmunder would expect and they got to know each other quite well in a short time. Henrik had experience of working on large buildings and was dexterous.

Best of all, he had a horse. His father had a farm, out Brunanburh way and gave it to him when he left home two years ago. Henrik was well thought of in Garstang. He was honest and hard working and seemed a personable young man to Agmunder. By noon on the next day they were both back at Agmunder's Ness Farm.

After introductions were made, during which Henrik praised Svala on her looks and her kitchen and then Erik on his sailing and fishing abilities, and Fjord on his teeth, much to Erik's amusement, Agmunder took him outside to look over the work he had planned.

'The beams will arrive in two days, by wagon from Garstang. They will help us unload, then we're on our own. I have tools enough and lifting equipment. Between us we will soon have a proper dwelling erected here,' he said finishing with his arms held out in front of himself pointing to an area along side the current house.

'So, you planning to add to the current house?' asked Henrik.

'Yes. Once we have the new house watertight we can move into it and make the canvas house more substantial too. I plan to use it for the animals in winter. So we have to build the new house as close as we can to this one,' he said making a cutting action with his hand right next to the bottom beam.

'Is there any point me making a start digging post holes, or will we have to know the size of the beams before I can begin?'

'I don't see why we can't make a start. I hate standing around waiting!'

Over the next two days they excavated four holes about two feet deep and a foot square. They cut smaller holes for the door frames at front and back. They were just finishing the 'safe' hole in the main room when there was a greeting from the hawthorn ridge as a wagon, laden with logs and cut beams, was pulled through by four horses.

'It's a wonder they got that lot through the hawthorns further south,' said Agmunder, genuinely amazed.

'Well, they're here and on time. Which is not always the case, I can assure you, Thane,' said Henrik, as they watched the wagon creak and groan its way the last fifty yards.

The driver and his three mates jumped down from the wagon. The mates started unleashing the cargo as the driver approached Agmunder and Henrik.

'Delivery of rough and sawn beams for Thane Amounder,' he said.

'It's *Agmunder*, but, that's me,' said the Viking.

'Six pence to pay on delivery, my Lord,' said the driver, actually knuckling his forehead to the Viking.

'Here you go,' said Agmunder giving him a purse that contained the right money already prepared for convenience.

The wood was lowered to the ground at the side of the wagon, not too far from where it needed to be. The two looked it over and thought it looked just fine. They said so to the driver who was pleased to hear it. Svala brought ale and bread for the workers as they finished, and after a brief rest, they jumped on the wagon waving and shouting goodbye and the driver cracked his whip and started their journey back to Garstang.

The wood had arrived. Their future house in a pile! There was nothing now to stop Agmunder getting on with starting the permanent building. He knew he still had to finish sowing the other half of the winter rye, but that could wait a week still. They spent the rest of that day moving the beams into the approximate positions they would need to be in before they were stood upright and lowered into the post holes. The two horses were ideal for this work and the two men with their animals soon had the wood laid out. They used a horse to pull a rope through a frame of poles like a capital A to raise the corner beams which neatly slotted into the holes and stood reasonably vertically. They could be adjusted until perfectly vertical with wedges, then the hole filled with small stones and sand packed down. By the end of that day he could envision how large his new permanent house would be.

'Fitting for a Thane,' he said, to no-one in particular.

CHAPTER 8

Late Autumn 781A.D.

There had been great changes in the eight weeks since Agmunder had returned from Garstang, *Thane of the Fylde*. The labourer, Henrik, had helped build the house, a process that took just five weeks. Henrik earned a small bonus by helping Erik with the fishing, while Agmunder sowed the rest of the winter field with Rye, with the help of Svala and Alsvior. Henrik was sorry to leave, but leave he must, because there wasn't anything now for him to do around the farm. So he returned to Garstang, after the building work was finished, but promised he would help in the future with any more projects that came up. He and Agmunder got on very well and he seemed to have a particular fondness for Erik and Erik loved having Henrik helping on the boat when he went fishing.

Now, in the cool of an overcast, mid September day, Agmunder's farm-house was finished. Timber beamed and willow walled, with white plaster and thick, warm, reed thatch atop the roof. Proper, lockable (from inside), front and rear doors of thick oak panels and a brick-built oven and hob in the kitchen. The canvas house had been sympathetically improved and now also sported a beautiful reed thatched roof and white plastered end walls. Inside the main house there was a mezzanine level above the warmth of the kitchen where they would sleep in the winter, warmed by the rising heat from the cooking fire. The animals would be sheltered from the worst of the weather by staying in the old canvas house wing of the 'big house' as they all thought of it.

It was easily the biggest house Agmunder had ever owned and possibly the biggest house Erik had ever seen. There was room to eat and sit and talk by the fire in the main part and plenty of room for Svala to prepare the food. In the days of the canvas house they were constantly moving something to make room for something else, now, they had room aplenty. Fjord seemed pleased that he could sleep near the fire at night without having to wedge himself between the bottom of the bed pallet and the wall.

The first day they woke in the new house, without Henrik there to help finish something off, was no different to any other on the farm. It was a day that Agmunder had something that couldn't wait and that he had to do immediately.

'Today, Erik, I have to ride to town to pay my winter taxes, it's what they call the vernal equinox today and I might as well get it done and out of the way. You can come along, if you'd like.'

'How will I get there, Father?'

'You can ride the goat!'

'Ride Dagny? Really?'

'Of course not, you can ride with me. Alsvior has carried both me and four bags of grain, weighing more than you do, to Garstang before.'

They got ready to go and made sure that Svala would be alright without them for the day. Fjord would stay to keep her safe although he would have preferred to accompany his masters.

There wasn't much to take to Garstang. Only Agmunder, his son and a bag of cash to pay the taxes. But, Agmunder, being a careful man also took his war axe when travelling with his taxes. He was sure there would be braggarts abroad who would like to separate a traveller from his wealth, but Erik couldn't remain on the farm all the time without seeing the wider world, and so they set off after breakfast.

'And this,' said Agmunder, who had been keeping up an almost constant commentary along the way, 'is where you would turn left to go to see Lars.'

'Who on earth would want to see Lars?' shouted a recognisable voice from the track just a short way ahead.

Erik, for one, was very happy to see Lars and jumped down from the horse before Agmunder had even begun to reign him in. He ran to Lars, who had been conspicuous by his absence in the last couple of weeks while both farms tended their crops on top of regular duties. Erik gave Lars a hearty hand shake, and they spoke as Agmunder watched his son.

He's growing up so quickly, he thought, looking at how the two interacted. Lars was pointing things out to Erik and they had a proper discussion about how things were going on the farmstead at Lars' Breck. They accepted an offer of ale and cheese to break their journey and spent a happy hour talking over the past fortnight with the big Dane. Erik stroked Skjolder, Lars' young dog, who loved the attention, while they chatted and nibbled.

There came a point that it became obvious that they had to get going, or they wouldn't be home before it was very dark and so, they said their farewells and Lars returned to whatever it was he was doing with the bushes by the road that passed Lars' Breck.

They rode the track to Garstang and tied the horse up outside the Dogtooth Arms and went in for a quick hello to the landlord.

'Thank you for bringing all that custom to my house, Agmunder. I shan't forget,' beamed the Landlord as they approached the bar, and he seemed genuine in his appreciation.

'It was a pleasure to repay some of your hospitality, a pleasure.'

'Who's this? Your brother? A tenant?'

Agmunder smiled, 'This is Erik, my son.'

'Hello,' said Erik.

'Hello, Erik. So, you've come to see the bustle of Garstang, have you?'

'Father says it will be an education.'

The landlord laughed, 'He's not wrong there, Erik. Mark you stay close to your father. There are still rough boys who think they can pick on strangers. Have a care, Erik.'

'I will, sir.'

After a quick ale and some bread and cheese, they left the horse tied at the inn and walked the short distance to the council building. It had had a new coat of whitewash since Agmunder last saw it. No doubt, paid for with proceeds from the raid on Knut's house. The two walked inside to find two lines of people.

Agmunder asked at the first table and was directed into the shorter of the two queues. They waited in line and eventually they were called forward by Weasel Face.

'Amounder, Thane of the Fylde, nice to see you back, sire.'

'It's *Agmunder*,' said the Viking.

'Not on my document,' said Weasel Face with a smirk, tapping his list.

'I've come to pay my taxes, it's the equinox.'

The man rummaged about in a box and produced a sheet of parchment that looked familiar.

'Here you are. Amounder of Amounder Ness Farm. I shall add 'Thane of the Fylde,' he said, as he dipped his quill in the ink pot. After a few seconds scribbling the indecipherable letters, he announced, 'Your tax bill for the winter will be three quarters of an ounce of silver.'

'That's half again what I had to pay in April. How can that be justified? I won't make as much from the rye.'

'You're a Thane now, Amounder, you can have a tenant who will raise you revenue. You can also claim ten percent of his crop profit too. I would look around if I were you and get someone on your land. It will help.'

'But I farm all my land, I have none to rent out.'

The second of the three men at the table spoke at this point, 'That is not entirely true, Amounder.'

'I am not a liar! I have three fields and the land around my house. I have never claimed more.'

'That is true,' replied the second man with a glance at the third.

'The council, in recognition of the service you did us in ridding the Fylde of the braggart, Knut,' said the third old man, 'voted you three fields worth of land and a plot to build a house. It's all covered in the taxes as my learned colleague stated.'

In traditional manner, Weasel Face spoke next, 'You can allow your tenant to build his own house on the land or *you* can build one for him and rent it to him.

The choice is yours.'

The second added, conspiratorially, 'You'll make a better profit returns if *you* build the house.'

'So,' Agmunder asked, 'I have twice as much land and can have a tenant from whom I can raise rent and a portion of his profits?'

'In a nutshell,' said the third, sticking to protocol.

'Oh, but you, Thane, you have responsibilities. You have to protect him from attack and give him all reasonable assistance to make sure he can pay his rent, that is, make sure he can farm his land. That might, for instance, mean you have to allow him to use your horse to harrow.'

'I see. Then, here's the money,' said Agmunder handing the men his silver pennies to the weight of three quarters of an ounce.'

The first man noted down the transaction on the parchment and the parchment was taken to the stamping table for him as he waited. Thanes don't have to attend the receipt table for themselves. Agmunder was pleased with the day as he left the council building with Erik following on asking all sorts of questions about who the tenant might be and where they might find one that they can trust.

'Isn't it obvious? We'll ask Henrik.'

Erik was so pleased with that suggestion. It had only been a few days but he really missed the young man's company.

'Can we go and ask him right now, father? Do you know where he lives?'

'I do know, Erik. But I think we'll have to think on it a while before we invite anyone. I will have to discuss it with your mother. Not only that, but we have to get back home today. It's getting dark already. We will have to go. But, we will return.'

They returned to Agmunder's Ness after two hours of dark had befallen the Fylde. It was a good thing that Muni shone brightly on the landscape and the track was easily visible now. The Thane talked things over with Svala, who agreed that Henrik would make an excellent tenant, and reminded Agmunder that he had expressed a desire to live in the area after he'd been helping with the house for a week or two.

'He said to me, "I would love to farm out here in the peace and quiet,"' said Svala, remembering the conversation she'd had with the youngster.

'We should ask him, Father,' said Erik, with enthusiasm.

'We'll need to build him a house first. Nothing grand, but suitable for a single man with a possibility that he might take a wife. Wouldn't want to lose a tenant because he couldn't keep a wife in the house we'd built.'

'Will it use up much money, Agmunder?' asked Svala, knowing he didn't have to answer questions about finances.

'We're fine. The new taxes and the house didn't even use up all the money from the harvest. We still have the money we brought and the award from the Knut hunt, too. We have enough to risk building a shilling house for Henrik.

'Where's the land?' asked Svala.

Erik too listened to the answer keen to learn how close his friend was going to be living, if he accepted.

'Just on the south side of the Skiff Pool, just beyond the hawthorns,' he thought a few seconds, 'We'll have to take out a few of those devilish bushes to allow better access.'

'Can we go to survey the land tomorrow, Father?'

'That's a good idea, Erik. I see you're keen to get this project moving. Is it because you want to see the rent coming in and our empire growing?'

'Ha!' answered Erik, knowing that his father was joking, 'I like the help in the boat, Father,' he answered untruthfully but cleverly.

The evening was pleasant with each member of the family talking through their idea of the future and general contentment was the feeling of the day. They looked forward to having a tenant and more crops to fall back on. There's safety in numbers. But first, they had to survey the land, mark out and clear the fields and level the plot for the house and build it! Getting a tenant farmer seemed like the easy bit compared to all that had to go before. Agmunder and

Erik planned to start in the morning. It was fortuitous that Svala had planted the remaining rye. At least they didn't have to put off their plans.

The morning light came noticeably later after the equinox. It had been creeping up on them slowly since midsummer's day, but the march of shorter days gathered speed during September and each day seemed obviously shorter somehow. Agmunder knew that it would be unlikely that they would have a tenant, Henrik or not, much before midwinter's day. It had occurred to him that if he, once again recruited the help of Henrik, they could build his house together. He had already expressed a desire to live in the area, it seemed natural to invite him to help mark, clear, build and ready everything.

After breakfast Erik was keen to get on. In his mind, Henrik was the tenant already. It looked like it might rain shortly, so they rode down to the site on Alsvior. They pulled a sledge of sorts loaded with stakes and rope and a hammer or two for marking out. When they arrived at the plot, after just a few minutes walk, the horse was allowed to roam the area and seemed pleased to have a change of grass to munch on. The two prepared to mark out their new farmstead.

'Have a look around, boy. Where is the flattest land? It has to be firm, but not hard to dig. This is where you will site the house. Think about sinking the posts and the condition of the floor inside the house,' instructed Agmunder.

Erik spent an impressive amount of time surveying the area. Agmunder thought that he would make a snap decision because he was so keen to get on, but Erik surprised him with his thoroughness. He went, first, to the highest point and used a stick to poke the ground. He looked around and then marched off a short way and tried again. Meanwhile, Agmunder looked into the position of the fields. The land between the high point and the river was reasonably flat, falling only a couple of feet from where he stood to the bank. He spent a few minutes pacing out various layouts and eventually had the best option in his mind as he returned to where the horse had dragged the willow 'A-frame' with their supplies on. Agmunder selected four stakes and the big hammer and paced out to the corner of the first field. As he hammered the first post in he noticed Erik going through the same actions. Erik took a post and a hammer and started to mark the position of the farmhouse just a little way from Agmunder. Within half an hour, Agmunder had the three fields staked out. They looked to be in an excellent position overlooking the river. The hawthorn made a natural northern boundary to one of the fields, without shading any part, and it lay next to the second. Due to a small outcropping of rock, the third field was a few yards separated from the other two, but seemed much the flatter and stone-free of them all.

'How are you doing?' asked the older man, as he returned his hammer to the sledge.

'Nearly done, Father.'

Agmunder strode over to where Erik had marked a rectangular plot, very accurately, four yards by five yards, on a piece of land just down from the highest point.

'Why here?' asked Agmunder.

'The highest point has very stony ground, Father. The ground next to the field, near the riverbank is quite boggy and might not support the house. Between the two, here, seems a firmer option, with few stones. There is a very slight slope which shouldn't be too hard to level. I thought here was good. It has a nice view of the river and the fields and,' he said pointing, 'from here you can see our house, which you can't from the top because of those hawthorns.'

Agmunder was impressed with his considered reasoning for the position of the house. He couldn't have positioned it better himself.

'Good,' was all he said.

'Shall I start clearing stones from the fields?'

'Let's have something to eat, first.'

They sat and had some barley bread and cheese with some smoked fish and some ale as the sun came out and their forms were cast in shadow on the new farmstead foundations. After lunch they did make a start clearing stones, though Agmunder remarked how many fewer there were than the plot he had chosen for his own farm. It seemed that this farm might be ready even before the winter celebration. As they returned to the farm Agmunder told Erik of his plan to go to Garstang to arrange for the materials of the house to be delivered. He would go tomorrow and expected Erik to look after the fishing and keep an eye on mum. Erik agreed, but Agmunder wondered how much of him wanted to go to the town again. He was proud how Erik never complained. When they got back Svala was bringing in the dried fish from the rack, planning to smoke them in the newly constructed canvas and willow smoking-shed that afternoon. Salted fish, she said, would keep a long time but the sooner you cured it the longer it would keep and the tastier it would be. So she never let the curing of fish happen too long after drying. Erik helped hang the fish in the shed as his father arranged his supplies and money needed for tomorrow's trip to town. Erik wondered if his father would bring Henrik back with him and asked when he had an opportunity.

'I will seek out Henrik, yes, and I will ask him to help with the construction of the farmstead. Rest easy, Erik, Henrik features in *my* plans for the farm too!'

CHAPTER 9
Agmunder's Ness

'Dull again!' exclaimed Agmunder as he rolled out of bed and poked his head out of the window skywards.

'At least it's not raining,' said Svala from the kitchen below, 'Breakfast.'

After his meal, Agmunder got his pack onto Alsvior and they set off for Garstang. He gave his own fields a long look as he passed them, thinking of the rye that would see the winter celebration before it thought about putting up shoots, and shortly, as he passed the newly staked out fields of the tenant's land, he wondered what the future held for them all. He wondered how long it would be before, from this small beginning, there was a village here, with him as the head. The Thane of the Fylde, residing in Agmunder's Ness.

'Will you be calling on Lars, Father?' shouted Erik from his fishing skiff a few yards from shore.

'My plans are mine, young man. I don't have to explain them to you!'

'That's a yes, then,' shouted Erik, pulling on the oars as the skiff moved away from the bank.

Agmunder smiled to himself. *What a happy family life we have. I would never have believed it could go so well!* He thought as he headed off through the break in the hawthorns, conveniently widened by the passing of the wagon that brought the wooden beams all those weeks ago. He rode as far as Lars' Breck and turned left down the lane. There was the usual welcome from Skjolder and, of course, Lars. They passed the time of day, Lars asking about how the new farm house was coming on. After explaining all that had happened since they paid their taxes, Agmunder told Lars about Henrik and Erik's plan to have him as tenant.

'Henrik is a good man, though I wouldn't want to get on the wrong side of his father, he's a stinker by all accounts.'

'I don't think that giving the lad somewhere to live and make a living is likely to get on his wrong side,' said Agmunder.

'You never know. He's a proud man and wouldn't want to think that Henrik was being given charity.'

'So, do you think I should make Henrik's first year a hard one, somehow?'

'That might be a good idea. If he talks about it with his father at the market, at least he will be saying how he's had to work hard for every penny, and not how easy it's been.'

'Then that's agreed. We will not help too much, but we will not hinder. He'll have to work hard, but we'll have his back,' said Agmunder.

The road to Garstang was quiet as always and soon he pulled up outside the Dogtooth Arms. He tied his horse ready for the stable lad to take him round the side for the night and took his things inside.

'A room for the Thane!' he shouted to the landlord as he piled his things on a table by the door.

'Greetings, Agmunder. Well met,' said the landlord coming over to shake hands in warm greeting.

'I think it's just for one night, Edred,' said the Viking to the Saxon.

'You're welcome to stay as long as you please, O' Thane,' said the landlord with a low bow.

'You mock me!' exclaimed Agmunder in jest.

'You can have your usual room at the usual rate, sire. Are you on business this trip?'

'Indeed, I have need of building materials and a tenant to fill the building when it is ready,' beamed the big Norseman.

'Expansion of your farm. It is good to see your enterprise growing.'

That evening Agmunder spoke to several people who frequented the inn. The lumber merchant's son was the first. Agmunder arranged for the beams and laths he required to be brought in the next week. As luck would have it another person staying at the inn that night was a reed supply merchant. He claimed to have the best reeds for thatching and the best prices you'd find anywhere between Garstang and Nottingham whence he hailed. Agmunder ordered a wagon full of those too. If the weather held and he could raise four labourers there seemed to be no reason why the farmhouse couldn't be finished before December clamped down its iron grip on the land. Six weeks was enough, with help. By the time midnight came and Agmunder was ready to go to sleep, he had made several deals and paid for the goods and services in advance. He was very pleased with how things were going at the inn. He was quietly satisfied that he hadn't had to step outside once all evening and all this had been accomplished. The only thing left to do tomorrow morning was find Henrik and a few willing labourers.

The next morning was mild and bright. Breakfast at the inn was the usual affair. Left overs from the night before and fresh bread and ale. Agmunder left his effects in the room and went to find Henrik and whomever else happened to sign up for the work he was offering. He started in the square, asking about for the blond gangly lad, and for other labourers. He was directed to another, smaller square outside the 'Sun Inn', where they told him that free men came to seek employment on a daily basis.

He waited outside the Sun Inn, and soon enough, several men arrived and were interested in Agmunder's offer. Two of them, Tom and Jack, were young men he'd employed in the war-band. They knew he was a good man to work for and quickly signed up. Another man was persuaded by them. Agmunder hadn't even spoken to him before he approached, asking where to sign. They had a quick chat and the man told him that Tom and Jack had recommended him as an employer. Agmunder signed him up. His name was Edgar. Finally, by a stroke of luck who should ride into the square, but Henrik?

'Agmunder!' he shouted, jumping to the ground, 'Looking for work?'

The two shook hands fiercely and smiled.

'Quite the opposite, Henrik. I'm hiring.'

'Well, count me in, whatever it is!'

Agmunder laughed, he liked Henrik a lot, 'All right, you're in.'

Henrik turned to Tom and whispered in what we would call a theatrical whisper today, 'What have I signed up for?'

'The new war-band,' said Tom with a straight face, 'We're the fyrd and we're going to conquer Lancaster, in the name of the Danelaw!'

Tom thought about this for a few seconds before Edgar could contain his mirth no longer and burst out laughing, quickly followed by the rest. Agmunder was pleased that his morning had been so fruitful. He had most of his supplies arranged and four good honest men to help build.

'I have an acquaintance, Will Tanner, who would be of use to you, sir. He's quite a bit older than me, but he is very dexterous and can turn his hand to anything if shown once,' said Henrik, 'He might surprise you.'

'If *you* recommend him, then he's hired. I have room for one more at thruppence a week. The same rate as the rest of you. I will supply your food and drink while you work for me. Henrik, I must talk to you separately at my farm when you arrive. Private business, separate from the work contract,' said Agmunder.

They arranged that they would convene at Agmunder's Ness in three day's time. The first of the supplies should be arriving by then and there would be the fields to clear and the ground to prepare. They said their farewells and split up. Agmunder returned to the inn and paid his bill, collected his things and sought his horse. After two hours riding he was passing Lars' Breck and decided not to call in, for a change. Lars saw him and waved from a distance while cutting wood. Agmunder was pleased with everything in his life. Alsvior carried him home without being steered once.

Two days later, as Erik was a dot on the Skiff Pool, fishing, the first of the deliveries arrived. The wood for the tenant's house. The wagon made it through the hawthorn hedge, even managing to widen the break yet further, much to Agmunder's delight, and stopped. The driver banged a large metal sheet to draw attention and within five minutes Agmunder was there to oversee the unloading of the materials. The men on the wagon set to work and within half an hour there were three neat piles of wood, thick beams, thin beams and laths, on the ground next to the marked rectangle of the house.

'That's thruppence for delivery, Thane,' said the driver, with a tilt of his head.

Agmunder paid him the three pennies in silver coin and the men remounted the wagon, just as the first of the labourers rode through the break in the hawthorns.

'Am I too late?' shouted Henrik as he approached.

'Not at all. We wouldn't have started without you. Welcome, Henrik. I knew you'd be the first!'

The wagon drove off through the break and the two men looked over the wood supply. They counted the beams, both large and small, and looked along the length of the laths to check straightness. Erik was soon on the scene. He seemed to be able to smell Henrik at a thousand paces. They were glad to be by the river in the sunshine. The work ahead was tough and lengthy, but the company made it bearable for all. At the evening meal Svala was very pleased, too, to see Henrik back on Agmunder's Ness.

They went down to the building site immediately after breakfast, to plan the day. After an hour another wagon came through the break. Agmunder looked at it surprised. It seemed to be yet another wagon full of wood supplies. He had all he needed, what could this be? He hoped that there hadn't been any mistake. The wagon driver saluted him and drew to a standstill. The driver jumped down and walked briskly toward where Agmunder still stood with a curious expression on his face. Agmunder could see he was older than him but wiry. Grey of hair and bearded, well attired but not built like a builder.

'Agmunder, Thane of the Fylde?' asked the man when he got within six yards.

'I am he.'

'Please allow me to introduce myself. I am Will Tanner, Henrik's acquaintance.'

Agmunder turned to look at Henrik, who nodded slightly.

Will continued, 'I have registered a farmstead with the council. With your permission I will raise a farm of my own, on your ness, a little to the west. Over there,' he said pointing.

'So this wood?'

'Is mine, and when I have built my own farm, I will be your tenant also. I can see the advantages of living in a community, although I like to keep myself to myself,' said Will.

'Has that too been arranged with the council?' asked Agmunder.

'It has. They were most keen to elevate this area's status to that of village!'

'Then, yes. Build, by all means,' he lowered his voice, ' You will have the same contract as Henrik, but don't mention it to him. He doesn't know this house we are building is for him yet!' smiled Agmunder, as he shook Will's hand to cement the deal.

The other supplies arrived later that afternoon after a morning in which Henrik, Erik and Agmunder cleared the three fields of Henrik's farm (Although Henrik was still unaware of the offer to come). Will, excited by being accepted as tenant, spent the time laying out his fields and the footprint of his dwelling. He asked Agmunder to come and sanction his site, so there would be no dispute. Agmunder looked along the lines of the fields and enjoyed the feeling of pacing out the field sizes to check they were within tolerance and correctly spaced. All was well, and he could see the pride in Will's eyes that he had passed this first test of Agmunder's critical assessment. Tom and Jack arrived on foot toward the end of the day burdened with heavy packs on their shoulders. The rest of the daylight hours were taken up showing them around the site and introducing them to Will and touring his site layout. As they were walking up to Agmunder's farm, Edgar arrived on a donkey with his things piled high in front of him, so high in fact that they could hardly see who it was riding the beast.

'Hello, everyone. Sorry I'm so late. I met a man, called Lars. He invited me to have lunch and, boy he can talk. So, here I am, willing and able, albeit late on.'

'Tomorrow,' announced Agmunder, 'is our first full day building these farms. We will begin at dawn and you will all earn your pay. But, tonight, we eat and drink to the future of Agmunder's Ness.'

Svala had a big welcoming spread put on. The table was loaded with breads, cheese, fish, chicken and eggs. Agmunder had brought another boar steak from Garstang and it was cut into thin strips for the workers and family alike to share. There was ale and a little wine too. The meal was accompanied by loud excited chatter. As the evening wore on and the chatter subsided a little, Agmunder asked Henrik to go outside with him.

They stood under the stars that had guided Agmunder in his seafaring days that now were of a different use to him as a farmer, in the cool air of late evening. Lars' fire could be seen and a drifting column of smoke rose to the inky blackness of the night from that distant house. Agmunder wished he had invited Lars to this revelry. As a close friend he should partake of this families joyous moments. He shook his head to clear these distractions.

'Henrik, I have something to ask. I don't want you to feel pressured, so if you think it's not for you, please, just say.'

'Oh?'

'Yes. I have invited you here to help build a new farm for a tenant, as yet undecided, and I know I can rely on you to do a good job and work well for your pay. When you were here last you expressed a fondness for the area and indicated to Svala and Erik that, one day, you might like to farm here on the ness.'

'I did. Erm, I would,' answered Henrik.

'Then, I have to ask you. When this farmstead is built, would you like to stay on as my tenant farmer? No special treatment, mind. Hard work and farm your own land. A contract will be drawn to split the profit of your labours as well as set the annual rent. If you are in agreement, make me a happy man and say you will be my tenant.'

Henrik didn't need to think about it, 'I will. I am. I... Yes!'

'Then, let us seal the bargain,' said Agmunder taking up his ale.

They drank to business, farming and tenancy and in the time it took Alsvior and Arvakr to pull Sunne's chariot across the heavens once, since yesterday, the number of official residents of Agmunder's Ness grew, from three souls, to five.

The building project went well. Will taking care of his house with some help from Henrik. Henrik's farm came on the quickest as he had the most help, notably from Tom and Jack and Agmunder, when he wasn't tending his own farm or overseeing Erik's responsibilities. Will surprised everyone by building his walls from a mixture of straw and clay-like mud that he called 'Cob'. The others, who had grown up in Scandinavian countries were used to building in wood and stone but had not thought of constructing anything in mud!

'Won't it fall down when it rains?'

'Will it wash away?'

'How will it support the weight of the roof?'

'How can you live in a *brown* house?'

Will just shook his head and carried on building. Admittedly he would have preferred to have a summer to harden the cob better before he faced his first winter but was sure that as long as he got his reed roof on the rain would not be a problem. The house looked different too. No beams showing at the corners and indeed it was not rectangular but more of a fat oval shape within the proscribed rectangular dimension footprint. There was a central post that took the laths that were built into the cob at the top of the walls. The reeds were spread about the pole radiating outwards from it to the wall, giving a conical look to the roof. On windless days, Will built small fires around the outside and within the structure to provide a little extra help with the drying of the cob. Large fires would dry it too quickly and create cracks. This would have been frowned upon by cob building purists, but he didn't think he had much option, and there weren't any around to offend anyway, so he did what he thought right. The brown cob wall had to be dry before November's damp air and wind got to rattle the foundations of his house. Will was very proud of his house and the others respected his choice of building method as they saw how strong it looked as it neared completion. They also noted that apart from the high work up the ladder that Henrik accomplished for him, Will did most of the work alone and produced a very liveable space in just under eight weeks. Between them the two new farms were ready to move into by the fourth day of December. That night they held a little party to celebrate finishing them off. It was tinged with sadness, for Tom and Jack and Edgar, who would leave in the morning, to go back to their families in Garstang for the winter. But, party they did, and Agmunder took a few moments later on to go outside in the chilly night air to look over the land under the setting first quarter moon. Three farmhouses, complete with fields, sown with winter crops, nestled on the ness. Agmunder's Ness.

CHAPTER 10
Winter Celebration

Agmunder made sure that Lars was invited to the winter celebration on Agmunder's Ness eleven days later for the December solstice. They would meet, to pass the longest night together, and fight off the ravages of the weather and the season. They would pack Agmunder's farmhouse and raise the rafters with their song, stories and merriment. Secure in the knowledge that the winter would abate and spring, and then the new year, would follow in March. Agmunder wondered if 782 would be as bountiful as the current year had been. Just three cold months to endure before the first showings of new growth appeared in the land. He had heard that it very rarely snowed in the Fylde, but took that with a pinch of salt. Although there was admittedly a good three months before the twenty first of March ushers in the new year and the spring, Agmunder was already looking forward to the new year.

The guests had arrived before the dusky cloak of night had been spread by the winter witch over the countryside and many torches burned to give light to the proceedings, as the last of the guests made themselves comfortable, but only after an extensive round of greetings and hand shakes had amused the massed residents for several minutes, Agmunder, as Thane and master of the house, stood and spread his arms for quiet.

'My honoured guests. Lars the Dane, Henrik, tenant farmer, Will Tanner, tenant farmer and mud house dweller, and my lovely family, Erik and Svala, and Fjord,' The dog barked. Everyone laughed, 'It gives me great pleasure to welcome you to my house at this special time of year. More important to us now than in past years. As farmers we live by the fickle seasons and the weather that they bring. We look with thanks on the year that has passed so far and forwards to the new one in the spring. We hope our crops spring forth from the ground to give us sufficient to eat and pay our cursed taxes. This day is the shortest, as you know, but that means that this night of feasting and optimism for the future will be the longest.'

There was a round of cheering at that last sentence and Agmunder cut the first huge slice off the roast boar on the spit before the fire. There was bread and cheese to pick from as well as cured fish and rabbit and chicken. Ale and a little wine were held in barrels outside by the back wall away from the fire, not through fear of any flammable properties, but rather to preserve their chill.

Lars stood up and raised his drink to the full stretch of his muscular arm.

'Agmunder. Thane of the Fylde. Good friend and landlord to his farmers. We salute you in drink at this festive time.'

There was much cheering and agreement and drinking.

Henrik stood, 'I thank the day that I said I would come to help the Thane on his farm. My life has changed beyond expectation.'

Will took his drink and stood, rather unsteadily, 'The farmer's life for me!'

They were getting less and less serious as the ale had it's effect.

Lars stood once more, thought better of it and sat down again, 'Look, this man,' pointing at Agmunder, 'saved my life.'

Agmunder looked at Lars. He couldn't remember ever saving his life. They'd been on the hunt for Knut, but Lars didn't have any close shaves on that particular expedition.

'Explain yourself '*the Dane*',' said Agmunder over his cup edge as he reached out for more chicken.

Lars continued, 'I had a small farm that was going down hill. I had an old dog that was about to die. I had no friends and no means of getting any. The people of Garstang, whilst civil enough, were distant and mistrusting, no matter what I did. My savings had run virtually dry and I had little to look forward to. Many years of the same, just scraping by... just, an existence. I was beginning to wonder if it was worth all the suffering to carry on. Then, the very day my dear old dog died. My only friend. I meet this man,' pointing again at the Thane.

'It's true, his dog did die,' nodded Agmunder.

Lars lifted his cup, 'I found that there were people who cared enough to call in to see me as they went to town. People who care about the plight of poor animals in cages. To share insights into farming methods and techniques. To include me in his plans and ask me along on his projects, to care for the people he knows,' Lars, the big Dane, wiped a tear from the corner of his eye, unashamed to show his gratitude for the friendship he'd received from Agmunder and his family, 'and welcome me to his farm and to share in his family's troubles and triumphs. I just wanted to say, thank you.'

The farmhouse was quiet after Lars finished. Everyone was thinking how much they owed to Agmunder and thinking on how happy these last few months had been toiling against the approaching winter with good friends and help when needed. The feeling of community and belonging was warming and kept their hearts filled with hope.

'I have a story,' said Henrik, as he leant forwards to grab some fish and a boiled egg from a platter in the middle of the table.

'Tell all!' said the Thane.

For a second Agmunder thought Henrik's face became white as a daisy, then he steeled himself and began to recount his tale, to the party round Agmunder's table on the winter celebration night.

'On my Father's farm there is a dark, weed-filled pond. A small body of water, maybe eight yards across. It lies in a steep hollow, surrounded by trees, willows, that bow low into the water when their branches are weighted by catkins. The water is dark and the green slimy weed that grows on the surface awaits unfortunate animals that slip on the muddy banks and find themselves entangled and drowned.'

Everyone was listening. Not a sound from the guests.

'I had need of water. My younger brother and I were cutting hedges in the field that stands by. My blade became dull and, well, that's a dangerous thing. So, I ventured to the pond to get water for my wet-stone, to sharpen the blade. As I crested the bank I saw a creature erupt out of the water and grab a weasel on the muddy bank below me, not five yards away. Now weasels are fearsome animals to their prey and they fight like the devil, but this one's life was snuffed out by the ferocity of the creature's attack. Swept away in the blink of an eye. The noise of the weasel's consumption masked my approach, and whatever it was, stayed. It did not run away and it did not become aware of my watching presence. I stopped and silently crouched, so that just the top of my head was showing above the bank beneath the trees disguised by the thick bushes at that part. I could still see, but wasn't seen. The thing looked like a monkey with no hair on its slimy green striped and spotted body. The ears were pointed and its back was knobby with bones, like the prickles of a stickleback, poking out of its spine. Thin, wiry legs and arms with webbed, clawed hands it had. It looked for all the world like a child's skeleton stuffed inside a frog's skin. It crouched while it ate, like a poacher setting a trap, and I could hear it crunching the bones of the catch it feasted upon. I watched as it ate every part, even the claws, and teeth. It looked around several times but seemed content that it was alone. For my part, as I watched the creature, I wondered how it couldn't hear my heart that was fit to burst through my ribs! As it finished its meat course a fish was foolish enough to come to the surface, as they do in spring, for a gulp of air. I expect the weed was choking the pond life that gasped for sustenance in the dark and cold watery world below.

The little creature jumped like a frog into the pond, so quickly it was almost like a lightning strike. It entered the water with a splash of green weed, exactly where the fish had shown itself to be and after a few seconds of thrashing about it, once again, crawled onto the shore, holding the hapless carp in its jaws. I watched, as in a trance, as the vile creature consumed the fish, every part.

There was a sound behind me and I turned to see. My younger brother Tostig, had come to find out why I was being so long fetching the water. When I turned back, the creature was gone, nothing. I waited to see if it would come back out from wherever it went to conceal itself and I even had a poke about under the weeping trees after a while, when the terror had released its freezing grip and the memory of the creature's hideous form had faded a little from my stricken mind.'

Henrik took a gulp of his ale and wiped the back of his hand across his lips. 'Later, I asked about in the village of Beranburgh, by the farm, and was told that I was lucky to get away with my life. If Jinny Greenteeth, for that is how she is called, had discovered me by her pond, that same lightning reaction, with which she despatched the weasel and the carp, would have been visited upon my slothful human body and I would have met my end in the pond that stands by my Father's field below the willows that weep in the presence of so much death. I packed my effects and left home on my father's horse that very night, and have vowed never to return to the farm, to stay far from the pond. I meet my Father in Garstang at the market from time to time, but I will not return to the farm. I was overjoyed when Agmunder asked me to move to the ness. Another seven miles separate me and Jinny Greenteeth.'

Henrik looked around the table at those who had witnessed his story. Will's eyes were like saucers, staring but focussed on something other than the room in which he sat. Svala had her hand over her mouth as she held Erik's head to her chest, hiding his face from such a cruel world. Agmunder's eyes were narrowed in thought and Henrik sincerely hoped he wasn't planning an adventure to kill Jinny Greenteeth. Lars' tears were dry now, and a faint smile played about the corners of his mouth.

'That is a very well told story, Henrik. I didn't know you were a bard,' said Lars as he began to clap slowly.

The sound of the clapping seemed to release whatever hold the story had on the others and they too began to talk and clap until the party was back to its boisterous noise, all except Will.

'We love a good tale, Henrik,' said Agmunder, smiling again, 'The best ones are those which are told so well they could be true. You had us all for a moment. Well done.'

'Thank you, Thane,' said Henrik, raising his cup in salute.

Will Tanner was still sitting quietly. He too was deep in thought. Agmunder touched him on the shoulder.

'Will, are you alright?'

'I was thinking about my childhood. I too grew up near Beranburgh, on the edge of the village. I was remembering a day when I was just five or six summers old. I was with my brother by a willow ringed, green-watered pond, similar in many ways to that which Henrik has just described. We played hide and seek in the trees. I counted to fifty, the highest I could go at that age, then went to look for him. But, I never saw him again.'

'What did your family do? Had he drowned?'

'My father and mother spent hours shouting for him and looking everywhere they could think of. Many villagers helped to search, too. They searched the trees and the pond, the fields, but found nothing. No remains. Not a clue to what had happened to my poor brother, Harold. Henrik's story brought it all back.'

'I am sorry you have been saddened by my story, Will,' said Henrik, patting the old man on the shoulder.

'My parents were so upset they sold their business, the tannery, to a Lancastrian merchant and bought a small farm near Garstang with their life savings. The memories of dear Harold in the old house were too much for them, I suppose.'

'And now you live on the ness as tenant to Agmunder,' observed Lars.

'Yes. And Happy I am to be such. Soon I will be able to sow my summer crop and look forward to paying Agmunder, our dear landlord and Thane, my tribute,' said Will, returning a little more to his usual self.

'At New Year, *I* will be off to see Weasel Face, to pay my taxes at the equinox,' announced Agmunder, the farmer.

The mention of "Weasel Face" inspired a round of laughter. Everyone knew exactly to whom it referred. It occurred to Agmunder that he didn't actually know the man's name, and decided to ask next time he saw him.

'Soon, I will endure the weather to travel to see John Smith at the Black Pool,' said Agmunder to Lars. I need some horseshoes before the spring planting. The track to Garstang is easy but quite stony. Alsvior will go lame if his hooves are damaged by rocks. My farms can't afford to have a lame horse, so an investment in shoes makes sense. I expect my hard-working tenants will want to borrow him for their harrowing. If I don't get shoes for the horse, I risk all these farms, not just mine. It is my responsibility to look after them all.'

'I will ride with you, my friend,' said Lars. 'My horse too needs shoeing, and if I remember rightly, it was me who told you about John Smith. It's only fair I go along to make the introduction.'

'You are, as ever, welcome to ride with me, Lars.'

Three days after the winter celebration the two met, on horseback, a little way south of Henrik's farmstead on the track where it faintly branches off south toward the Black Pool. They took the little-used path and rode slowly toward the blacksmith's workshop on the edge of the mere. It took them the best part of the day to make the trip in the cold, late December wind. The horses trudged with their heads held low out of the blustery gusts that raked the wild countryside. Agmunder and Lars wore their winter cloaks against the worst of the weather, though they travelled light. By the time twilight was approaching they were in sight of the blacksmith's buildings. There was a house, curiously built of cob, with a reed roof in the circular style. It was reminiscent of Will's dwelling at the ness. There was smoke visible, coming out of the top of the roof. Though it was blown almost horizontally from the hole from which it emerged by the rising wind. The smithy itself was of more familiar beam and plaster construction. The roof was wooden shingles and the orange glow from the window apertures told of industry within. As they circled the water, a dark and forbidding expanse of rough wavelets, they rode temporarily directly out of the wind, which afforded some respite as they neared their goal. Agmunder was pleased to see that there were stables next to the smithy, hopefully for the berthing of both the horses and their riders during the night. During the ride both men had had ample opportunity to think on the possibility that they might be sleeping outside. Agmunder found it hard to see temporarily, as his hair was blowing playfully across his vision. Lars had *his* long hair in a ponytail that whipped his face but at least afforded him a view of where they were headed.

'Who's idea was this trip?' shouted Lars through the wind.

'Who was foolish enough to volunteer to come along?'

'Why can't horses just walk, what do they need shoes for?' Lars laughed in the gale.

They made it to the blacksmith's stables before nightfall. John Smith was a huge man, as blacksmiths often are, with red hair. He emerged from the smithy just as the men were dismounting their horses.

'Lars! I haven't seen you for such a long time,' said John, the smith.

'It's been too long, Jack,' said Lars.

'I thought you said he was called John?' asked Agmunder.

'Jack is how he's known. His name *is* John. In years gone by he was known as "Fiery Jack". Neither because of his red hair or because he works with fire.'

'Why then?'

'Because when he'd had a couple of ales, his temper knew no bounds!'

Agmunder looked from Lars to Jack.

'In my dotage I am brave enough to say *no* to the ale,' said Jack, with a grin.

Lars continued, 'Jack, this is Agmunder, Thane of the Fylde. He has three farms on the ness, "Agmunder's Ness", no less. He has a horse to be shod, as do I. May we rest in your stables with the animals for the night?'

'Thane of the Fylde, eh? Do you think that I would risk my reputation as a good host to sleep a Thane in my stables? Lars Larsson, you and the good Thane may spend the night in my house as my guest, and no mention of payment, do you hear, old friend.'

Agmunder turned to Lars, 'I thought you said you had no friends?' he asked with a smile.

'The stories we tell at the winter celebration are always exaggerated, Agmunder, you know that,' answered Lars, with a slight smile in the corners of his mouth.

They entered Jack's house, which was mercifully warm and draught free. His wife, Gretel, heavy with child, had a large pot of stew on the go. Agmunder remarked on how much was in the pot, to Jack.

Jack said, 'You never know when customers, or travellers, will seek shelter from the weather, so I always keep a big stew on the hob,' a glance to his wife, 'Or, rather, Gretel does.'

Gretel got out six large wooden bowls. Agmunder did a head count, four people present. Strange.

Gretel ladled the stew into four of the bowls and filled the fifth with bread. All was set on the table in the centre of the room and ale was brought in a keg that had been outside where it had been making good use of the opportunity to keep cold and set it on the floor next the table by Jack's place. The metalwork around the barrel was beaded with moisture in just a few seconds, which then ran down the sides of the keg into a small but growing ring of water around its base in the dust of the hard clay floor. Just as John Smith seated himself on the stool at the head of the table there came a knock at his door, which then opened and another large man entered looking for all the world like Thor himself.

'Take a seat, Grim,' said Jack, as Gretel ladled more stew into the final bowl. Obviously the man was expected.

'Thank you, Gretel,' said Grim with a thick Norse accent.

The blacksmith cleared his throat, 'Grim, here, lives just a little way to the west along the edge of the Black Pool. He's skilled in the art of blacksmithery, but wants to bring Christianity to the Fylde. He is planning to build a church to unite the prayers for those on land, and those on the sea, by constructing it right on the coast, due west of here, in the spring. His church roof will be made of an upturned longboat. Quite ingenious, and fitting, I think. He has the bell made already. Forged it from bronze,' he said, picking up some bread and his spoon.

The man, Grim, didn't say a word. Perhaps not keen to converse with pagans. *Who can be sure of what goes on in the minds of these religious types*, thought Agmunder.

The meal was hearty and warming after their journey and, to be honest, Agmunder was glad they were staying in the house and not sleeping in the draughty and unheated stables. Being a Thane had its advantages.

In the morning the sun managed to show through the clouds and the wind had dropped considerably. Agmunder, looking around the landscape could understand why the smith had settled here, it was a beautiful part of the Fylde. Very flat. He could see across the smooth water, all the way to the dunes that lined the sea.

'He's ready, Agmunder,' said Lars, at his elbow.

The Viking lead his horse to the smithy to be shod as the Dane took his turn to admire the view over the mere. Agmunder rejoined Lars at the water's edge. There were few tall standing plants, like bulrushes, the constant wind across the low land keeping what vegetation did grow to a few inches tall at best. Lars allowed his horse to drink while they waited, the sound of Jack's hammer on the metal in distant rhythm with their heartbeats.

By mid morning both the horses were re-shod and ready for the trek back to Agmunder's Ness. They paid what they owed to Jack and got ready to leave. As they mounted up, Grim came to them. He held up a bronze Christian cross. 'Carry this and you will be looked after, whether you believe, or not,' he said.

Agmunder took the cross and looked at it critically. It was very well made. He wondered how someone with such skill could consider giving it up for this new religion. *He's got commitment*, he thought.

'Thank you, Grim,' is all he said.

Grim gave another cross to Lars, who nodded as he looked at the workmanship.

They set off as soon as Grim turned to leave. The horses started their journey in the flat, easy terrain of the southern Fylde and, before the sun was half way to its meagre culmination, they started into the more familiar, more stony, ground of the central lands. They picked up the main track, just west of Lars' Breck at noon and went their separate ways, promising to speak soon. Agmunder got the customary welcome on his arrival, not least from Fjord, and told his family all about his meeting with John Smith, previously known as Fiery Jack, and Grim, the would-be preacher, over a lunch of chicken broth and bread.

CHAPTER 11
Spring Equinox

Agmunder looked at the sunrise over the fells. The sun was progressing nicely Northward along the horizon day by day. In ten days it would be New Year's Day. He wondered what the future held for him in 782. The crops were doing well and would be ready for harvest in mid to late June. Followed seventy or eighty days later by the summer field's crop of barley and beans. *The taxes owed next week will deplete the coin in the savings hole, but the winter crop bonus later in the year will more than replenish it. Especially with the extra revenue coming in from the tenants*, thought the Viking as he surveyed his fields and looked over to the other farms nearby.

The tenants were contracted to pay their rent all in one go, including the ten percent of their crop value, at the September equinox. The spring taxes were due by the end of March. If the debtor strayed, even one day, into April, they were deemed to be a fool, because they had to pay a fine of five percent on top of what they owed.

Agmunder asked only for payment in September from his tenants. This meant that they didn't have the struggle of paying him when they had no crop to sell in spring and they had time to sell their crop before the debt became due, in late September. The winter months had been good to the farming community of Agmunder's Ness, with few storms and just a dusting of snow that lasted nearly a whole day. There were just two days in February when the ground lay white all around to the depth of three barleycorns, an inch. Today, the sixteenth of March 781, the land was flushed with signs of new growth. The fields were greener and there were Snowdrops by the river in the lee of the bank next to the place Erik beached Waverider. The days were lengthening and Agmunder was pleased that the information he had been given about the pleasant winters on the Fylde had proved, in this first winter at least, to be true.

There was much to do on the farm. As well as preparing for the harvest in June, the fallow field had to be prepared for the planting of the barley and beans in early April, just a fortnight away. The goat and the horse would have two months of restricted movement until they could take up residence, after the harvest, in the field that currently grew the rye. Next time he sowed the winter crop, Agmunder planned to split the field with wheat and rye in equal measure. A fourth crop to tend and another seed option for Svala to grind her flour from. The longer growing wheat would give them another harvest to deal with in July, but he had time to farm now. He had seeds of a hardy wheat strain that even grew in southern Denmark. He had hopes that it would flourish in the milder climate of the Fylde.

'Hey!'

Agmunder's thoughts were broken by a shout from the river. He turned to see a skiff, similar to Waverider, with two people on board, a man and a woman. The craft was low in the water, laden with many items.

'Can I help you?' shouted Agmunder to the couple.

'We're from the Lancaster area, and we are looking for Amounder's Ness, a village hereabouts that we've heard of. We'd like to get there before the end of this morning. We have sailed down the coast from the harbour at Glasson. We stayed the night with a monk on the coast by the estuary and set off this morning at first light. Do you know of the village?'

'Well, yes. This is Agmunder's Ness,' answered the Viking.

There was great excitement in the boat. Then they seemed to calm a little.

'Do you think we could come ashore?'

'I don't see why not,' shouted Agmunder.

The boat was skilfully handled and beached quickly onto the muddy bank of the Skiff Pool. The man threw the anchor stone onto the bank and helped the woman down making sure she didn't get wet. Once they were both ashore and the boat was secure the man once again addressed Agmunder.

'Thank you. We heard that the Thane Amounder is seeking tenants and is a fair man.'

'Oh, he's the fairest, but he likes people to call him Agmunder,' answered the Thane.

'We have skills in farming. We have left a farm just north of Lancaster to settle here and start a new life in the fair ness. Our experience should be useful to the Thane, and we hear he has a good contract with his tenants,' continued the man.

The woman spoke, 'We heard he's also skilled with the war-axe.'

'That he is. Particularly when he has to protect his village,' said the Viking Thane.

'Then lead us to him, that we can offer our tenancy and prove our worth,' said the man.

'I cannot lead you to him. And you do not need to prove your worth.'

'What? Is he away? Is he so desperate for tenants that he will take anyone? How do you know so much of Thane Amounder's mind?'

'Because, I *am* the Thane. This, is *my* land... And it's Agmunder!'

The two immediately dropped to their knees and bowed their heads to the ground. Agmunder could hear mumbling but couldn't make it out.

'Please, rise. We do not stand on ceremony here. I don't know what life was like on your old farm, but you won't find the residents of Agmunder's Ness wasting precious farming time bowing and scraping to the Thane. Please... Rise.'

The two rose slowly as if they expected it to be a trick and they would be thrown to the floor at any moment for not showing the correct subservience or daring to speak to the Thane himself. It took a full minute of sincere reassurance for them to calm down and relax a little.

'I am Michael, and this is Anne,' said the man as he composed himself.

'I am pleased to meet you both. I am Agmunder, Thane of the Fylde,' taking the opportunity to pronounce his name once more for the confused couple.

Agmunder took them for a short stroll, showing them the layout of the village farms and asking them if they had permission from the council to ask for a tenancy.

Michael read him a document that he said granted someone called Michael, whom Agmunder assumed was this Michael, permission to seek tenancy in Agmunder's Ness, from the shire council at Lancaster. There was a huge red wax seal on the document that, to illiterate persons, certainly looked impressive. Agmunder decided to trust them on their word and ask Lars to read the document the next time he came to visit.

'Do you have any preference where you would like to set up your fields for your crops?', Agmunder asked as the strolled.

'Oh. We don't farm crops, sire. We farm pigs,' said Michael.

'Pigs? Aren't they rather smelly when kept in one place?' asked Agmunder.

'They are, and that is why we would ask that we have a plot as far east as possible to keep their pong away from your lovely home, Thane,' said Anne.

'Well, I suppose that you could have the area on the bank of the Skiff Pool to the south of the hawthorn ridge. Just a bit further down from Henrik's farmstead. He'd like a neighbour. He's a good man, but there's no woman in his life as yet, it must be a bit lonely at times.'

'Oh, you're never lonely with pigs about,' said Michael to the nodding Anne.

The couple were very thankful and set about immediately looking at the area. They left Agmunder, promising to come up to the farm when they had marked out their plot. They had brought the equipment, and all their belongings, in the boat.

Agmunder walked back up to his farm and thought about the couple. They were very happy in each other's company. Almost too happy for ordinary folk. Agmunder guessed that they weren't married. Or at least not married to each other! They had an air about them of new lovers. He wondered if they would bring some sort of trouble, but shrugged it off. They wanted to live in the Ness and they had important skills. Besides, he would have pigs as tribute and who could resist eating well?

Will Tanner was in the yard helping Erik make a larger hook for fishing. The fish in the Skiff Pool often got off Erik's current hook and it was thought that it was just a little too small for the size of fish that frequented the shallows near the bottom end of the pool. Will had skills with metal and was showing Erik how to fashion the eye of the hook using a hammer and a block of metal as Michael and Anne entered the yard and introduced themselves, "prospective tenants of the great Thane, Agmunder". This made the two laugh, especially Erik. The youngster was admonished by Michael for not showing the correct respect for Agmunder, which made him laugh even more. Michael only saw the funny side when Will explained that the great Thane of the Fylde and master farmer, benevolent ruler of the empire was, in fact, Erik's dad. After a few seconds chuckling at this situation Michael suddenly stopped laughing and made a half bow to Erik. This action set them off laughing again and Michael seemed very put out for a few moments before he grasped the fact that it really was as laid back as he had been told by Agmunder.

The Thane heard the discourse from within the house and came to the door.

'Don't mind those two, Michael. No respect for the Thane!'

'I told him. I told him. I did...' said Michael, still not fully grasping that they were still joking.

When they had both entered the house, Agmunder asked Michael and Anne to sit at the table. When they were sat he introduced Svala and asked her to bring some ale. He explained the tenancy agreement and their obligations and their benefits, before declaring that they were now tenants, if they wanted to be. He would get the necessary documents to make it legal the next time he went to Garstang. For he next few minutes he very carefully explained that the tenants were all treated like one family. They all lived together on the ness and each was familiar to the others. They did not stand on ceremony and he, certainly, didn't expect to be bowed to. It took a while, but Michael eventually understood that he could be respectful without having to make a show of it.

'I have to ask,' said Agmunder, 'How are you two related?'

'Well we... that is, Anne and I... you see... Well, it was like this,' started Michael.

Agmunder couldn't waste time pussy-footing about, 'Are you married?'

'No.'

'Are you able to *be* married, in law?'

'Yes,' said Anne, clearly happy to say so.

'So, what's your story?' asked Agmunder, relaxing a little now that difficult question was out of the way.

The couple looked at each other and Anne gave a subtle nod to Michael.

Agmunder understood that Michael had just been given permission to tell the real story, rather than one they had agreed on when they ran away. He appreciated that and prepared to hear their tale.

'We were both married and we both worked on the same farm. It wasn't ours, we just worked there, do you see? Well, we wondered how we could ever be together because we want to be, don't we?'

Anne nodded and Michael carried on the explanation, 'My wife was a terrible bully of a woman, didn't give me a moment's rest from the day I married her. Well, she died when one of the pigs bit her leg. The wound swelled up and went green in two days. She couldn't walk and after a short while in bed, maybe two more days, she passed away. We had a proper burial. That was in March last year. Anne was still married to a man who was a brute. Used to hire himself out for fighting and suchlike. I was terrified that he should find out that I was sweet on Anne, though I couldn't help being so.'

He smiled at Anne, who squeezed the hand she was holding on the table.

'So, what became of this man, Anne's husband? Will he bring trouble to the ness? I can't have that, you know.'

'No, no, no. There will be no trouble. He was killed outright. A vile man called Knut Huss, Huse, Husser, something, came to the farm to employ Anne's husband one day. Said he had use for him in the Fylde. They rode off and by all accounts they didn't even reach this Knut's house before there was a skirmish and he died protecting his employer as the coward, Knut, rode away.

'Knut Husasson, was hunted down and executed by *my* war-band.'

The couple thought about the statement for a few seconds before Michael stood up from the stool and offered Agmunder his hand, 'Then we have you to thank for being able to be together. We will honour you till our dying day, Thane Agmunder.'

The Thane was pleased that Michael had pronounced his name correctly, though he still hoped the ceremonial tendencies would subside in a few days.

Anne got to her feet and curtsied as Michael bowed. Agmunder allowed them this moment of deference, it seemed almost appropriate given that he was their saviour, in a small way. They sat again.

'Why did you come here? You had a position on the pig farm,' asked Agmunder.

'There were many people at the farm who thought that somehow we'd done away with our spouses and said they wouldn't bless our union in marriage. We had to go somewhere to start afresh, where people would take us for who we *are* and not for what *might* have happened. Neither of us have any other family that survive, we didn't have to leave any loved ones behind to come here. The choice was easy,' explained Michael, as Anne nodded beside him.

'Then, you are more than welcome. Michael and Anne, make your home here with us. Have you got any stock? A pig... or two? I presume you'll need two pigs to make piglets?'

'We spent our savings on a fine, pregnant sow, and a man to bring her here on a cart. We are to meet him in Garstang and come here, or sell the pig, if we could not be your tenants,' explained Michael.

'There is one thing, Thane,' said Anne, shyly.

Michael continued the point, to save her embarrassment, 'We have converted to the new faith. When we do get married it will be by a Christian service and not a pagan one. We thought we'd better state that up front, Thane.'

Agmunder prided himself on being a good judge of character and saw these two as good and honest people. A couple that would be a credit to the community. The couple both looked to the ground, as if this was a deal-breaker and Agmunder was expected to throw them out of the house and off his land. They were pleasantly surprised, therefore, when Agmunder said, 'I know of a church that is being built on the coast, not too far away, by a good man of my acquaintance, named Grim. I like to count him a friend. When his church is finished, I am sure he will be more than happy to marry you.'

If that surprised them, then what Agmunder said next was totally unexpected.

'If I may, I would like to attend. Anne will need someone to give her away if you have no other family. As your landlord and Thane, it would be my duty but also a pleasure to perform the honour.'

Life on Agmunder's Ness had suddenly become busier than ever before. Michael and Anne set about preparing the ground for a building where they could live and an enclosure for their stock. They needed to erect a fence around the entirety of their plot to keep the pigs from wandering. Agmunder visited regularly to see how they were getting on, as did Henrik and Erik. Will Tanner, as he said, kept largely to himself.

They all leant a hand from time to time. Agmunder and Erik had to excuse themselves to finalise preparations for sowing their summer crop. Alsvior was put to work harrowing the field. The horse and the goat were moved to Henrik's nearest field, a longer walk for Erik to get the milk in the morning, but with a chance of seeing his friend, that was no burden. The day after the equinox, Agmunder paid his taxes in Garstang, without incident, and verified that Michael had the right to be a tenant. Luckily, though, because Michael didn't yet have a completed dwelling on the land, or for that matter a single pig, Agmunder didn't have to pay anything for their part of the taxes until September. He found out that when the total number of tenants reached five, he would pay a different tax, that of "the Manor", that would be all inclusive and fixed. This meant that if he had six or seven or more tenants, he would not personally be responsible for any more tax. He also found out, as he had promised himself to do, that Weasel Face had a name, and that name was, Maximilian. *Max the Tax*, he thought wittily (for him). Apparently his father was from Italy. Agmunder's one night stay at the Dogtooth Arms was raucous and welcoming, as ever, and the excess of drink had him rising to leave quite late in the morning, much to the amusement of the Landlord. Agmunder got to wondering, as he rode the familiar track back home in the warmth of early afternoon, if anyone that lived in the Fylde was actually born in Britain.

'Good trip, Agmunder?' asked Henrik, from Michael's field, as he helped work on the perimeter fence.

'All business was accomplished without a hiccough,' said Agmunder.

He rode over the where Michael was working and tossed a bundle of documents to him. Michael caught the sheaf and looked with concern at the Viking.

Knowing it would cause concern, but unable to resist the joke, Agmunder said, 'You are now an official tenant, Michael the Swineherd.'

'That's the last time I hear that lowly name, I hope, Agmunder. Were you able to arrange the change I requested?' he enquired timidly, hoping for an affirmative answer.

Agmunder allowed the silence to expand until it was almost overwhelming poor Michael.

Eventually, Agmunder put the man out of his anguish, 'Of course. I have had your name changed to be in keeping with your "farmer" status. On the tenancy and on my deeds, you are registered as Michael *Shard*, an approximate contraction of Swineherd. That's the best Max the Weasel and I could do for you.'

'Michael Shard,' Michael said out loud, feeling the name in his mouth, 'Shard. Shaaaaarrrrrd.'

Seeing Michael's face and worrying that he might not show appreciation for the work Agmunder had done on his behalf, Anne said, 'Thank you, Thane. It is a fine name, and I for one will be pleased to be known as Mrs. Anne Shard, after the wedding.'

At these words, Agmunder said his goodbyes and rode up to his farm, where, as usual, Fjord came bounding up to him in welcome as the Viking slipped from Alsvior's back, glad to be home.

By the middle of April all of the arable farms had their summer crops sown. Michael had his pregnant sow and was already thinking of expanding. He'd realised that the journey to Garstang would be significantly shortened if there was a way across the Wyre at the bottom of the Skiff Pool. He envisaged getting a barge with a flat top that could follow a thick rope strung between two tree trunks sunk into the river banks at each side. He said that pig farming was largely waiting for them to grow big enough to be butchered and apart from feeding them every day, he would have enough time to ferry people to and fro until he became too old to physically manage the weight of the barge in the river. He mused that what he really wanted to do was build a bridge and charge people to use it, but for now at least, the barge would have to suffice as there definitely wasn't enough traffic to warrant a bridge at the moment. But, he argued, with Agmunder's Ness growing as fast as it was, it wouldn't be long before it would be a full time job ferrying people across the water to save them six hours on the trip to town.

Agmunder came down to see how the fence was holding up to the inquisitive pig.

'Yes, she's been very keen to explore the new surroundings, and I'm no help. What she needs, at the moment, is a familiar face and I'm new to her. I'm spending as much time with her as possible at the moment so she gets used to seeing me around and settles down a bit. It's also handy being on hand when she starts chewing the fence down. She'd be out in an hour if I left her at the moment,' he said as he kept a keen eye on the sow's movements around the enclosure.

'She'll settle down when the piglets arrive, Mr. Shard,' said Agmunder slapping Michael on the shoulder.

'That's another week or so yet, Thane,' said Michael as he headed off into the enclosure to distract the sow, as she started dismantling one of the posts holding the fence up.

Agmunder shouted after him, 'Till then you have a full time job, Michael.'

He returned to Henrik's farm to relocate the goat. He'd noticed that she'd completely eaten the grass in the circle of her tether in the last two days and planned to move her a few yards down the field edge. Henrik met him as he turned down the path that was becoming quite well trodden already.

'I saw smoke earlier, in the west. Close, too. Somewhere on the coast I think. There could be a landing party. I was thinking of riding out there to find out,' said the young farmer.

Agmunder scoured the horizon for signs of life. Nothing to be seen. He went down the field and moved the goat's post several yards further down and hammered it in two feet with a huge hammer they had made to help with building Michael's enclosure.

'I will go with you,' said the Viking, as he passed Henrik on his way back home. 'When?'

'Now!' he called, 'I can't afford to let anyone threaten the peace of the ness.'

Henrik didn't argue, but turned and went to get his horse and provisions for the scouting trip. It was already quite late and it would be dark before they had a chance to get back.

Agmunder returned to his farm and by the time he was provisioned, and had explained to Svala and Erik what they were doing, Henrik was waiting at the end of Agmunder's path mounted on his horse.

CHAPTER 12
Thunder Clouds

They rode west, hoping to make the coast before nightfall. They planned to sleep close by, then scout out the invaders in the morning light. There were trees along the coastal area that would shield the light of a fire to cook with, which would also keep them warm overnight. Importantly, the trees would dissipate the column of smoke. Hopefully, they wouldn't be discovered on their approach, by whoever it was that had arrived on the ness. The way was not an oft travelled one, and the horses stumbled and faltered at each step. The land to the west of the thorn ridge was rocky and also boggy in parts. It was deceptively difficult to make any headway and soon they realised that they were not going to make the coast before it became too dark to ride. Without the trees to cut wood from they had nothing to burn, so the problem of building a fire, whilst being exposed, never arose. They tied the horses together with each nose fastened to the other's tail, side by side but pointing different directions, so that neither horse could walk off in the night without being held back by the other, who wouldn't like going backwards. The men made a wind break of their cloaks and settled down on their bed-rolls for the night.

'We will ride out at first light. We must get to the coast as soon as we can then move slowly north. If they show cooking smoke in the morning, it will indicate that they don't know we're here,' said Agmunder, almost to himself.

They spent the evening in quiet conversation. Once or twice they thought the wind brought the sound of a whinnying horse or two. That inspired fresh conversation and much speculation. The night was dry and reasonably warm for mid April.

There was no sign of frost in the pre-dawn gloom of the Fylde, as Agmunder and Henrik got their things together and mounted up, ready for the uncertainties of the day ahead. The horses were reluctant to start out before they could see well enough and took some encouragement to get started. But soon the sky lightened enough for them to lose their anxiety and, as the ground became less stony and firmer, they made good time. The pale sun rose ever higher over the fells far to the east, in a sky covered in a sheet of thin cloud, that made the whole sky almost white. To the west was a tell-tale wisp of smoke rising maybe two miles distant, by Agmunder's estimation. He was pleased the camp was relaxed enough to make smoke.

They made the coast before the sun was very high, even before the air lost it's cool dampness. Agmunder regarded the beach, that he'd hoped would give them better, smoother passage.

'It looks like were riding along the edge, then,' he said as he and Henrik saw that the coast here was completely made of smooth boulders and rocks the size of coconuts. There was no way a horse could walk on that surface. They would have to continue on the uneven, hard surface that they had ridden since making it out of the boggy ground. Neither of the men were looking forward to the ride back. The beach was a disappointment but what they saw after just a mile worried them deeply. They stopped the horses and dismounted as soon as they saw it.

'Well, it's not a wreck,' said Agmunder.

'No. It looks in fine condition.'

'A ship that size... A minimum crew of what, twenty?'

'Let's hope they're just here for supplies,' said Henrik, glancing at Agmunder for a clue.

'Let's hope, indeed,' was all he said.

They had a discussion about whether to take the horses. Agmunder argued that without them, they could be quieter and get closer. Henrik's point of view was that the party from the ship had horses, they had heard them in the night, and so without theirs they would be easily outrun. Each point of view had its own merit and they could not decide. As it turned out, they didn't have to make the decision. As they were still in discussion a voice, quite nearby, said 'There's a horse here! And another! Hey – Two horses!'

Before the men could react they were confronted by three Vikings, presumably from the ship, with spears. Agmunder cursed his luck, the men were probably a hunting party looking for boar or a deer in amongst the trees.

'Hello, who do we have here?' said the largest of the Vikings, eyeing Agmunder and Henrik, hoping they would make a run for it, then they could have some sport.

Agmunder thought the best plan was to be friendly and try to get into some conversation.

'We were trekking across the land and we saw your smoke. We came to see if you needed any help.'

'If you'd run aground,' added Henrik.

'So, you've seen that we have a ship. Lucky we caught you spying before you reported to your lord.'

'He *is* the lord!' said Henrik, rather to Agmunder's annoyance.

'I am Agmunder, Thane of the Fylde,' he said, glancing at Henrik.

The three Viking raiders looked at each other and the leader took the others aside. They spent a few minutes in conversation, deciding what to do, but none of them took their eyes off Agmunder and Henrik. Agmunder knew what they were going to do. Henrik guessed what they were going to do. It came as no surprise to either of them when the leader approached them.

'You will accompany us, to speak with Captain Thor.'

The other two Vikings untied their horses and lead them, whilst Agmunder and Henrik were shown which way to go with a jerk of the spear. The walk was over half a mile. After the first five hundred yards, walking in the gloom under the tight-knit branches of the trees, they emerged from the woodland edge and walked in fairly easy meadow-lands. The going was not boggy or rocky at all, with nice short grass, dotted here and there with early wild-flowers. The smoke was still visible and so they didn't need steering with the spear over the open country. The Vikings remained silent on the journey, doubtless waiting for the captives to make a break for it. Agmunder and Henrik had decided to offer no resistance and see what the captain had to say. In less than half an hour they approached the camp on the edge of the dunes overlooking the sea and the longship pulled up out of the water, resting at an angle, on the pebbles of the beach.

'What's this?' said the first other person they saw, who was driving a stake into the ground, with a goat on a rope attached to it. They made their way along a beaten path through the grasses that grew in the lee of the slight coastal ridge.

'Found them snooping around in the woods. Nice horses,' said the tallest.

The other man nodded and went back to tending the goat.

They dropped down to the shore and into the camp proper, and were told to wait. The leader went into a tent as the other two stood watching the captives. After a few seconds one of the other raiders took the horses to be tied up behind the tent. As he finished the deed, the leader came out of the tent, followed by another Viking. A large man with a sheepskin jerkin over his shirt and woollen calf bindings on his lower legs, criss-crossed with leather ties in a diamond pattern. He had an axe slung over his shoulder and his beard was plaited into two horns tied with thin leather laces at the ends. His ice-blue eyes looked at the captives from beneath the rim of his pointed and horned helmet.

'Which one of you claims to be Thane?' he demanded.

'I am Agmunder, Thane of the Fylde.'

'Then state your business. Why did you approach my camp without announcing yourself?'

'These men came across us just as we had dismounted to water the horses, we weren't near enough to shout a greeting,' said Agmunder.

'We didn't have chance to announce ourselves before these men challenged us,' added Henrik.

'And why would you be approaching our camp anyway?' asked the Viking.

'We came to see if all was well,' answered Agmunder.

The Viking looked around at the camp surrounding them, 'All is well.'

'We are glad to know it. Is there anything we can do to help you?'

'We don't need your help. You are a Viking, Agmunder, I see it. Did you ever need help when you were on foreign soil? I doubt it. I think that you, as I do now, would consider the offer of help an insult!'

The Viking adjusted the hang of his axe, which made Henrik look very worried. The man took a pace closer to Agmunder, 'I am Thor, Captain of that vessel and of these, my men. We came to see if there was anything here worth sending a settlement party to this green land for. I must say that on first viewing the land is lush and fertile, flat and probably easy to farm.'

'Captain Thor, I would welcome you to visit *my* farm and see how we have managed in the last year,' said Agmunder, thinking that the friendly angle might still be the best option. 'I arrived here a year ago, and have had great success with the crops in this mild climate. I would welcome more tenants to start their farms in the ness hereabouts, with pleasure.'

'If I wish, I will come to see your farm, and if I wish, I will take it from you, Thane of the Fylde. We are not interested in becoming slaves to your tenancies,' said Thor.

'We farm in peace. Violence is something that, for me, is in the past now,' said Agmunder.

'Peace is something that is dependent upon those who come to visit. It's not something *you* can expect to control without violent conflict,' replied Thor.

Turning abruptly, the captain walked back to his tent and went inside. The flap fell down to hide his retreating form and the camp suddenly seemed tense. The outcome of this visit looking less and less likely to be in Agmunder's favour.

'Follow me,' said one of the Vikings.

After a few minutes of sitting, tied to a stake, with their hands secured behind their backs and their ankles tied. Agmunder said, 'Well, that didn't go too well. Though, I suppose Captain Thor was courteous enough.'

'What can we do?' asked Henrik.

'We will have to wait and see what unfolds and hope that we will be released before anything too alarming befalls us.'

'Did you see where they took the horses? If we get a chance we must get them back, if we are to have any chance of getting away,' said Henrik.

'They went behind the tent, then I couldn't see. I hope they're tied up just round the back. The raider that took them wasn't long, was he?'

The two sat and watched the activity of the camp. There were about fifteen people in total, which possibly was all there were. The longship was not one of the big ones, although it was an ocean-going one.

'We have to look for an opportunity to get away. They don't seem to be bothered about watching us at the moment,' said Agmunder.

They sat a while longer, and were brought some soup by the cook's lad. A boy of about twelve. He didn't say a word but gave them a bowl each and a small round roll of bread between them. They ate in silence, and difficulty, with hands tied, as the evening became dusk and the fire became a more pronounced source of light in the landscape.

Suddenly, there were shouts and the camp became very active. Men ran here and there and Agmunder could see they were arming themselves in a hurry. Before he had thought to convey this to Henrik, who was facing away from the activity, several horses charged into the camp and fighting broke out between those on horseback and those on foot. Agmunder and Henrik knew that this was the most dangerous time for them. They would be helpless if anyone came to kill them now. They had to hope that the men of the camp were too busy repelling the attackers to bother with them.

Agmunder turned with difficulty to follow the action, wondering who could be attacking. He didn't have to wait long to find out. The next horse to charge into the clearing by the fire was ridden by the recognisable form of John of Kirkham, the captain of the men he had hired to chase Knut to ground. He was swinging a long-poled axe into the back of a Viking that was running directly towards Agmunder, knife in hand.

'Captain Kirkham!' shouted Agmunder above the din of battle.

The man reined in his horse, and, at great risk to himself, dismounted and rushed to where the two were tied. He quickly released Agmunder and was cutting through the leather bindings that kept Henrik from standing when two more Vikings burst, howling, through a row of low bushes, about ten yards away, and brandishing their weapons, came charging toward them. John and Agmunder turned to face them, while Henrik, in panic, tried to get a hold of the small knife John had been using. Twice he got a finger to it, but twice it escaped his grip, nudged further away in the dirt.

'Here!' shouted John to Agmunder, as he threw a seax over to where he was stood, defenceless, against the approaching Vikings.

Agmunder caught it well and dodged to the left as the first Viking swung his axe toward Agmunder's head. The blow missed and the Viking continued, by inertia, to pass Agmunder, his axe continuing its swing toward the ground as he passed. The seax, in Agmunder's expert grip, slashed out to the right and caught the Viking under the chin. He let go of his axe and grasped his throat stumbling on top of Henrik, who let out a shout, thinking he was being attacked. John, who was nearest, sheathed his weapon and using both hands, pulled the fallen body off Henrik and went back to freeing him with the small knife from the floor, all the time being guarded by Agmunder. As John finally got Henrik free, there was another gurgling shout, as Agmunder dealt with the other attacker. He went over to where John was helping Henrik to stand and clapped the captain on the shoulder.

'John, it is good to see you. How many of you are there? We have counted fifteen here in camp,' Agmunder shouted over the noise of the fighting nearby.

An arrow thudded into the post Henrik was recently released from. Agmunder raised an eyebrow to his friend, 'You have an admirer, Henrik!'

Henrik rushed to where the fallen axe of Agmunder's first kill lay in the sandy ground and picked it up. Although he wasn't experienced in fighting it's surprising what a man will do under pressure.

'There's ten of us, Thane,' said John. 'Rode out last night from Garstang. We'd had news of this raiding party and determined to come to your aid. We thought you'd be coming to Garstang but we learned from your wife and your tenant, Michael Shard, that you had come out here, just the two of you. We made best speed to get here.'

As Henrik turned, looking at the edge of the axe, there was a shout from behind them and they all turned to see Captain Thor charging out of his tent, toward where John was remounting his horse.

'John!' warned Agmunder, but it was too late.

John was stuck between being on foot and being fully mounted and couldn't react in time to the sudden threat. He was struck with a spear through the ribcage. An expert throw by Thor, from three yards away, as he launched the weapon from the run. The spear passed right through John's body, projecting far enough to injure the horse, which bolted from the camp, whinnying and tossing its head wildly as it went. The horse dragged John as far as they could see before, on the edge of a ridge, the spear dislodged and he and the weapon fell to the ground with a crack and a thud. The horse continued out of sight.

Henrik ran at Thor as the Viking pulled a dagger and turned to face him. Henrik wondered what chance he had against this fierce, experienced Viking captain and stopped before they were too close together. The two were in a stand off. Neither wanting to give up his position to attack the other. Although Thor was clearly the bigger man, Henrik had the advantage of better ground and the slight slope. Thor wasn't stupid, and thought quickly how to better his opponent. Agmunder grabbed the axe that the second attacker had swung at him and approached Thor, with a weapon in each hand. The captain watched the two men warily, knowing that one of them would make a move and then the other. He couldn't easily defend against two men, so started backing away. He raised his dagger to give a more fearsome appearance as he backed up toward his tent. As he did so, Edgar came riding into the small area by the fire. Agmunder's men glanced to check that he was one of their own. Seeing this distraction, Captain Thor quickly turned and ran into the darkness. He was gone.

'Edgar!' shouted Agmunder. 'Is my whole War-Band here?'

Edgar replied, 'Glad to find you well, Thane. We are about the same men you commanded. Tom and Jack, his brother, are here somewhere fighting on foot. And Lars is mounted to the west side. He took on the first two men we discovered and despatched them both with a single swing of his axe!'

'Lars is here? I must find him,' said Agmunder.

'I'll see what happened to the horses,' shouted Henrik as a spear came out of the dark and planted itself into the ground by his right foot. He pulled the spear out of the ground and with a comment of, 'Handy!' went off to see what had become of the horses, tucking the small knife into his belt. The sounds of battle were subsiding now and although it was nearly completely dark, Agmunder could tell by the shouts that Thor's scouting party had been overcome by the men of the Fylde.

'Keep one alive,' he shouted over and over as he made his way through the camp to find Lars, 'Try to make it Thor!'

Lars was on foot by the time he was discovered standing over no less than four slumped and sprawled Vikings at the foot of a small rise that backed onto the pebble beach. His horse was munching happily on the stiff grass that grew nearby.

'Lars! Well met, my friend,' said Agmunder, to the Dane.

'Greetings, Thane,' he replied, smiling and wiping the blade of his axe on a fallen enemy's trouser leg.

'Having fun?'

'I am, now I see you're alive...' he quickly looked Agmunder over for injuries or blood, seeing nothing, he added, 'and well.'

'I've been lucky. We have to capture Captain Thor.'

'I'm free,' said Lars, looking around him, grinning, 'I've finished here.'

The two set off, Lars following Agmunder's lead, into the grassy area away from the beach that Thor had headed off into after the confrontation with Agmunder and Henrik.

'He's a big man. Experienced. Old enough to be weary from running and fighting.' said Agmunder as they searched the bushes and grass topped dunes.

They couldn't see very well in the dark, moonless night and returned to the camp where the fires had been relit by the war-band, or stoked to provide light, heat and protection. The remaining men of John of Kirkham's troop were inspecting a pile of weapons and bounty stripped from the fallen by the light of the fires.

'This,' shouted Lars as they approached from the darkness, 'is Agmunder, Thane of the Fylde. He is now our commander. John, your has been killed, sadly. Brogged, by spear, between the shoulder blades by their, Captain Thor.'

They entered the camp, unchallenged and joined the others looking at the weapons they had captured.

'How many did we settle?'

'We have counted fourteen dead, Lars.'

Agmunder took up the narrative, 'Just one left alive then. Their captain is still out there somewhere. He is on foot and only had a dagger when we last saw him. Though it is possible that he knows of the location of more weapons. This is his camp after all. Keep a sentry on tonight, change every hour. Keep alert. We will track him in the morning.'

One of the men, someone Agmunder hadn't seen before, immediately took a spear and went to stand with his back to the fire looking out over the land, from the highest dune, protecting his eyes from the brightness and peering south into the darkness. Another man, Tom, chose to guard the other side of the camp and took up a similar high position looking east. The three quarter waning Moon finally rose large and orange over the fells. As it rose higher, through successive sentry changes, the light added to that of the fires, and the countryside around became more visible, bathed in its pale light.

The camp was busy even before dawn. By first light the horses were readied for the journey back to the town and four of the party: Agmunder, Lars, Tom and the man who had been first to sentry, a foreign man from eastern Europe called, Gothman, prepared to remain behind, to track Thor.

As the orange Moon paled above the grey horizon over the Irish Sea, far to the west, the top edge of Sunne, breached the gap between two fells to the east. Into that brightening glare rode the returning war party, laden with bounty, bound for Garstang.

'Well,' said Agmunder, always keen to share thoughts, 'Which way did Thor go?'

'If I were he,' said Lars, hitching his axe into place in his belt, 'I would have put as much land between us over night going east.   If he went north, or south, along the coast, he would only have one option if we found him, and that would be to turn away from the sea, inland. If he goes east,' he said pointing,'He can turn south or north or carry on east. We have more land to search and he has more to hide in.'

'Agreed,' said Agmunder.

Tom added his thoughts, 'If he just kept going east on foot, he will soon be caught by the war-band returning to Garstang later this morning. He may have thought of that too.'

'A good point.' said Lars.

Agmunder thought out loud, 'If he knows anything about the Fylde he wouldn't go north-east. That would leave him trapped on the ness. So, south-east is the only sensible option for him. Moving into the heartland of the Fylde with options of a road to Preston, Kirkham or Garstang, though he'd be foolish to go there, from the Black Pool.'

Turning to the other three, who were already making ready to mount up, he made the order to head south east toward the Black Pool, and Jack Smith's, at best speed.

They heeled their horses to a quick walk, all four of them in different directions as they left camp. It wouldn't do to miss Thor if he was hiding just a few yards away. After what seemed like an hour, but was no more than fifteen minutes, they were satisfied that Captain Thor had headed off in the night, trying to get as much distance between him and the war-band as possible. Under the light of the Moon, that could be quite a distance. They had to hope that they could find his tracks in the dry dirt as they rode.

'To the Black Pool,' shouted Lars, and they all turned south-east and left the camp, and the longship high and dry on the beach, behind.

They rode as fast as they could whilst still being able to keep a look out for tell-tale signs of a man's passing in the night. If Thor had been travelling by day it would be harder to track him. Being able to see easily made avoiding obstacles much easier. Even the most careful night traveller stood in a bit of boggy ground, or trampled a small bush or snapped an old dry branch and left an easy trail. Thor had been no different and it heartened the men to know they had guessed his moves correctly. There was a tree that stood alone by a small pond. It stood to the south of the water. Presumably, the dark pond, in the moonlight, looked like the shadow of the tree on the ground and at its edge, in the muddy bank, were two fresh foot holes and a churned area where someone, a big man, presumably Thor, had backed back out of the sludge and regained firmer ground before making his way around the tree to the right. There were tell-tale damp patches in the dry clay leading off that way. Agmunder thought that for it to be dark enough to make that error it would have had to have been between midnight and three hours later.

'So he's between three and six hours ahead, but at least three of those hours, for him, were in the dark.'

They rode off quickly in the direction of the Black Pool, with renewed determination. They now knew they were heading the right way and it was only a matter of time before they would spot a figure in the distance. The path toward Fiery Jack Smith's smithy was becoming more definite, worn, maybe by Jack himself going to the coast to catch fish for food. This would help them, but also the fugitive, Thor. They moved to a gallop along the track, adding to its worn surface as the four horses passed. Agmunder estimated that they would be at the smithy very shortly. There was every chance that Thor was already there.

'Ho!' shouted Gothman, pointing as he rode.

They looked to where his outstretched arm pointed. On the track, just half a mile ahead there was a small rise and a hobbling figure of a large man was cresting that rise.

'Maybe he's twisted his ankle in the pond,' said Agmunder. 'He's limping.'

They caught up with Thor as he sat down on the side of the path. He had heard the horses approaching and decided to take his chance at a peaceful meeting.

'You killed all my men. You have my ship and my weapons, save this.'

He threw his dagger into the dirt of the track before Lars' horse.

'What were you doing here?' asked Agmunder.

'We were a scouting party. Just looking about, you know. What's the land like? Any good for farming? Is it a rich area or just empty land? That sort of thing. My lord expects me back by harvest. He will come,' Thor answered.

'And we will be ready when he does,' said Lars.

'You'd better be, for my lord is also my father.'

Lars wasn't impressed, 'What kind of a name is Thor, anyway? How conceited to think that a mortal man could bear the name Thor!'

'It's a name I use when I'm out on patrol. It's not my real name. My father is not particularly religious. He would never have given me such a name.'

Agmunder spoke up, 'Well, do you want us to keep calling you "Thor"? What's your proper name?'

'I am called, Jorgen,' said the captain with resignation.

'Ha! Jorgen?' laughed Lars, looking at Agmunder, who shrugged.

Lars continued, 'It's a Danish name. It means "Farmer".'

Agmunder turned to look at the Viking captive, 'Farmer?' he asked with incredulity in his tone.

'Yes. I told you I was scouting for farmland. I wasn't lying. My father has tasked me with starting a new life for myself in a green and empty land. I had heard tales of this area and made it my first call. I see rich land and a flat landscape fit for the purpose of arable farming. I plan to plant barley, beans, oats, rye and wheat. I would register at the council and do it all properly.'

'You sound like Agmunder here,' said Lars.

Agmunder spoke, 'This ness is mine. I am Thane of the Fylde and control all the farms in this area. I am landlord to three tenants at a place known as Agmunder's Ness, by the Skiff Pool, on the River Wyre. You cannot farm here without being a tenant of mine.'

'I would be a tenant, Agmunder, Thane of the Fylde,' said Jorgen, worried that Agmunder had given him so much information. He must be sure it wouldn't get to the wrong hands. Either Agmunder trusted him, which he doubted, or he was done for.

'But there's the matter of your party killing John of Kirkham, a well respected man.'

'It wasn't my fault. My men...' he tailed off.

'But it *was* you,' said Lars, calmly, 'It was you who speared him to his horse.'

They could tell that Jorgen understood that he himself had, in fact, killed John.

As Lars spoke, Gothman made a show of going off to deal with the horses, but as he went from Jorgen's sight he circled back, stealthily and silently on the hard ground of the track, until he was right behind the sitting Dane.

'I don't know what to do with you,' said Agmunder.

As Thane, he was responsible for minor crimes and justice on Agmunder's Ness and parts of the Fylde nearby. Sitting before him was a murderer.

'I can farm. I can be a tenant, and I can farm for you, Thane,' said Jorgen in desperation, looking from Agmunder to Lars and back.

Behind him, Gothman raised his axe above his head and looked at Agmunder.

Agmunder spoke to Jorgen, 'I feel that your killing of Captain Kirkham has forced my hand rather, in this matter. He was a well respected man, a captain of the Fyrd,' he paused, 'and my personal friend.'

This last made Jorgen gulp, 'But they attacked *us*!' he shouted.

Agmunder looked into Jorgen's pleading eyes and then flicked his eyes up to Gothman's with an imperceptible nod. The blade swiftly fell to cleave Jorgen's helmet to the rim. Jorgen's body slumped heavily back onto the hard track, bright blood seeping from the gash into the dry, gritty dust of the surface.

'Get a horse,' commanded Lars, looking at Henrik.

Henrik went to where the horses were stood and brought both the animal and a length of rope from his pack. The rope was tied around Jorgen's foot and the horse was mounted.

'Drag him a good way off the track into the bush. Leave him for the crows to pick clean, then join us at John Smith's workshop, by the Black Pool, along this track,' said Agmunder, pointing south.

'I thought that Vikings were burnt with their ships?' said Henrik.

'Viking warrior *lords* are, but this is a farmer! Besides, I have a use for that ship,' said Agmunder, as he kicked his horse into a walk along the track towards Jack Smith's.

As Henrik urged his horse off into the scrub surrounding the group, the body of Jorgen dragging behind through the grasses and over small bushes, the others mounted up and prepared to ride the short distance to the blacksmith's house. They rode slowly, discussing the possible consequences of the execution of

Jorgen. He was, supposedly, the son of a lord of Denmark. He might send a war-band to find out what happened. From what Jorgen had said, his father knew where he was scouting. There would be a day when Agmunder had to answer the questions of Jorgen's father. But that day was in the future and there was interesting work to be done on the Fylde. As they came into view of the blacksmith's workshop, Henrik joined them. Trotting up from behind.

'Ho! Agmunder.'

He drew level with Agmunder's horse and slowed to match speed, 'There was a shallow boggy gash in the ground about half a mile from the track. Part of a small creek, I think. It was ideal for rolling a body into. The water and the crows will render Jorgen down to bleached bones in no time, if he doesn't sink into the mud first,' Henrik reported, with a broad smile.

'Well done, Henrik. Good thinking.'

'You know his father will come looking?'

'Of course,' said Lars, 'You haven't met Fiery Jack Smith, have you, Henrik?'

They rode to the buildings on the edge of the mere. Not much gets past the inquisitive nose of John the blacksmith, and before they had approached more than two hundred paces he emerged from the workshop, wiping his brow with a cloth and shouting greeting to Lars and Agmunder. *A good memory and good eyesight!'* thought Agmunder, as they rode the final few yards.

They dismounted and gave the reigns to Henrik to tie the horses up, as the three older men, Agmunder, Lars and Gothman, shook hands with Jack Smith. Gothman went to help with the animals.

'Have you been dealing with the scouting party up the coast?' asked John, of the Thane.

'You miss nothing, Jack!'

'I miss my sleep,' he said, 'Gretel has had our son. We have called him, Marton after Gretel's father.'

'A son. Well done,' said Lars.

'Yes, congratulations, Jack,' agreed Agmunder.

'Grim has agreed to christen him when his church is built.'

'It is about that, that I have come,' said Agmunder.

'Come inside and have some stew, Thane. Tell me what's on your mind. If I can help, I will be more than happy.'

'It is I who bring the help, Jack. Is Grim about?'

They went into Jack's house and Agmunder and Lars congratulated Gretel on the safe birth of the baby Marton. Grim was sat at the table with a bowl of stew in front of him and another was waiting for Jack at the head of the table.

'Please sit, Thane, Lars,' said Gretel expertly getting another bowl of stew with the baby carried in a sling on her chest as she worked.

'There's two more of them out there,' said Jack, as Gretel got to work readying more places at the table for the others.

The stew was filling, hot and delicious, as always. Agmunder paid for the meal with two silver pennies, amid protests from Jack. He insisted until Jack cheerfully relented, and the conversation turned to the reason for their visit.

'Grim,' started Agmunder, 'I understand that you wish to build a church on the coast?'

Grim looked up, 'Yes, Thane. I have planned it for a long time and will accomplish it when time serves. I pray, daily, for deliverance of the means, good Thane.'

'The means, master Grim, is sitting on the beach by Captain Jorgen's camp.'

'You speak in riddles, my Thane. What do you mean by that?'

'There was a scouting party that came ashore about six miles north along the coast. Shall we say that we rid the Fylde of their threat? Nevertheless, they had a twenty man longship. Now, I have no use for such a vessel, but I thought I had heard of a man hereabouts that wanted to use an upturned longship as roof for his chapel?'

Agmunder could see a tear of joy come to Grim's eye, as they sat in the gloom of the house. A tiny sparkle in the darkness. The man put his hands together and offered a short, silent prayer in thanks for the deliverance of the ship.

'The ship is safely beached at the moment and is in perfect condition. This was no wreck. We will deliver it to the coast wherever you wish, Grim. Consider it a present from the Thane.'

John spoke up, 'I will make a small fire and erect a red flag on the coast where Grim tells me to.'

'You are a good friend,' said Agmunder, 'I will deliver the ship in seven day's time, winds willing.'

'We will be ready,' said Jack, looking at Grim, who nodded, as he shook Agmunder's hand.

CHAPTER 13
The Keel Roof

Over the last week, Agmunder and the other farmers of the ness had busied themselves with their duties on the land. All except Michael, who had piglets to deal with, and a protective mother sow to stay clear of while doing it. A week to the day after they had been at Jack Smith's, Agmunder visited Michael in the early morning as he tended the mother and piglets in the enclosure to the south of his dwelling.

'Today we go to deliver the longship to Grim. Do you have any sea faring experience?'

Michael looked up from a piglet that he was inspecting, 'I do not, good Thane.'

'In that case you can keep an eye on all the other farms. I am taking Erik in your place. Henrik and Lars will attend also. We should be back by nightfall tonight.'

'Very well, good Thane.'

Agmunder waved to the approaching Lars and they rode together to Agmunder's farmhouse to collect Erik. With Erik riding with Agmunder they set off from Henrik's farmstead on the track to the west. They travelled through the thorns and continued on their course until, by midday, they were in sight of the ship on the beach. The tide was high and it wouldn't take much to re-float the ship. The wind was light but from the north west. Ideal for a southerly journey. Henrik had no experience as a sailor, but Agmunder had another plan for him. They had to get back home from wherever grim had decided his church will be, and so, the horses had to be taken down the coast, following the ship. This was Henrik's task today.

'I estimate that we will be there before the sun is half way down today. Maybe two hours? Three?' said Agmunder as he lifted Erik into the ship. Erik immediately started preparing the sail for use, untying ropes and sheets, handling the yardarm, though he was too small to lift it. The steerboard too was currently stowed in the ship and movement about inside the vessel was awkward. Lars and Henrik lifted the anchor stone into the bows, careful not to drop it in. Agmunder put his shoulder to the keel at the front of the ship and felt the weight of it.

'These pebbles will act like rollers under the ship,' he said, 'It should be easy to slide her into the sea.'

The three men got ready to move the ship. It was a shame in some ways that the beach wasn't smooth sand, they could have used the horses to pull the ship into the water, but, they did have the advantage of the pebbles easing the friction. The three men took up position at the front of the ship and heaved. Slowly the ship began to slide across the pebbles and smooth, weed-covered boulders below the hull. In a minute or two the back end of the ship was floating in the sea and in another two minutes the bows floated free of the beach with the three men pulling on ropes to stop her getting away completely. Henrik returned to the horses and bid them a safe journey.

'We shan't be going too far off shore, Henrik,' said Agmunder, as Lars climbed aboard.

Agmunder gave the ship a push away from shore and climbed over the bow-rail to take his position by the bow.

It looked strange being in a longship without the shields along the sides, and with only two other people in it, but there was work to be done. First they set the steerboard in position and showed Erik how to hold it straight as they went to sort out the sail.

Lars and Agmunder hauled on the ropes that raised the sail-bearing yardarm to almost the top of the mast. They tied it off and his father went to relieve Erik of the strain of trying to turn the ship. As Agmunder heaved on the tiller, and with Lars pushing on an oar onto the sea bed, the ship slowly turned south and, with a pull on the left hand sail sheet that nearly had Erik sprawled on the deck, the wind filled the sail and they were off to see Grim.

They made good time, Henrik having to keep the horses at a good walking speed on the sandy trail at the edge of the beach to keep up with them. The wind was fair and drove the eager vessel southwards along the straight coastline. After about a mile, the pebble beach that Henrik had to stay off to allow the horses to walk safely, gave way to golden, flat sand that stretched as far as he could see to the south. Henrik steered the horse pack onto the smooth sandy beach. *This is going to be an easy ride,* he thought. Agmunder kept the longship about five hundred yards off shore to protect the steerboard in the brown and shallow sea. He could see from the type of waves that lapped the shore, and from the colour of the water, dulled by sand stirred up from below, that the sea bed was smooth but a very shallow slope beneath them. He estimated that they probably had only two or three feet of water beneath the keel, maybe less, even at this distance from shore.

As the sun dropped toward the half way down point, they spotted a red flag on the coast ahead and smoke beginning to rise from a fire. They would be there in less than half an hour. Henrik moved on in front of the ship, now at a canter, waving to the gathered people on the beach as he rode. Henrik wondered where Grim and John Smith had got so many helpers from as he neared the red flag atop a dune. Shortly he reached the crowd and from the longship Agmunder could see them making their way to the water's edge.

Looking up at the pennant at the top of the mast Agmunder could see that the wind had moved more westerly, perfect for their approach to the shore. He steered slightly out to sea, maybe just two hundred yards more and then, with a huge heave on the tiller, he swung the ship directly east, toward the gathered crowd of people. With the wind directly behind the ship picked up a little more speed and nodded its way through the waves as they approached the sandy shore.

There was a knock and a grinding, shooshing sound and they lurched to a stop. Erik was in the bow and readily caught the rope thrown from Henrik's horse which stood up to its fetlocks in the wavelets that calmly smoothed the sand. Erik made the rope fast around the bow-post and Henrik attached the other two horses to his end and began to work the animals to drag the ship onto the beach. The people, that Grim and Jack had brought to help, carried one of several smooth logs and placed it in front of the ship's keel to act as a roller. Between the shape of the ship and the smoothness of the beach, and the row of helpers on each side, mindless of their wet feet, this worked very well and soon they had another roller in place as the ship crawled from the sea onto the sunny beach.

Henrik was controlling the horses, in the main, but in the intervals when they were not required he was to be found chatting with a young woman who had brought bread and cheese for the crowd to eat. Standing among her baskets, Henrik and the woman talked rather more than helped. Once or twice Agmunder looked over to where the two stood, as he went about the business of getting the ship up the beach, and smiled to himself. He had never known anything sway Henrik from the task at hand before. It could only mean one thing.

The dunes, that were to be the only barrier between Grim's church and the sea, were not too far from the high water mark and soon the ship was brought to a standstill with its bow resting against the first dune of the coastal ridge.

Grim stood atop the dune and indicated a flattened and marked off area just beyond, with an outstretched arm.

'This, is where I will build my church. Dedicated to those that ply the waves and those that wait at home for their safe return,' he called to the crowd, who cheered.

They set to with renewed vigour and the ship was stripped of everything that made it seagoing. The mast came down and the yardarm was removed. Then the mast itself was released from its pivot and thrown onto the beach. The steerboard was cut loose and lowered over the stern-rail and laid on the sand next to the mast (Useful wood).

All the ropes of the rigging were simply cut from their moorings and coiled for use later. Everything that wasn't attached to the ship was thrown onto the pile. The twenty oars. An axe. Two shields. A thick sheet of canvas from the foredeck. Two plain horn mugs and more rope.

When everything was removed from the longship that wouldn't be needed when it formed the roof of the church, they started to move it into position between the dunes. The rollers were not as useful here in the soft, windblown sand and the people had to employ a levering method using the oars. Within an hour, though, they had the hull wrestled between the dunes and laid alongside the flattened area.

'Is there anything else we can do to help?' asked Agmunder, as Lars and Erik untied the ropes and coiled them.

'My people here will help me construct my chapel,' said Grim.

'Then we will be on our way, we are sorry to leave you, but it will be dark before we get back,' said Agmunder.

'Look,' said Erik.

They looked. He was standing in the bow of the longship, holding an impressive shield aloft. A circular Viking shield, with a plain wooden board, nice shining steel rim edging and a brilliant white central boss.

'Please,' said Grim, 'Take it as a memento and a symbol of our thanks.'

Lars rode his horse to the side of the ship and Erik, with the shield, climbed on in front of the Dane.

'Thank you, Grim. I will return soon to see if there is anything I can do to help, but for now I must return to my farm. There is the spring harvest to deal with.'

Agmunder rode over to where Henrik was in conversation with the young woman, still.

'Are you coming back tonight? You have a farm and responsibilities on the ness, Henrik.'

'Oh, yes, Thane,' he said. Then, turning to the woman he added, 'As soon as I can, I'll be back to help, Eleanor.'

Agmunder rolled his eyes to the sky.

The couple looked at each other and smiled.

The next few days were busy on the farms as each sowed the seeds of their summer harvest crops. Taking it in turns to harrow their field with Alsvior or Henrik's horse, Alfred. All except, Michael who was still busy keeping his fences in good order after the attentions of the sow. Even Henrik, plagued with thoughts of his encounter with the girl on the coast, knuckled down and saw to his farm's needs without stinting on what had to be done. They all worked hard and had little time for conversation, or other distractions, as they toiled to get the crops sown.

Agmunder was particularly glad that the business with Thor was out of the way, but, like Henrik in particular, thought a lot about returning to Grim's church to help out there. And so it wasn't long after the crops were in the field and the others cleared ready for the year ahead that Agmunder and Henrik found themselves in the saddle heading south again through the break in the hawthorns with the flat horizon ahead of them. To the right as they rode Agmunder's thoughts were taken by a small hill, bordered on the eastern slope by yet more brambles and hawthorn bushes. He had never explored this area and decided that once their work at Grim's Keel Chapel was complete he would make his way up and see what the view was like.

They rode for the whole morning and soon saw the impressive chapel in the distance. The coast at this point was low, flat and bleak. The roof stood clearly visible on the horizon even a mile distant. Henrik was grinning, his thoughts betrayed on his lips. Conversation had been sparse and short during the trip, both men consumed by their private thoughts.

'Agmunder! Henrik!', shouted Grim at their appearance over the small dunes just inland of the chapel's position.

'Well met, Grim,' hailed the Viking as they drew to a halt by a pile of split logs.

They dismounted and shook hands with Grim and several of the workforce that gathered round them.

Agmunder regarded the work so far. The keel was inverted and firmly supported by six huge beams. Two at the front, two centrally placed, and the third pair at the rear of what once was a ship. The sides were seven or eight feet above the levelled ground and the whole stood twelve or thirteen feet to the top of the roof. The keel. There were smaller beams outlining the position of the entrance at what was the stern end of the ship, on the western end of the chapel. The hull being aligned west to east, door to altar.

'Impressive,' was all that Agmunder said before stooping to lift the end of a board that was being stood upright by one of the helpers, a man that Agmunder thought he had seen at Jack's smithy one time.

Henrik found himself looking around for the bread stall. It was not there. He approached a man he had worked with when they brought the ship ashore.

'Have you seen Eleanor?'

'She's away at the market in Kirkham this week, my friend She's been gone four days. He thought a little, 'She said, if you arrived while she was away, to tell you that she will be back soon.'

'Oh. Good. Er... Need a hand?'

'You can grab that axe and help shape these beams,' said the man, 'Good to see you have your priorities right!' he laughed.

Henrik coloured slightly as he hefted the axe and joined the man, whom he soon found was another 'John', and set to cutting tenons on the end of the beams. The afternoon was fine and warm and the work kept Henrik busy until a voice over his shoulder said, 'Hello, Henrik.'

He turned to see Eleanor, smiling in the sunshine. All the emotion of separation and longing over the last few weeks overflowed and he dropped the axe and quickly took the young woman in his arms. He hugged her for what seemed an age before releasing her to look at her face in the bright afternoon light.

'It's been so long since I've seen anything so beautiful,' he said at length.

'It's been five weeks,' said Eleanor with a smile.

This factual statement seemed to lessen Henrik's demeanour. The smile fading slightly on his lips.

'But it's been five weeks too long,' she added, returning the smile to Henrik's face as he hugged her again.

'I never want to let you go,' he said in her ear.

'You'll have to. The Thane approacheth.'

'Eleanor, so nice to see you,' said Agmunder as he got near enough to speak without shouting. Eleanor bowed slightly, 'Thane.'

'Henrik has been like a puppy left at home this last month,' he said.

'Five weeks,' said Henrik.

'See what I mean?' laughed the Viking.

Eleanor looked into Henrik's eyes, 'I've missed him too.'

They set about the work on the chapel for the rest of the afternoon, Henrik happily working close by Eleanor, as he continued to help John shape the wood frame pieces. Over the next five days and with the dozen or so people helping Grim to build his chapel it wasn't long before the work was almost completed on the Keel-Hull-Church. Agmunder, who had given of his time and expertise as he prepared to leave, was roundly thanked for his efforts by Grim and those he'd worked with.

'It is a shame, but I have to see my farm. I've enjoyed helping to build your church, Grim.'

'Your help has been gratefully received, Agmunder. God will bless you, whether you believe or not!'

'Thank you, Grim.'

Agmunder prepared to leave and noticed that Henrik was noticeable by his absence. He looked around and found him working on the bell support frame, behind the smaller of the two dunes. Something that would have made more sense to be done nearer to the building site. He was hiding!

'Henrik.'

Henrik looked up, his face almost a mask of guilt.

'Henrik, I am going back to my farm. I suppose you think I expect you to come with me. But, your farm is in order and they still need help here. Maybe more than your farm needs you for a week or two. Please, stay as you wish, but return in a timely manner. Bring your woman if you choose but return in ten days at the latest.'

'Thank you, Agmunder, Thane of the Fylde,' said Henrik, bowing in gratitude for the extension to his stay.

'Your life is your own, Henrik. I like having you around and you're an attentive farmer. But, for you, the important things are here at the moment. Enjoy another few days working here, and being near to Eleanor.'

'Thank you. I will.'

'You're a good man, Henrik. Farewell for now.'

Agmunder returned to Alsvior and made some last adjustment to his saddle, then mounted and rode north on the track, with a wave to the assembled workforce.

CHAPTER 14
The Hill

As he rode his mind returned to the hill that he had seen as he rode down to help 'Keel Grim', as the preacher was becoming known. He couldn't put his finger on it, but there was a draw for him to visit the hill and see the lay of the land thereabouts. He adjusted his direction almost unconsciously, taking the left path at an almost invisible fork in the track just north of Jack's smithy. It was a path he'd noticed before on their return from Jack's though he'd never wondered where it led.

The evening came on quickly as low cloud gathered on the western horizon, snuffing the light from the low sun prematurely. Agmunder took shelter in the lee of the hawthorn bushes and by the last of the daylight took some twigs, dry windfall splinters that had been sheltered under the hawthorns, to make a fire, returning to chop a few stout branches down as the flames took hold and grew. As the warm late May night drew in, he fried fish in goose fat and broke bread as the stars came out over the fells. He sat gazing at Venus, close to the western horizon at dusk, as she sank towards the sea. In Leo the lion, a fearsome beast, close to the star Regulus, Jupiter shone his steady light. Agmunder noted fiery Mars to the left of Jupiter and wondered what omen that signified. The King of the gods consorting with the god of war as the goddess of love looked the other way. To their left, the half phased Moon shone her helpful light. Agmunder watched the planets, the Moon and the stars until the building clouds covered Jupiter's creamy face with misty tendrils, and then he settled down to sleep.

The next morning was cloudy, but not too chilly, as he set off to explore the hill. He found a break in the hawthorns where there was evidence that someone had passed through before, but not for some time.

The faint path led steadily up the slope until it suddenly became quite steep and he had to encourage Alsvior to speed up a little as he took the incline. It took only five minutes to ascend to the top of the escarpment, for that is how it turned out, not a hill as such, but a ridge in the land. Beyond the ridge the land sloped down to the seashore in a gentler slope. From the top, looking east, Agmunder could see the land spread out below him as far as the fells. He could see smoke on the horizon to the south east. *'Preston!'* he though to himself. He'd never been, but had been told it's thriving, bustling town streets should be seen by anyone with a hunger for adventure.

To the south he was pleased that he could see smoke rising from what must be the cooking fires at Grim's Keel-Church. His mind wandered to Henrik and Eleanor. They would make a lovely couple. *Very complimentary*, he thought.

Looking north west there was a line of cliffs that Henrik had ridden below on the beach as they delivered the longship. To the north and north east, there was just the low flat land and, on a clear day like today, the Cumbrian hills on the horizon beyond the bay. Much more like mountains than the one on which he stood. However, there was an impressive view and a useful advantage from any direction, in time of attack. He wondered if he should get a tenant to run his farm and build a fortress here on the edge of the ridge. Cement his domination of the area. He wondered if the council would allow it.

After a few minutes though, he had made up his mind. Although he came to the Fylde to lead the quiet life and farm into his old age, life has a habit of changing one's plans and moving off in a different direction. It made a lot of sense to build a stronghold. Especially after the threats of Jorgen about his father coming to avenge his death. They had dismissed that as bravado at the time, but in Viking society fathers have a duty to despatch those that kill their sons, especially those higher up in society. It was a real threat. Agmunder had responsibilities to his tenants and the people of the Fylde as their Thane, to protect them from violence. These were responsibilities which he took very seriously.

With the thought of a stronghold, his own castle, in his mind, he remounted his horse and headed north along the ridge that sloped gently down to the flat land ahead. He turned right onto a faint path when he reached the bottom of the higher ground and headed towards the familiar thick line of thorn bushes to the west of Agmunder's Ness. He was surprised to see that the path led to an almost imperceptible break in the thorns and an easy way through to the fertile land leading to his farm. By midday he was home, much to the pleasure of Fjord, Erik and Svala. They ate lunch outside and talked about the things that had been going on in his absence and how things were going at Grim's Keel Church. Agmunder told them about coming back via the hill that was almost hidden from view from their place on the ness due to the very line of hawthorns that provided the passage towards it. He didn't mention the thoughts of building a fortress. He might have felt he needed to justify the building and didn't want to raise the possibility of Viking retribution raids to his family on this happy occasion. Svala watched him eat. She could sense that there was more to the tale and resolved to find out that night, after Erik was asleep.

Agmunder had a walk around the farm in the warm late may afternoon, with Erik in tow. They looked at each field and discussed the crops and the weather and the harvest plans for nine week's time. They checked on the goat and the chickens and then Erik was sent to see to anything that Alsvior might need. He'd been put in his paddock area on return to the farm but needed to be brushed, and settled. The hooves needed to be checked for stones and buckets of river water added to his trough.

Late in the evening, as Svala and Agmunder sat quietly by the light of the fire, she asked, 'What else is there to tell, husband?'

'What? More about what?'

'Agmunder, this afternoon you said lots about where you had been, and plenty about what you had accomplished, but nothing about what you felt. I could see in your eyes that there is much you didn't share at the table.'

Agmunder thought a while in silence staring, lost, into the fire. Svala waited in silence. If he decided to tell her, he would. If he decided not to tell her, that was up to him.

'The position up on the hill is excellent. Easy to defend and with such a wonderful view of the land,' he said at length.

Svala remained silent. There was more and she didn't want to interrupt the information. She was patient and liked to marshal her thoughts before making any statement.

He continued, 'I was thinking of getting another tenant to run Henrik's farm. Making Henrik my lieutenant in residence here, with Eleanor, once I've built a stronghold on the hill.'

Still she waited, though her interest in Eleanor was piqued by this statement.

'I think that Jorgen's father will send a war-band, if not this year, then next, certainly. We need to be ready. We can't afford not to be ready, and we can afford to build. We have enough of an income from the tenants and the farm. This is good land and our crops flourish. We have most of our gold coins and plenty more money to come from the crops each year. I know we came here to farm, but trouble will follow and we have to be ready to resist.'

Svala sat in silence, lost in the fire's dancing flames. Eventually, she asked, 'Do you think we have that long? If it were Erik that had been killed you would be on the sea before the news had stopped ringing in your ears!'

Agmunder took this as an agreement and said nothing more on the subject. He reached over and pulled the wolf-skin cover off the bed and covered them over where they sat, still looking at the slowly dying fire.

The sun rose bright in a clear blue sky and a wind whipped little waves swiftly across the skiff-pool, bulrushes bending in the stiff breeze. Agmunder led Alsvior from his field and prepared to leave.

'These things are best settled as soon as practical. There are a few days yet before we have much work on the farm. I will ride to Garstang today to make enquiries about building a fort on the hill. I will call to see Lars on the way back. I will be home tomorrow if not sooner.'

With that he mounted the horse and rode off at a canter. Svala watched him go, sensing the urgency in his shrinking figure.

Agmunder thought to himself, that he wished he had visited the hill sooner. He hadn't given much thought to the very real threat of Jorgen's avengers until he stood atop the hill and saw how good the command of the land was. At that very moment he had been filled with a sense that he had to build a fortress to protect what he had. The farm on the ness was a splendid place to live, but was indefensible, and vulnerable to attack. So close to the water. An arrow shot or spear's throw from a longship on the water could set fire to the thatch. There were too many places down stream that could hide a landing party. He remembered how quickly Knut's boat had been hidden behind the stand of brambles. No, he had to command the land and to do that he had to have his fortified dwelling on the highest bit of land in the area. The time had come for Agmunder to truly be the Thane of the Fylde, and to do so meant he had to be invincible in his own land.

He arrived in Garstang mid-morning, having found that Lars wasn't at his farmstead. He found him at the inn. There was much joviality in the welcome he received from the landlord, Edred, and Lars. Many locals were pleased to shake his hand in friendship and respect equally.

'I am here on business!' Agmunder announced to his friend.

He explained about the thoughts he'd had on building a fortress on the hill, and Lars agreed it made sense. He had been thinking on the possibility of a war-band coming from Norway for the last few weeks too. He offered help in building the fortress.

'You need to be able to summon your fyrd, Agmunder. Maybe a beacon would be prudent? You could light it only when the fyrd were required, thick, black smoke in the day, bright fire at night. I can see the hill from my farm as can many in the Fylde. I'm sure the tenant farmers on the ness would see it too, even through the screen of hawthorns. We need to prepare for the day when sails are seen on the sea,' he mused.

'I have to get official permission first, Lars. First things first.'

'Then there's no time to waste. Exercise your right to urgent council and get started. Today!'

'That's why I'm here. Would you come with me, friend and advisor?'

'It would be an honour, as always, my Thane.'

The two made the short walk to the council building in just a few minutes and were allowed straight to the front of the existing queue by the bowing populace that thronged the hall getting their licenses and paying their taxes and whatever ordinary people did in the council offices.

Weasel-Faced Max said, 'Amounder, how can the council assist you today?'

Agmunder, with enthusiastic assistance from Lars, detailed his plan to oversee the ness with a stronghold on the hill. He explained about the farming rearrangement and made enquiries about formally appointing Henrik as his second, to take care of the farms in the Agmunder's Ness area. All went well and apart from the fee, which was rather higher than either Agmunder or Lars had though possible, it was agreed. The wily Max had detected Agmunder's desperation and hiked the fee, a good salesman for the council.

Although the council wanted four gold coins for the land, Agmunder paid just three of his Norse coins to the official at the square table, with another promised when the fort was completed. He was given a stamped parchment giving him title to a circular area, five hundred paces in radius, from the highest point on the hill. He was advised that when the fort was built he had to return to register it by name, and pay for the deed of course, as he was to build on generally unowned ground. The first owner of such land got to name it for registration and future tax payment purposes. This amused Agmunder, and he began to think about what he could call his hill fort. He hoped that a name would become self evident as they worked at its construction.

Clutching his registration document and the title to the land, he returned to the inn for the night, pleased that in name at least, he had got something done so quickly. The land was his and the building could commence. Tomorrow morning he could place some large wood orders and arrange delivery to the hill next month. July would be free to build in, but by August he would be needed on his farm. There was no way, he thought after due consideration, that Henrik would be able to sort out all of Agmunder's crops, as well as his own, after just a few weeks on the farm. But, happily, he contented himself with the thought that building could begin on the hill. The hill with no name.

June started well enough, with excellent weather for the delivery of materials to the hill top. The wagon followed the path that Agmunder had gone home on from the hilltop. Avoiding the impossible climb up the hill's steep front. They skirted round to the north and drove the load up the slight but steady incline. Agmunder joined them as they passed the hawthorn patch, emerging through the break in the bushes as they turned west to begin the long climb. From Agmunder's Ness the only sensible way to approach the hill was through the breck, the passage through the hawthorns. *Maybe,* he thought, *I should call my new possession Breck Hill? Lars would like that,* he mused further, *it would be a connection to his farm at Lars' Breck.*

'Well met Thane,' shouted the wagon driver.

'Indeed,' answered the Thane.

'I have not seen you since I delivered the wood for your farm, Thane. I trust everything is going well?'

'As well as can be hoped, thank you.'

After this initial round of pleasantries they travelled mostly in silence, watching the way ahead for obstacles and potential difficulties. Agmunder, lost in his plans and thoughts of his fortress design.

There was a moment when the load shifted suddenly on the wagon as the incline increased sharply with uneven ground beneath the wheels and the horses faltered, but in general the long haul up the steady slope went well and they arrived ahead of their projected time. Even the horses appeared glad to be able to stop pulling the load. They stood looking at the ground in search of something to eat as the load gang hit the chocks with their heavy hammers to release the wood. There was a cacophonous sound as the logs rolled off the side of each of the wagons into an untidy pile at each side. There was the squeaking sound of the odd beam shifting into a more comfortable position for a few seconds before everything went quiet again and Agmunder was satisfied that the preparations for building his fortress were properly under way. They were joined on the hilltop by Henrik who had ridden out from Agmunder's Ness to see the site for himself on his horse, Alfred. He looked at the raw materials on the hilltop in satisfaction and slapped Agmunder on the shoulder in congratulation.

The load gang worked over the next three hours to position the beams as directed by Agmunder ready for the building workforce to arrive in the morning. As the clouds moved in from the west, Agmunder saw that everything was as he had asked and they rode together on the return trip until they parted their ways at the stand of hawthorn. Although cloudy he was sure it wasn't going to rain in the next few days to spoil his building plans. Agmunder and Henrik said their goodbyes to the wagoneers and slipped through the breck towards his farm as the empty wagons turned south to skirt round the river on their return to Garstang. They were to return in two weeks with the first lot of stockade spike poles.

On their return to the farm they were pleased to see that Eleanor was waiting for them, standing with an older man who was holding the reins of a fine looking horse. He was older than Agmunder but younger than Michael Shard. Agmunder hadn't seen him before and wondered who it could be. Eleanor appeared excited about something.

'Ho, there!' shouted Agmunder in greeting through the gloom of the thickly clouded evening.

'Welcome home, Thane,' shouted Eleanor, turning to the older man and talking animatedly.

Henrik had brought Eleanor back from Keel-Grim's building site when he returned. The work there had gone well and the building was, externally at any rate, almost complete. After a serious but short conversation between himself and Agmunder, about the proposed changes to operational arrangements on the ness, he had readily agreed to take over the running of Agmunder's farm as soon as the fort accommodation was ready to move into. Meanwhile he had been given the task of finding a tenant for his own farm that would still require tending.

'I haven't told you yet, Agmunder, but, we have found what we consider a suitable a tenant for my farm,' said Henrik, with a glance at Eleanor as he dismounted.

Eleanor raised her hand that was clasped in the hand of the stranger. Agmunder approached closer and noticed a similarity of features between the man and Eleanor. Her father, he assumed.

'Agmunder, this is my uncle,' said Eleanor.

'Of course,' said Agmunder shaking him warmly by the hand. He remembered that Eleanor's Father had died of an infection contracted tending vegetables on a farm near the fishing port of Preston. Not a thing he should have forgotten, he admonished himself.

If Agmunder had any reservations about Eleanor's uncle, Thomas, in conversation with the three round the table over supper that night he learned that he had been a farm manager for a wealthy landowner the other side of the river to the south of Preston at a place called, In translation, Waters Town (Eauxton in the Angle tongue) although it wasn't much more than a few houses and the manor, by all accounts. This seemed to be a very good person to have nearby. Not only was he fully experienced in farming, and on a larger scale than the whole of Agmunder's Ness, and had a superb horse, but he would be trusted to do right by the couple in charge as he was family and it was obvious that he thought the world of Eleanor and was rather taken with Henrik, too.

By mid morning the following day, Agmunder's party assembled on the hilltop. Agmunder stood on the hill, next the piles of wood, with Lars, Erik, Michael, Henrik and Thomas, who was keen to become part of the community. Even Will Tanner, who preferred to farm alone and had kept largely to himself since coming to farm on the ness, had joined them. They stood admiring the vista to the east and watched as the work-party crossed the land toward them, a gang of what looked like thirty or so men loaded with equipment and more loaded on three horses with them. The fortress would be built on a good vantage point, they all agreed. It was another hour before the work-party had ascended the steep slope to sit breathless for a while on the ground. A drink was passed round as they recovered from the climb.

They brought spades and ropes and hammers and saws and chisels and a whole assortment of equipment that Agmunder knew would all be very useful in erecting his fortress. The ground on top of the hill was relatively rock free and covered in waving grass that came up to their calves. Even exposed as it was to the worst of the westerly winds that swept over the raised ground the grass endured and thrived. Despite the huge amount of equipment, no-one had brought a scythe or sickle, and so the building started with them marking out the outer wall with pegs and rope in the long grass. Soon, however, the grass was flattened with the passage of many feet. From even a short distance it was obvious where the fort was going to be. It wasn't going to be large. Enough for a family to live in and room for food reserves to support the fighting men for a week if need be. Sieges were rare in Viking times. Most battles were pitched and short, the raiders coming for immediate gains, not land or property. There was room to sleep twenty, and with another twenty on duty there could be a fifty or so people comfortably in the fort if need be. Enough to see of an attack of three longship crews.

'Any wooden structure can be burned, Agmunder,' said one of the workmen as they took their lunch in the hot sun of the early afternoon on that first day.

'I am planning to roof the buildings with a thin layer of sand mixed with lime. It will protect the roof from fire arrows. I plan to pitch the roof quite steeply so they will slide off onto the ground. Anything lower down the inner walls we can deal with ourselves before it catches hold. But the main purpose of the fort is to garrison the men until they go to fight. We will try to meet the attackers from our position of superiority, rather than waiting for them to arrive. The roof plan is a precaution against surprise attack,' explained Agmunder to the interested men that listened.

Several of the men nodded at this and there were a few exclamations from those impressed by the planning. By the end of the first day there were four huge, twelve foot tall, posts, secured into post-holes a yard deep at the corners of the sixty foot square. There were gate posts in place on the side facing the steep slope. It made sense that the entrance gate would be on the most difficult side to approach. There were smaller posts every three yards between the large corner posts onto which the horizontal wall bearers would be attached. Finally, as far as the outer wall went, there would be a complete covering of straight tree trunks standing side by side vertically, eight feet high with pointed tops. A stockade, similar to Michaels pig enclosure, but on a much larger scale, designed, not to keep animals in but men, out. There would be a kitchen, store room and sleeping quarters for the Thane and his family and a sleeping quarters for the fyrdmen, which would double up as weapons repository when not occupied. Outside the walls there would be a ditch making the walls over eleven feet tall when viewed from its depth. A formidable obstacle.

CHAPTER 15
The Beacon

By the winter celebration Agmunder and his family were settled in the fortified house standing on top of the bluff overseeing the land below. The crops had come in strong and profitable in another lucky year of fine farming weather. Henrik had taken to his new job and his new woman was indeed a most welcome addition to the inhabitants of the ness. Svala particularly was happy that there were more women about, and was sad to leave to live on the hill, in some ways. Michael had provided a pig for the winter solstice feast and everything was going according to Agmunder's plan. He sat looking into the fire on his sixth night in the new house on Breck Hill. He had decided that the fort needed a more fearsome name and after much thought, throughout the building of the fortress, had decided on Warbreck Hill. A name that communicated the purpose of the building, the means of entry and its commanding position. He had planted more strategically placed, hawthorn bushes slightly down the steep slope to hinder approach yet further, and designed a break in the bushes where the path to the gate passed through.

The metal basket that held the dry wood sticks and moss, that would be lit in times of trouble, had been supplied, at some little cost by Jack Smith, who had come personally to oversee its installation. The basket, that was fastened to one of the corner beams, stood some sixteen feet above the ground level of the fortress. The walls and walkway directly below were protected from catching fire by a shield of thin iron, that shed the embers over the fortress wall and into the ditch, which held a small amount of water following rain and was nearly always damp to some degree. Jack Smith had stayed two days after fitting the well constructed beacon basket and had left only this morning to return to his family for Marton's first winter celebration tomorrow evening. He was pleased that Grim would be in attendance with Agmunder. Agmunder asked him to look out for the lighting of the beacon on the celebration and Jack said it would make him proud to see it.

The beacon was out there now, in the dark, suffering the cold and wind of a late December night. Metal, icy cold, beneath the tightly secured canvas cover that kept the wood dry against the worst of the Fylde weather. Its purpose was to summon the fyrd in the event that a Viking raiding party arrived to relieve Agmunder's Ness of its wealth, or to the same end, if Jorgen's father's war-band came to avenge his son's death.

Agmunder sat still looking into the fire in his living area of the dwelling, as he thought further on his preparations. He had twenty spears on order from Jack. There was a house sale in Garstang next month. The owner, a wealthy man, had died of some pox or ague. His household was being broken up and sold off to the highest bidder and Agmunder had heard that he had an impressive collection of swords, axes and daggers. He aimed to buy a selection. Although the fyrd brought their own weapons, often they weren't of good quality. Agmunder was determined that he would be able to meet any raiders, like for like on the field, at least in terms of weaponry.

Svala was busy in the cooking area preparing something for the winter celebration, a cake or a bread of some sort. Agmunder still staring into the fire, lost in thoughts of empire. Since coming to this island Svala had joked several times that he was here to build an empire and they would have to call him Caesar. Her joke was starting to ring true, he thought. In just two years he had progressed from living in a glorified tent on the shore of a river in an unpopulated part of the country, via becoming Thane and landlord to four farms, to having a fortress, command of the local militia and five farms with a second in command installed in his flagship farm on a piece of land known by his own name – Agmunder's Ness. He allowed himself a smile at the flames that danced in the hearth of his hilltop castle. His smile faded – He hoped he would never have to rely on its attack repellent construction. In his heart he had come to seek the quiet life, in all honesty. But life had decided otherwise for him. Vikings don't get to choose their own path. He considered that what he had said to Svala over the evening meal earlier was true enough. She was now singing contentedly in the kitchen. They had some breathing space. Jorgen's revenge wouldn't come in the winter. The Vikings holed up over winter unless they had travelled somewhere before the sea became too dangerous. Basically, what he was saying was, 'If they aren't here by November, they won't be here until April.'

April. He remembered that voyage in April that brought them to this land. The waves crashing against the boat and the wind howling in the rigging, whipping the seawater across the deck like horizontal rain. He remembered the relative warmth and dryness of the foredeck covered in a rough canvas cover with the three of them snuggled up like foxes in the den in winter. He wished that life could always be as simple as it was at that time. Just him, Svala and Erik, keeping warm while the elements existed in what seemed like another world, just a wolf pelt and a canvas thickness away.

Then he thought of the things that had happened to him in the short while that they had been here. He had made good and loyal friends, Lars and Jack, and Grim. He had good and honest, hard working tenants, Michael and Anne, Henrik, Will Tanner and now, Eleanor and her uncle, Thomas. Then, and it was unusual for a Viking to think of such things, but there was Alsvior and Fjord. Excellent, hard working and faithful, dependable animals. His life was complicated it was true, but all the more rich for the things that the complication had brought along the way.

The Viking life is much more instant, he thought, few possessions, and likely to end at any moment. He had much more to lose now, and many more possessions than he had ever had before. Although he was a successful Viking he had never felt as accomplished as he did now. Looking around himself at the well-finished interior of the fortress' living quarters he thought back to the raiding days of his youth when he only saw such buildings fleetingly as he rushed through the door to kill the occupants and take anything of value. At the time he pitied the people who lived and died in one place and had all their possessions laid out ready for anyone who wanted to take them. He didn't think that kind of life would ever beckon. But now it did. He looked in his heart and knew that this was what he wanted. Friends, family and to build Agmunder's Ness into a community. A jewel in the Danelaw's frontier.

The night of the feast was a special night. The first guests to be entertained at the fortress and the first lighting of the beacon planned for later in the evening. The fyrd would not come, they knew that the beacon would be lit in celebration henceforth, on the winter solstice, as part of the celebration, and on significant other days and to remind them of its presence and direction. A form of training exercise, wrapped up in ceremony.

After the main course of the feast had been consumed, the conversation turned to tall tales, as usual. Each story-teller trying to outdo the previous orator. The tales were told in strict rotation around the table, starting with the host. The stories, edging on the unbelievable, with just enough probability to make the listener unsure about whether it could be true, were told and the guests were suitably enthralled in the telling. Henrik told his story of Jinny Greenteeth of course. This was only his second winter feast on the ness, and the story was still fresh. Besides, there were people around the table that hadn't heard it before and their reaction was an amusement to those that had. When Henrik had finished there was the customary silence as each considered the tale. A respectful silence. Then, Eleanor's uncle, Thomas, sitting as he was, next to Henrik, cleared his throat, waited for a modicum of attention and began to regale the assembled guests with his own tale.

'The events that I am about to recall for you tonight relate to the death of my dear brother Edwin. Forgive me, Eleanor, for any upset I bestow.'

Eleanor nodded and kept her head bowed, her hands in her lap below the level of the table.

'By the Chorley hundred border, there is the village of Waterstown, or Eauxton as the locals call it. The woods thereabouts are deep and dark. The sunlight strives to meet the ground but seldom makes a dent in the enshrouding darkness. My brother, Edwin, Eleanor's dear departed father, loved to hunt the boar that snuffled and dug for sustenance in the dark earth beneath the bushes that thronged the tree-trunk packed forest that stretches as far as the river Dee, to the west. Of a Sunday, he would take his horse and his three prize boar-spears to hunt. The spears were ten feet long, with a square pointed tip a foot long, nearly three inches wide at the base. His beautifully decorated boar hunting spears were the talk of the town on many a Sunday night, after he had ridden back in, with his impressive kill dragging behind his exhausted horse.

This one time, close to the winter celebration, one late autumn morning, he asked me to accompany him. He had me ride with him on three occasions before, but we never found any prey on those hunts. Speaking of previous hunts, he joked with me that I brought him ill luck. We rode deep into the forest until I swore we had passed into another land. Dark, gloomy, damp and eerie. The very sounds we made seemed to deaden as they left our mouths. Edwin was just telling me that it was supposed by the local elders that the boar took the soul of the hunter to bolster its own bravery and strength for future encounters, if it made a kill. Then, there was a rustle in the bushes and a boar the size of a horse came out. Fully five feet at the shoulder if it were a foot! Such a beast I had never seen before, neither have I seen such an animal since. Save for once.

Edwin jumped down from his horse and grabbed his best spear. It had a bar through it about four feet from the point. This, he had told me once, was to stop the boar crashing right down the length of the weapon and goring him even in its death-throws. He levelled the spear at the animal's hairy, shadowy form and the boar, seeing him for the first time, charged through the undergrowth at full speed. My brother thrust his back against a young tree for support against the weight of the animal's attack. The distance between them was halved in less than a heartbeat's pulse. As Edwin swung the spear upwards to meet the animal between its charging shoulders, to pierce the spinal cord, the boar seemed to see the danger and lowered itself to slide in the slippery leaves. This took Edwin by surprise as the boar completed the final few feet under the murderous form of the weapon.

The enraged animal hit poor Edwin with full force in the lower abdomen and took his legs with its gleaming white tusks. Edwin was thrust backwards, with a splintering sound that could have been the sapling tree or Edwin's legs. The driving momentous weight of the charging beast crushed my brother into the tree that he had hoped would provide him some protection with another, sickening sound. The boar tossed its head and got to its feet as Edwin bled copious amounts onto the forest floor. The spilled blood bright, despite the gloom, decorating the autumn leaves on the forest floor. The boar tossed its head, dislodged its tusks from my brother's rag-doll body and made its way back into the brush, emitting a contemptuous snort.'

Thomas adjusted his position on his stool, took a drink of red wine from his horn cup and carried on with the tale as he shook his head.

'There was nothing I could do for my dear brother. He died at the foot of that tree with his spear still gripped in his hand. I took him back to the village and there was much mourning.

Against the advice of my neighbours and friends, I went out the next day, armed with Edwin's spears, riding his horse, looking for his killer to exact my revenge. I had been in the woods for just half an hour when I came across the very beast, snuffling about in a small clearing. He wasn't hiding, almost as if he knew I would be looking for him and wanted me to find him. The boar stopped rooting for mushrooms and eyed me from across the small glade. I slipped from the horse and readied the spear. I expected the animal to charge, but it merely raised its head, fixed me with a hard stare and moved slowly toward me. My heart raced as I waited for the charge. I noticed a tatter of Edwin's trousers still caught on the left tusk. I was determined to finish the beast off. When it got to about fifteen feet away, just too far away from the spear point for me to strike with a good lunge, it stopped and raised its head again, looking into my eyes.'

'Don't do it, Thomas,' said the beast as clearly as you can hear me, 'Don't.'

'I was sure I heard the voice of Edwin issue from the animal before me. My emotions broke, my resolve to kill was quelled. I dropped heavily to my knees in the leaves, and presently, I let the spear drop among my tears on the deep layer of fallen foliage. The beast drew near, until I could feel its hot breath on my arm. I raised my face to look it in the eye.'

'Edwin is with me, now. Go home. Look after little Eleanor as your own.'

'With that, the boar trotted off into the bushes and I never saw it again. I returned to the village and resolved to look after Eleanor to the best of my ability in honour of my brave, departed brother. The best hunter I have ever known.'

Thomas lowered his head and set the cup down on the table before him. There was the usual silence of respect from the other guests. Shortly, a murmur began as the guests discussed parts of the tale. It was slightly disrespectful to speak of Eleanor's father's death with her present, but generally the story was well received. They shared pork from the carcass of the pig that Michael had provided (it was not the old sow – He couldn't bring himself to finish her off. There was a boar who was very aggressive toward Anne, and it was a pleasure to despatch *him* for the feast.) The guests were stirred from their mealtime conversation by Agmunder, who asked them all to join him in the courtyard for the lighting of the beacon.

This was the first time the beacon had been lit. The night was cool but not cold. A clear sky with little wind, the stars of the winter constellations familiar scintillating points in the inky black sky. A perfect first lighting night. The guests filed out into the courtyard to see the firing of the beacon. Wrapped in blankets and thick cloaks and shawls they waited, chattering excitedly, feeling the anticipation warm them against the cool night air. They watched as

Agmunder scaled a ladder with a torch in one hand.

Henrik put an arm round Eleanor's waist in the darkness and pulled her to him as they watched the Viking ascend the ladder to the walkway above.

'I hope you weren't too saddened by the telling of Thomas' tale?' he whispered to her tenderly.

Eleanor fixed him with a glint in her eye, 'My father died of the ague after he cut himself with a rusty blade chopping turnips!' she said, quietly so as not to be overheard.

Henrik allowed himself a smile in the darkness. He'd been hoodwinked by Thomas' winter celebration story, and listening to the conversation going on around him, he wasn't the only one.

'This,' said Agmunder, as he stood on the battlement walkway by the corner beam that supported the metal basket of the beacon, 'is the first lighting of the beacon on Warbreck Hill. I hope it is lit on this night for many years to come as part of the winter celebration welcoming the turning of the seasons with warmth and light that can be seen throughout the Fylde. You will join me in hoping it is never lit for its more sinister purpose? May we live under its light in peace.'

With that he touched the torch to the lower part of the tinder and the goose-fat smeared wood. The flames quickly licked up the branches and sticks and took hold with sudden bright fury.

The assembled friends cheered in the light and clapped as the fire took hold and the light grew in intensity. A beacon indeed. Within just a few seconds the light was so bright that the assembled crowd had trouble seeing even the brightest familiar stars of Orion.

When the beacon was fully ablaze the host and his guests watched for a few minutes, before returning to the warmth of the house. They continued in their revelry even as Erik tended the beacon, keeping an eye on the embers with a quantity of water nearby. He looked out over the Fylde in the darkness, specks of light here and there, kept warm by the heat of the brightly burning beacon and naming the towns he could see.

The next morning Erik was found asleep on the walkway, wrapped in his blanket against the cold, with the beacon still smoking and occasionally bursting into sporadic flame from the glowing embers when the breeze freshened. There wasn't much material left in the beacon basket. Jack's self cleaning design had worked well and Agmunder leaned over the stockade to view the pile of cold, damp ashes in the moat-ditch at the base of the wall. Pleased, he woke Erik and thanked him for keeping watch all night. In future the beacon could be left to its own devices, supervision was not required. The two came down from the wall and headed inside for breakfast.

Life in Warbreck was different to living on the farm. No crop to attend. Fewer chickens. There was still the goat to milk and Erik had to make trips to Agmunder's Ness to collect meat, from Michael, and to fish in the river from the familiar comfort of Waverider. Back at the farms, Will Tanner had started growing a strange vegetable, which he said was called, turnip. Henrik recognised the name from Eleanor's account of her father's real death, but no-one else had seen or eaten the vegetable. Will couldn't believe it, the turnip was staple in many parts of the country. Where, he wondered, had these people been, to avoid the turnip all these years? He explained that it could be stewed and was quite flavourful. It could also be eaten raw if you had a raging hunger. Will had also planted a few apple trees, but warned that they took a few years to mature enough to bear fruit. Also, in the fortress there was the ongoing duty to scale the wall and look out over the land for signs of trouble.

The view from the beacon, which naturally had been sited at the point with the best view so it could be seen from as many locations as possible, was superb. Erik could see all the land from the hill to the fells in the east. He could see the fire at Jacks smithy, Lars' smoke from his little copse, Preston and Garstang. Looking north, he could trace the Wyre as it made its way to the sea, up where Knut was buried and the monk prayed for his soul. Further to the left, north west, he could see a ridge that marked the shore where Jorgen came ashore. He could see down to the sea if he looked west, but knew that it was an illusion, there were cliffs there with a drop of over a hundred feet to the water. Looking south west he was sure that he could see the keel-hulled church. It was distant but there was a definite black blip on the flat horizon. He would watch for smoke, that would betray Gretel's cooking, later in the day. Erik was charged with attending the lookout position and scouring the land once an hour every day, while he was in the fortress – Other duties took him to the village on the ness in the mornings. He didn't complain. Being told he was old enough to bring food and ride Alsvior alone made him feel important and proud.

In the next few days Agmunder received messages, or spoke in person to everyone who he'd asked to watch out for the beacon on the winter celebration. They all said that the beacon was clearly visible, several also commented that the smoke was also quite visible in the morning, despite the fire being almost out. Agmunder was pleased with this news. His beacon was a great success, visible in all directions for a day's ride at least. He just hoped that there would be no need to light it in circumstances other than celebration. The next time it was likely to be lit was in three months at the spring equinox, New Year celebration. Agmunder hoped this was the case, for although the crossing was dangerous in April, it was not impossible that the journey could be made in mid-March, if there was a pleasant spring. As a farmer he shouldn't, but Agmunder found himself hoping that this spring was harsh, cold and windy, and New Year's Day, 783, would arrive in storm and tempest. He had never shied away from his responsibilities and couldn't understand this feeling of fear. Vikings didn't feel fear. What was wrong with him? He wrestled with self doubt and the inner turmoil of his happy home, and good life, and the nagging certainty that Jorgen's father was out for his blood. Despite Agmunder's most fervent hope, the next time the beacon was lit wasn't in celebration.

CHAPTER 16
The Blessing

By mid February the worst of the winter had already subsided, much to Agmunder's annoyance. It looked like an early spring was in the air. Here and there were signs of life, though nothing so grand as a snowdrop. *They* wouldn't be seen until the middle of April at the earliest. No, the signs of life that held Agmunder's attention were the steadily growing bumps in the bellies of Eleanor and Anne. It was not uncommon for people to be with child at the time of their wedding, although those of the new religion frowned upon it somewhat. Grim, on the other hand, welcomed all life to his chapel and celebrated people above everything else. Agmunder decided to take his mind off the impending visit from across the water with a double wedding. He had promised to waltz Anne up the aisle and now, it seemed, he was to be joined by Thomas, wheeling the lovely Eleanor alongside him. He had planned to have the weddings during the slack time in May, but, rutting animals and humans alike can't help falling pregnant, and babies wait for no man or season!

Erik had confirmed that it was indeed Grim's chapel that he could see on the horizon from the fortress. Agmunder visited Grim to ask if the weddings could be performed with any possibility in March. Grim was overjoyed to have weddings to conduct. He had thought that he would have been preaching Sunday services to fewer than half a dozen people for months, maybe years, before anything as grand as a wedding came along, and here we was, arranging two at once! The chapel was nicely finished. Compact but serviceable. Erik climbed onto the top of the roof to inspect Grim's bell that had been installed by Jack Smith, just the week before. From the top, he could plainly see Warbreck Hill with the fortress atop the ridge, standing proud, on the northern rise in the land. Warbreck Hill marked the southernmost point of Agmunder's Ness.

'So, we shall say the third Sunday in March for the wedding ceremony of

Michael and Anne Shard, *and*, Henrik and Eleanor Gunnerson,' said Grim, showing his teeth in a wide smile, 'The equinox and New year.'

Agmunder collected Erik from his vantage point on top of the chapel and together they rode back to Warbreck. Erik was proud to have borrowed Henrik's horse for the journey and was looking forward to delivering Alfred back to the farm that evening, hoping to get permission to stay over in his old room for the night from Agmunder on the way back.

The weather didn't deteriorate for the whole of February and March swept in windy but mild. Preparations were going ahead nicely for the weddings. Agmunder saw to it that there was plenty of mead and wine and Michael promised that there would be no shortage of pork for the wedding feast supplied at a bargain price – Business was business! He had looked at the cantankerous old sow as he made his promise, with something approaching sorrow in his eye. She was starting to make a nuisance of herself with the younger females, perhaps it was time she went to the table.

Agmunder had been getting on very well with Thomas too. He was a man serious about farming and his experience would certainly help Henrik to take the reigns at the farm. Thomas had already increased the land usage on Henrik's old farm and shown Henrik how to make better use of the land on the big farm. Life at Agmunder's Ness was very comfy at the moment. There were times when Agmunder forgot all about the threat from across the sea and simply enjoyed life.

The day of the wedding dawned bright and still. A perfect day for a ceremony, especially one that involved a good long trek and outside revelries. The wedding party conveying themselves to Grim's chapel, which he had called after Saint Anne, in honour of its first bride, consisted of Agmunder and Svala, Michael and, of course, Anne. Henrik, Thomas and Eleanor, Erik and Jack Smith with his wife, Gretel carrying Marton, and Lars Larsson made up the rest. A good few people. They had enough horses to ride, with Erik riding with Henrik. They arrived at St. Anne's chapel before noon. The morning worshippers had stayed on to help prepare the chapel for the wedding with Grim. They had brought the winter celebration decorations from their houses. There were dried hop fronds, all the way from Kent, and baskets of bread. No flowers so early in the year, but there was a sheaf of dried corn to represent the farms and a net to represent the fishermen. The decorations were meagre but well thought out. The bridal parties seemed pleased.

As Grim, or Keel-Grim as he was becoming known, ushered everyone inside the upturned hull, the doors closed on the assembled people and it was very cosy and intimate.

Candles were lit to dispel the gloom and Grim began the service. It wasn't long before the parties spilled out into the sun again and amongst cheering and clapping they prepared to make the journey back to Agmunder's Ness, to the big farmhouse for the celebrations. The wedding party took a direct route missing out the detour to Warbreck. Within two hours the whole singing, clapping, raucous collection of happy people, some on horseback and others on the decorated log wagons, had made it back to the farm and the merriments went on well into the night. Agmunder had employed some musicians from Garstang to entertain and there was a juggler that used batons of fire, much to the delight of the assembled party-goers. The juggler held no charms for Fjord, who stayed inside... near the pork.

Lars took Agmunder to one side, 'A wonderful day, friend.'

'Yes. It couldn't have gone better.'

The two walked out of the house together and sat on a log looking over the river to the spot where Knut had launched his boat. It seemed like a lifetime ago.

'When will they come?'

'When they're ready.'

'If it were me, I would come when you wouldn't expect it. Or with sufficient numbers that you haven't got a chance!'

'That's what I know, deep down,' said Agmunder, looking up to his friend's face, 'I try to fool myself that he will wait for the good weather, or that he won't come at all.'

He shifted his weight and looked again toward the far bank of the Wyre.

'He will come... *I* would come, and soon!'

The new year's celebration and the trip to Garstang to pay an enormous amount in taxes, to the pleased looking, weasel-faced Max, came all too soon. The day spent away from the vantage point of his fortress worried at his mind. Agmunder, looking to the sea at every opportunity from the ramparts of Warbreck, was almost obsessed with keeping a lookout for his enemy.

Svala tried to convince him that the day may never come, but Agmunder knew that the moment he let his guard down was the day his family perished. Failing to be vigilant was to endanger everyone recklessly.

The next day, at breakfast, Erik said, 'Father, would you prefer to live in this shadow or get it over with and go back to life as it was?'

'A good question, my boy. I have thought a lot about that very dilemma. On the one hand, while he hasn't come we are safe, but have to live with that shadow. If he comes, we could win the battle and he, like Knut, would be a past chapter in our lives. But, what if he comes with an unbeatable force? Or catches me by surprise on a trip to Garstang, or a trip to Jack's or Grim's?'

'We are prepared, father. We have the weapons and the beacon to summon the fyrd. That's all we can do.'

'You're right, Erik. That's all we can do. That and wait.'

Agmunder thought. If they were going to come and try surprise they would be on the way. If it were he, he would risk the journey early, to arrive before anyone thought it were possible. He was expecting them in the next week. The damned weather had been calm and warm for the last three weeks, the only thing in their favour was that the wind was a westerly and difficult to navigate the North Sea against the wind. His doubt persevered, '*Difficult, but not impossible*,' he told himself.

He ascended the ladder to the walkway by the beacon to look out again over the landscape of the Fylde. Seaward? Nothing. Northward? Nothing. To the east from the river? Nothing. Looking south? A small party was approaching. Nothing to worry about. A mile off yet. He looked carefully. As the horses moved slowly closer at a walk he began to discern more details. It was Grim and Jack Smith. He watched as they approached yet closer, only leaving his vantage point as they got within shouting distance and he had welcomed them from the walls. He climbed down quickly and he and Erik opened the gate to welcome the visitors.

'Welcome to Warbreck, Jack, Grim. Please, come in and rest.'

'Thank you, Thane. We have been on the road for two hours. Your fortress was visible for the whole journey, I thought we'd never arrive!' said Jack.

'I thought it would be New Year's Day before we arrived,' added Grim.

'This is a pleasure to see friendly faces.'

Grim said, 'I was talking to Jack about offering to bless your home for the new year and he said he would come along to check on the beacon.'

'Good luck for the New Year, my friends. Well, the beacon works perfectly. We have lit it twice now with a full charge of firewood and it burned bright and smoky with the spent ashes and falling embers being ejected into the ditch. Not a single problem has been encountered in its functioning, Jack. Your clever design works perfectly. Thank you.'

Jack bowed and said, 'I am pleased. I thought it would work, I have a similar system in use at the smithy for one of my fires. I came mainly to keep Grim company, and to see you, my friend.'

'Well, would you?' asked Grim.

'Would I what?' asked Agmunder.

'Would you like me to bless the house?'

'Oh, I see. Well, yes. Yes I would, Grim. Thank you,' then turning towards the building, 'Svala, Erik, come out here.'

The two came out, followed by Fjord who bounded up to Jack and was made a fuss of as he eyed Grim, a stranger.

'Don't mind Fjord, Grim,' said Erik, 'He'll know you're a friend when we speak nicely to you. You see.'

Agmunder said, 'Grim has offered to bless the house in the religion of the cross, Svala. Would that be acceptable to you?'

'Of course, my courteous husband. It would be an honour.'

'Then that's settled, Grim. Please, proceed with whatever preparations you need to make. Svala will bring us some fare and drink on this third day of spring.'

Svala nodded and went into the house, pulling Erik with her to help. She wanted to get back outside as soon as she could. It was her house too and she didn't want to miss the blessing.

Agmunder spoke to Grim.

'It is a kind thing to bless the house, Grim. Svala has mentioned an interest in your religion. Since we came to this land we have embraced the local culture and shunned the Norse ways. Having the house blessed will strengthen our feeling of belonging. Thank you.'

Fjord nosed his way over to the man of the cloth and with wagging tail looked up at him, almost as if he were remembering his face.

Erik came out of the house with a wine skin over his shoulder.

'See. I said Fjord would be OK.'

'That you did, Erik,' said Grim, patting Fjord on the neck and shoulders.

As Svala came out with a tray of bread, eggs, chicken and cheese, Grim smiled and started to get the things from his horse that he'd brought in a roll tied behind where he had sat to ride.

He quickly put the roll on the floor and went over to where the others were starting to pick food off the tray to eat. They sat on the smooth ground in the sunshine and talked as they ate.

The chapel was getting a good number of worshippers on a Sunday and business was good at the blacksmith's shop. No-one touched upon Agmunder's worry. It was a pleasant afternoon and they didn't want to bring the mood down – Though, they all knew that Agmunder's mind was never far from those thoughts.

When the food was gone and the news shared, they prepared for grim to bless the house within the fortress walls.

'There's not much to the actual blessing,' he had said as he unpacked his roll, 'The Bible, obviously, is the most important thing. Simply having it here will impart goodness and peace to the whole area. You have welcomed us in and so my God will reside in these walls, whether you believe or not.'

Agmunder wondered how many times Grim used those words to deflect the unbelievers, 'Thank you,' he said.

Grim said a short prayer and sprinkled a little of the holy water from his vial over the threshold of the living quarters. He continued urging his god to inhabit the house and bring happiness, peace and prosperity of heart to those that dwelt within its walls. Beseeching Him to protect them against their enemies and protect their souls against the influences of the devil.

'And that's it!' said Grim, almost like a salesman who had completed a deal.

'Thank you,' said Svala and Agmunder together.

'My pleasure,' answered Grim, shaking Agmunder by the hand.

'Please, stay the night with us here. It's a long ride back and you must have had enough time in the saddle today,' said Agmunder to both men.

'I wish we could, Thane,' said Jack, 'But I have horses waiting for shoes and Grim, I believe, has a service to conduct tomorrow morning at St. Anne's.'

'Very well. Please then, take some meat and more cheese for your journey. I expect it will be nearly dark before you arrive home this evening.'

The food was brought as the men got their horses ready for the return journey. Erik lifted the bag up to Jack as he sat looking out of the gate as Agmunder opened it for them to leave.

'It is always a pleasure to spend time in your company Agmunder, and with your lovely family,' he nodded to Svala, 'Peace be with you here.'

He kicked his horse and it moved out of the fortress gateway onto the path that led down through the hawthorns and onto the plain below, followed by the waving figure of Grim.

Agmunder climbed onto the battlements to watch them depart. He was still there, deep in thought, an hour later when they had disappeared from view to the human eye. It was late March and there was still no sign of *Jorgen's revenge*, as he'd come to call them privately to himself. He looked north west for a few moments, noting a slight sea mist that wouldn't help if they were out there. Still lost in the same wild imaginings that had crowded his thoughts as he had watched Jack and Grim ride away, he scoured the land again. A movement on the northern horizon caught his attention. He snapped out of his reverie and scrutinised the tiny dot. As it got larger he could make out that the rider was galloping quickly. A lone rider travelling fast usually meant news, and it was rarely good news when the horse was being pushed so hard. Agmunder was one who believed in positive action and quickly ran to get Alsvior ready to meet the rider. He flung open the gate with a shout to Erik, and mounted up. He yelled something that Erik missed as he charged out of the gate and down the track between the bushes. Erik shut the gate and climbed to watch. In the few seconds it took to scale the ladder Agmunder had wheeled the horse to the left and was galloping across the grassland toward the other rider on the track. Erik watched as the two closed distance between each-other. This could be very bad.

'Ho, Agmunder!' shouted the rider, becoming recognisable as one of the fyrd that had helped track down Knut. He reined in to a halt.

'Matthew Pilling. Well met?' answered the Viking as he drew his horse to a halt beside the other man.

'Indeed not, Thane. I have ridden two hours at this pace to bring you news. I have heard today that a longship put into Glasson, a village on the coast. It's just a few miles down the Lune river from Lancaster on the eastern shore of the bay. They, claimed to be trading in peace but their cargo was worthless. In the taverns the crew were asking questions about how to find a village called *Agmunder's Ness*. We thought you should know.'

Agmunder listened in silence. His mind reeling. How had they sailed by without him seeing them? Were they armed for a battle, or did they bring a message? Were they a raiding party, or just the vanguard of a larger fleet to be met and led to him?

'How many men?' he asked.

'A medium sized ship. Thirty crew, sire,' answered Matthew.

'Maybe they think thirty, well deployed, will be enough. They don't know about Warbreck. Ride with me and have a meal. Stay the night with us. I will bestow a pig to thank your efforts as we talk more on this matter,' said Agmunder wheeling his horse and walking on back toward the fortress.

'I have heard about your castle on the hill, Thane. It will be a pleasure to see it from inside.'

'For all our sakes, I hope so, Matthew. I hope, so!'

CHAPTER 17

The Near Revenge

The gate of the Warbreck Hill fortress closed behind the horses as the two men rode inside. Matthew looked around, nodding his approval, as Erik took his reins. Matthew fetched his leg over the horse's neck and slid to the ground. Erik walked the horse to the stable to be watered. Thoughtfully he tied her up outside the stable, in the shade, but in the breeze. He knew it would be too hot to stand inside, even in March, for a horse that had run extensively, at a gallop.

When he returned to the men in the courtyard, Agmunder was pointing out the defensive positions that could be manned in time of attack. Erik didn't think this was good news – He had been right about the message.

Svala prepared a good meal for them all that evening. Salt pig and turnip too. Agmunder had a taste for the strange looking vegetable. They sat around the table and discussed the way forward. Agmunder didn't feel so bad about missing the ship's arrival. Matthew told him that it had sailed into port just after sunrise two days earlier. That would have been easily missed in the misty mornings they had had recently, especially before dawn. Nevertheless, they were here and making enquiries. Matthew wasn't sure that many people up in Glasson knew the location of Agmunder's Ness, even though it was becoming a much talked about subject for disenchanted tenants with greedy landlords and workers looking for a better life.

Nevertheless, most knew it was in the Fylde and smoke would give them away, they can't stop cooking! The only chances they had were the facts that Agmunder knew the crew were looking for them and the crew didn't know about the fortress with its warning beacon.

'If I fire the beacon tonight,' said Agmunder musing aloud, 'the fyrd in strength will be here by tomorrow noon. But, is the threat from thirty men strong enough to overwhelm this fortress? Do I need so many men?'

'Surely, it is better to be too strong than one man too weak, Thane?' asked Matthew, as Svala nodded to herself.

'It is, Matthew. But, suppose they don't come for a week? You know Vikings, they get a sniff of easy pickings and they're easily distracted. They could raid towns up and down the Lune for a fortnight before they decide to come down here.'

'They could, it's true. Or they could be on the way right now, Thane.'

In a rare moment showing his anxiety, Agmunder stood immediately from his stool and went out to check the horizon. Matthew and Erik quickly followed their master and soon all three of them stood looking north, straining to see in the gloom of evening. Although there was a thickening mist over the water, the land horizon was clear and there was no sign of smoke from a landed crew to be seen in any direction. Checking all around, they could see the cooking smoke from Garstang, Lars' farmstead, Jack's smithy and Grim's chapel, and of course, the several smoke trails rising from Agmunder's Ness to the north east. But nothing new or unusual. Hopefully, that meant the raiders were still up in the Glasson area. Agmunder's personal anxiety level climbed down a peg or two and he relaxed a little, knowing they were not under direct threat. For now, at least, they were safe.

'Look!' shouted Erik, pointing west.

The two men turned and saw a new pillar of smoke beginning to rise less than two miles away on the coast, just a little further up from where the cliffs eased their way back to sea level.

'They're here, then!' said Agmunder, solemnly, anxiety clicking back up a notch.

'Shall I light the beacon now, father?' asked Erik, enthusiastically.

'Yes, Erik. But take out all the goose-fat smeared sticks and completely remove the canvas sheeting – We don't want too much smoke while it is still daylight. They don't know the beacon's purpose, but they may still see it if they venture even a few hundred feet inland past the dunes. If we keep the fire smoke free we can lessen the chance of discovery.'

'Let's hope they have decided to fish for their supper tonight, and stay on the beach,' added Matthew.

The beacon was stripped of smoke making materials. It would be dark soon and making smoke wouldn't matter. But, there was a chance that smoke would be seen from the beach before darkness completely hid it from view. Agmunder was a careful commander. Before the night had fully fallen there was a bright blaze seen in the countryside of the Fylde, and diligent fyrdmen for miles around were preparing to ride out to aid their Thane at daybreak.

Neither Agmunder nor Matthew got much sleep that night. Both insisted on taking turns to keep watch for anything suspicious abroad in the night shadowed landscape. The silvery scene stretched from the fortress to the silvery sea, which shone for the first three hours of the vigil, beneath the setting crescent moon. Although they remained vigilant, neither giving in to the temptation to close an eye, nothing disturbed their peace that night. Dawn came eventually and the two stood, gazing to the west, on the ramparts together, as wisps of smoke betrayed the enemy camp.

'They're out there, Matthew.'

'Yes, Thane. Do you think they will come today?'

'If I was their leader, I would. The less time they give us to prepare the better their chances. We have to assume they know we know they're here.'

'That's what I thought. The fyrd will be on the way by now. We have to hold out for just a couple of hours before the first of them arrive,' said Matthew.

'It will be sooner than that. Look there,' said Agmunder smiling and pointing. He knew that the first person to arrive would be Lars Larsson. He could tell it was him, he was the only person he knew with a piebald horse. You could tell Lars' horse for half a mile or more, and in the morning sunshine it was plain to see. Suddenly it became apparent that Lars wasn't alone on the track as another horse became visible. Henrik. His two best friends were fittingly the first to show up for the muster.

Agmunder called to Svala to prepare a welcome for the first of the fyrd, his trusted lieutenants. He climbed down from the wall and opened the gate himself, in welcome. Matthew stayed on the battlements keenly searching the land all about for the arrival of more militia-men. Agmunder called up to him to reward his efforts during the night vigil.

'Matthew, you did me good service in the hunt for Knut and last night, again. I will make you a captain today, in recognition of your hard work and loyalty.'

'Thank you, Thane. I will not disappoint.'

'That, I doubt not!'

The lieutenants rode in to the fortress with smiles concealing their worried hearts.

'Agmunder!' shouted Henrik, good-naturedly, 'Lars stayed at my... er, your, farm last night. He arrived shortly after dark. It was all I could do to keep him from riding over last night!'

'But, Henrik was the first one to mount up and spur his horse this morning, before first light!' answered Lars, grinning.

The three clasped each-other's arms in greeting and clapped each-other on the back.

'How is life in the fortress?' asked Lars.

'A bit stressful of late, my friend,' answered Agmunder.

'People out to get you will have that effect,' said Henrik spotting Erik coming out of the house.

Erik hadn't heard the new arrivals and was nearly at the stable before he happened to look up and see his friends. He dropped the bucket he was carrying and the contents splashed all over the otherwise clean and dry floor of the courtyard. He ran over to them as quickly as his eight year old legs would carry him. He threw his arms around Henrik first and eventually, Lars. Fjord joined in too, bouncing about like he'd got the biggest bone for tea.

'Erik, we have to talk seriously with your father,' said Henrik.

'I know. I'll be just over here, cleaning up this mess,' he said and they all shared a smile.

Agmunder started off the conversation with his commanders,

'They're on the coast, two or three miles away. If I were they, I would come today. We have to hope the fyrdmen will arrive very shortly. The beacon seemed to be effective – You two arrived smartly enough.'

'Show us the land,' said Lars.

The three men climbed onto the wall and looked out over the terrain. They scoured the west for signs of the approaching war-band of Vikings. Nothing visible yet, though Agmunder was convinced that they were approaching.

They scanned the vista from north to south, where the fyrdmen could be approaching. They picked up three definite and two more possible horses walking quickly on the tracks that criss-crossed the plain ahead of them.

'Looks like we'll have five or six more men within half an hour, Thane,' said Lars.

'Indeed,' he paused a second, then pointed, 'or seven.'

'Your beacon has done its job, Agmunder,' observed Henrik.

Over the next hour, nine more arrived to serve their Thane at Warbreck. The fortress hummed to the sound of conversation, the din made by men's preparations and animals. There were now fifteen people within the stockade walls, all working to prepare for an attack that may come at any moment. As the minutes passed, Erik stood atop the wall, watching for the slightest glimpse of movement in the west. He took a moment off occasionally to sweep for the fyrdmen approaching from the east and south too, so the gate could be opened for their entrance and shut again quickly.

Another six arrived in the next half hour and Agmunder was pleased with the response. Friends had assured him that he was popular in the Fylde and said people would follow him, but there was always a nagging doubt. This turn-out confirmed that what people had said was true. He was humbled.

About five minutes after the twenty first person had entered Warbreck's gate there came a shout from the wall. It was Matthew, who had relieved Erik in the look-out position, telling him that his father wanted him to go into the house to help his mother.

'Ho! Enemy sighted,' shouted Matthew as Erik started down the ladder, 'To the west and on foot. Walking. Unknown number at present. About a mile!'

Agmunder, Lars and Henrik joined Matthew on the wall to assess the situation. After a few minutes he had the measure of the approaching force. The Thane turned his back on the enemy and addressed the assembled fyrdmen below.

'There are about thirty men expected to attack shortly. Get your weapons and get up here on the wall. Bows and arrows and spears will be the best means of repelling them.'

Erik came out of the house with some strips of cloth, maybe for bandages or making fire arrows. Agmunder called to him, 'Make the water available in case they send fire, Erik.'

The fortress scurried into life again and within less than a minute the wall was lined with the fyrd, armed appropriately to repel the attack. They wore helmets with a strong nose-piece. The helmet was fashioned out of one piece of steel, with the nose piece riveted on. No horns though, the Saxon fyrd preferred plain and effective. Thick coats, quilted against a weak sword blow. Some had a circular wooden shield with a metal boss, but most had a weapon in each hand, standing behind the stockade wall. Agmunder hefted his helmet into place and tied the chinstrap. He was a Viking and he wanted the attackers to remember that. His helmet had no nose-piece to hide the face of their enemy, but the horns were polished white and gleamed in the sun, as did the silver capped tips.

They watched as the approaching group moved into line astern formation to make hitting more than one difficult with arrow or spear. Agmunder expected to go through the ritual of having to talk to his foe before they launched their attack, so he wasn't concerned too much about this tactic.

When the group of attackers had closed to about a hundred paces they stopped and knelt in the grass. A small target for the inaccurate bows and out of range of even the best spear throw. One of their number separated from the group and approached into shouting distance. Speaking Norse, he addressed the fortress.

'Agmunder. We have come to avenge the killing of Thor, son of Lord Hrothgar Jorgenson, lord of Hundvag and Bouy. Wronged father and our master. He sends his regret at being too old to travel himself to settle this wrong, but commands us to appraise you of his mind. He gives you little regard and knows that you will be defeated. He hopes you have a swift and pleasant journey across the Bifrost bridge later this day, even as your earthly body is consumed by crows.'

Through accident, or fear, one of the fyrd let fly an arrow. It sailed through the sky, watched by all present in its graceful, deadly arc. It fell to ground not five feet from where the messenger stood. To his credit he did not flinch, but rather stared at the arrow with disgust, as if measuring the skill of his enemy by this one missed shot. He continued as if nothing had happened.

'My lord said that your men would be out of practice, living a sedentary life on their backs in the warm sun has made them soft!'

Henrik looked as though he was going to shout something back in return, but Agmunder quickly put a hand on his shoulder to quieten him.

'Talk is for old men and women,' said Agmunder, quietly, 'The real test will come when steel meets shield. Nothing he can say will change that outcome. Whatever he says to us will not hurt as much as our spears will hurt them as they approach. Let them have their moment of bravado.'

'You think you're safe within your wooden walls, but know this Agmunder, son of that three legged, one eyed, flea covered, dog, Asmunde. One of your men is in our pay and will strike you in the heat of battle. You are not as safe behind your wall as you would believe.'

This rather went against what Agmunder had just said to Henrik. It was possible that he could say some very worrying things.

'Don't listen to him my stout warriors,' Agmunder shouted hoping that his own doubt didn't show, 'There is none of you whom I wouldn't gladly fight alongside at any time. He is grasping at straws. Why would he warn me? A stupid move – It's just a tactic to unsettle us. This is just words. We will see what he's made of when the arrows fly!'

This was met with a cheer from the men within the fortress. Agmunder was glad of that, but resolved to keep an eye out for anyone suspiciously edging close to him in the battle. Now it was Agmunder's turn to answer. There was a protocol to the pre-battle and Agmunder had to adhere, or risk looking weak to his men.

'You, out there in the grass like snakes. I speak to you. Jorgen came here to take what was not his and to kill those he feared, though they were unarmed. A coward's fight. When confronted he ran, when caught he buckled – As you will buckle.'

This was his chance to hit them with some words that might not weaken them, but would boost the fyrdmen's resolve.

'When I came to this land I was looking for peace, it's true, but these men have shown me that when it matters they are the equal of any Viking. Indeed the little band that flattened Jorgen's men were only nine in number where Jorgen had fully fifteen men at his rediculous command. I was there, and saw how his men were cut down like August wheat in seconds by a sorry band of boys and old men. We might be part time soldiers but we're fighting for our home, our families, our friends and our life. So, come. Do your best – It will *not* be good enough.'

There was another huge cheer from the men assembled on the wall, some banging their shields with their swords and axes in a frightful noise, as those in the field below them started to spread out into pockets of three or four men. Each pocket moved outwards while the commander stayed in the spot by the arrow. When they were separated by ten paces from each-other the eight small pods of Vikings began to move toward the fortress.

'Archers, let them advance ten more yards. Make sure you have their distance before you let loose. Spear-men, mop up the remainder. Do not leave the fortress unless instructed by me, Henrik or Lars. Remember that Matthew is this day made your captain. Listen for his commands too.'

'This is my voice,' shouted Matthew, 'mark it well, our lives may depend upon it.'

Although his speech was quite short, the advance of the enemy was swift. As the last syllable issued from Matthew's lips, the first of Agmunder's archers let fly their deadly arrow and the zip of the goose feathers in flight came to a sudden end, with a shout. One down.

Then the other archers let their arrows fly and shortly there were bodies lying in the field. It was going well, so far, for those in the fortress.

Agmunder watched the skirmish unfold from the wall. The attackers had only hand weapons. No archers. He thought this strange and wondered if the fortress had been a big surprise for the raiders. Then he saw them, another wave of thirty men coming up behind the first as they fell. He saw the archers on the wall were shooting arrows into the injured and even the dead in their anger.

'Archers, save your arrows. There are more live ones for you. Look!'

The archers slowed but did not stop wasting arrows.

Matthew took up the task. He walked quickly along the wall tipping the elbows of the archers with a shouted word, 'Stop!'

He got some angry looks from the soldiers with concentrations disturbed. But they stopped once told. Matthew's face convinced those who may have disobeyed.

'They have reinforcements. There are at least twice as many as we thought. Archers, count your arrows, I want a tally,' shouted Matthew, rising to the responsibilities of his promotion.

The tally was quickly taken. They still had over three hundred arrows. But, Agmunder was right to be cautious. What use was the fortress if they couldn't defend it? After the battle they could go out and recover many arrows that struck soft earth and use them again, but if they ran out there would be a sorry reckoning.

Outside the wall, the Vikings were regrouping and falling back to meet the reinforcements. They were out of range of the archers temporarily, but everyone knew that would change shortly.

'As before. Wait for them to get well within range. Make each arrow count,' shouted Lars from his position on the far end of the line on the wall. He was checking the gate side of the fortress to make sure that none of the attackers had sneaked round the sides during the first clash, when an arm came over the stockade wall between the spikes. He rushed to grab the hand that was searching for a grip to pull its owner over the wall and pulled it up quickly. He let go and there was a short silence before the sound of someone landing in the ditch. There was a squelch and some groaning as Lars looked over the wall to see the Viking had fallen on his helper and the two of them were struggling to sort themselves out. If circumstances had been different it might have been quite comical, but Lars was in no mood for laughing. He grabbed a spear off the nearest of the fyrdmen and hurled it at the two attackers scrambling over each-other in an attempt to get clear of the ditch. The spear passed through one and into the other. The two bodies so joined rolled slowly until the spear rested on the ground. Their feet and hands quivered for a few seconds, the one beneath seemed to be reaching for something, before there was a visible deflation of the chest and both lay still in the mud.

'Two, trying to get over the wall, back here,' shouted Lars across the fortress to Agmunder, 'I spitted them.'

Then the battle started afresh. Arrows whizzed through the air and the shouts of injured men once again filled their ears. Unusually, in *this* battle, there was not the *ching* of ringing swords and the *thud* of axes finding shields. Just the zipping of arrows.

'Hold!' commanded Agmunder, 'They're pulling back. Save your arrows.'

The sound of arrows fleeting through the air stopped immediately this time. *Good*, thought Agmunder, at least they learn fast.

The Viking attackers had lost about half of their number and one of them had been the commander who had given them the fighting words before the action. He had charged the wall in a mad attempt to scale it with the three warriors carrying several axes each. It seemed that they were planning to embed them firmly into one of the stockade's tree-trunk poles, to make a scaling ladder, but all three had been cut down by a spear throwing expert, Edwald, who got all three with just three throws. *Good idea, though*, thought Agmunder, *if they hit the axes in hard enough they could grab the handles to climb and put their feet on the heads like the steps of a ladder. We will have to watch out for that trick in future.*

'Agmunder!'

The shout brought him back from his thoughts. He looked round and saw that Henrik was pointing out into the field. He had a strange look on his face. The Thane looked and saw the Vikings retreating across the field. They were grouped and helping their injured. There was no urgency in their retreat, though. They were just walking away as if they were having a break to plan their next move. They were not beaten. They were not running. They were not, by any means, finished.

'Where are they going?' asked Matthew.

'Probably to think about how to get in,' said Agmunder turning to more pressing things.

'You five,' he said, pointing to a group of men that happened to be near the gate, checking their weapons, and dipping into the water bucket with their horn cups, 'Go out and retrieve our arrows. Don't be long.'

The men unbarred the gate and went out almost immediately. Agmunder was impressed with their speed and proficiency at collecting the arrows. In less than fifteen minutes the men were back with two hundred usable arrows, six bloodied spears, and the gate barred again. While they were gone, Agmunder had sought out Erik and Svala. As requested, they had remained inside the house during the attack, and Agmunder was pleased they were alright.

'Can't I watch, father?'

'You can watch when you're a little older, Erik. A fort under attack is no place for a small boy.'

It was mid-to-late afternoon before they saw smoke rising from the coast.

One of the new fyrdmen that Agmunder hadn't seen before, but that he had watched make some good kills, pointed to the smoke, 'The attackers are back at their camp.'

Agmunder saw through the flaw in his logic straight away. The smoke was proof of only one thing, there was a fire in that direction. They couldn't prove who was by the fire or where it actually was. He would keep the warriors on the walls, and keep them vigilant. He took a penny out of his pouch and held it aloft.

'You there, brave fyrdmen on the walls. We are expecting another attack. This penny for the first man to spot them returning.'

The men, who had been chatting idly and even sitting down with their backs to the wall, looking inward at the activities within, stood up and scoured the land for signs of the returning attackers.

Satisfied, Agmunder turned to speak to Lars.

'The fyrd fought well, Lars.'

'That they did. It would be a different story if we were outside with the Vikings, though.'

'Agreed, we have a very strong advantage in here. Lars, do you think there is anything in what he said about there being an assassin inside?'

'No, Thane. I think they would have given themselves away in the first skirmish. People like that are rarely calm. The anxiety gets too much and they either panic and react too quickly or collapse. I've seen examples, when we knew who it was to watch, information learned by some means best not spoken of in polite company. The man concerned was supposed to kill the commander of the fyrd at Lancaster castle when I was stationed there for a while. We watched him over the hours leading up to the battle and his arrest. He was a bag of nerves. Any slight noise and he flinched. He hardly spoke to anyone. He was serious of face, even at the lunchtime revelries. He was so tightly wound with the heavy orisons of his charge that he visibly wilted when I challenged him.'

Lars made a sweeping gesture with his hand, encompassing all within Warbreck, 'All these things I have been looking out for in the men here and only one person has displayed these traits. One person in this fortress has been humourless to the extreme since the proud boast of the Viking commander. One person has been snapped out of his thoughts by a shout.'

'Who is it? We shall question him,' said Agmunder looking around with a stern look on his face, eyebrows wrinkled.

'You, Sire,' said Lars, with a smile. Then he added with mock seriousness, 'Agmunder son of esteemed Asmunde, have you been sent to thwart the Thane?'

At that point Agmunder's face cracked as the relief swept through him. His friend was having a joke, but at the same time calming his Thane's worried mind. There is no assassin. He could see that he had been distant and humourless in his worry.

To help diffuse the tension, Lars added, 'There is no-one here who is not wholly with us, Thane.'

'So, when should we expect them back?'

'I would return in the evening just before sunset, as long as clouds don't form to hide the sun's disc. We would have to shoot directly into the sun. They would have the best light to attack in. There will be more of them next time too. They will bring everyone. They will also have a plan, which we know not. We need to be vigilant of their movements. They may have spotted a weakness. Unlikely, but a possibility.'

'I will relate this to the men.'

They walked to take a position in the centre of the fort where they could be seen by everyone and gave those assembled a few pointers for rebuffing the next attack.

Two men, Harold and Aethelwierd, volunteered to man the back wall, to keep any enemy warriors sneaking round to the gate pinned down in a crossfire, one at each end of the wall by the corner beams. Agmunder agreed to this suggestion, if Lars hadn't seen that arm coming over the wall there could have been a death or two inside the fort, and that, Agmunder was determined would not happen.

It was a bright, sunny afternoon and Agmunder couldn't help hoping for some cloud in the west to shield their eyes from the setting sun. As the golden orb of Sunne dropped closer to the horizon he expected the warning shout to go up, from the penny greedy men on the wall, at any moment.'

Cloud was forming over the sea, but it was thin and high. The rays of the sun would not be hindered by their thin veil.

CHAPTER 18
The Return

They had guessed the attack time perfectly. The sun was low enough to be causing squints among the lookouts posted along the wall, but it was not so low that the light would fade quickly. There was about half an hour of sunshine left before the bright orb would sink below the golden sheen of the Irish Sea.

'Ho! They're back!' shouted an archer, with a huge red beard, by the far end of the wall.

Everyone sharpened their attention and peered, blinking into the sun, looking for movement in the bushes and grasses. There was a large party approaching. They were a good distance away but made no attempt to conceal themselves. Their spears were vertical and their shields were across their fronts, making a good silhouette, when the eyes were shielded from the glare. Everyone prepared for the next attack, as the Viking's walked ever closer.

'Same plan as before, men,' shouted Agmunder to the busy collection of militia within Warbreck, as he flicked the penny piece reward to the bearded archer, who caught it with a 'Thank you, Thane.' and a smile.

Lars joined in, 'Wait until you can't miss. The angle will be better and you won't be looking at the sun. Keep an eye out for them trying something new.'

'Yes,' agreed Agmunder, 'Shout if you see anything unusual or different from the last attack.'

Turning to Lars, he said, 'Hopefully they will just have decided to try with more men.'

'They had the plan to sneak round the back and make the axe ladder last time, though. They may still have that in mind.'

'Well, we have collected all those arrows and spears back. That's a bonus. If they bring more men, we're ready,' said Agmunder, slapping the big Dane on the shoulder.

There was a shout from the wall as an arrow arched high into the sky coming toward the fortress. Everyone watched it as it fell within the compound and stuck into the ground. There was a message attached. Henrik retrieved the parchment and brought it to Agmunder.

'It says. Oh, typical. It says, we haven't got a chance, we should give up now. All they want is am...amud, oh...me! And then they will let everyone else go!'

'You believe that?' asked Lars.

'I don't believe anything a Viking says in battle, I used to be one, I know what they're like.'

Lars smiled at that comment, the men looked uneasy.

Agmunder climbed onto the wall and addressed the messenger, who stood slightly closer than the assembled war-band. He thought he'd use the opportunity to raise his men's morale once more, as they prepared to face the Vikings a second time that day. Agmunder knew well that the moment just before battle is always a nervous time for the inexperienced, and old hands, alike.

'You've brought your shopping list to the wrong shop! We have no eggs or butter!'

The men within the walls laughed a little.

'Who wrote this? I see no children in your ranks. Honestly, the hand writing is... What's this?'

He was now holding the parchment aloft in the breeze, looking at it, 'Mink? Muck? Ah... Milk. No milk here either, old man.'

The men laughed harder.

'What we *do* have are spears, arrows, swords, daggers and enough courage to put them to good use. Run along home now. Really, you should have stayed in Glasson where the unarmed people are afraid of you.'

The men cheered loudly.

'And Agmunder has a G in it... And a capital A would have shown respect. We will teach you some respect this day.'

Another cheer from within the wooden walled fortress.

While Agmunder was delivering this last insult, Lars and Henrik had been coaching the archers and had made them ready. The Vikings slowly advanced ever nearer and as Agmunder's hand, that had continued to hold the message high, fell, the archers let go their arrows in a single wave and notched another arrow immediately and shot again at the same target, only, assuming they would have retreated a little.

The first wave of arrows caught only four Vikings, who could not easily move sideways because of others crushing them inwards. The second wave found more targets, maybe nine. The front row was trapped in the push of warriors, trying to edge further back but finding resistance from the ranks behind them. The first blow had been struck. Ten percent of the attackers lay dead or injured in the first exchange. Whatever the Vikings had planned for this second attack, Agmunder was heartened by this first blood.

There was a shout, from the many voices of the Viking group and they charged toward the fortress.

'Take careful aim, we have plenty of time!' shouted Matthew, reassuring his men.

Agmunder turned again to Lars, 'Is that the best plan they can come up with? Try for a surrender and then run at the walls?'

'Let's hope so!' Lars answered, smiling and hefting his spear in his right hand.

The Vikings were well within range of the archers as they let go their third volley. It seemed that half the remaining front row of running Vikings went down and half the second row fell over them. The third row managed to stop, but could not advance until the pile of human arms and legs sorted itself out. This gave the archers time to nock an arrow, aim carefully and send another fifteen attackers looking for the Bifrost bridge. The remaining Vikings looked unsure, an unusual thing. They renewed their efforts and clambered over the injured and fallen before them. They resumed their charge, although there was now less than half of their original number.

Some of them were now close enough for the spear-men to heave their heavy weapons at them from the walls, pinning several to the earth and providing yet more obstacles in the way of the charging mad-men behind them. Agmunder wondered what exactly they were going to do when they reached the fortress stockade wall. They wouldn't be able to climb it, and there were few bowmen left on their side. They weren't far away and he wouldn't have long to wait.

The first of the lucky had made it to the ditch. They didn't enter the moat, but stood on its bank, a higher position, hurling their spears over the wall and into the fort. Each thrown spear was announced by those on the wall with a shout of, 'Aware!'. Some threw directly at those manning the wall.

The spear-men didn't have much hope of being effective or of making much difference to the obvious outcome of this battle. The pointed tops of the stockade wall were three to four feet above their heads, with archers, spear-men and their commanders watching from above.

'This is crazy!' said Lars.

'I'm glad I have a fortress wall between us, though!' said Agmunder, as the archers picked off the standing men that appeared to be looking for a way through the wall after launching their spears.

Agmunder had a sudden, terrifying thought, 'Is this just a diversion?' he yelled at Lars.

They turned round in unison as the thought registered, to see what terrible fate had befallen the guards on the back wall, half expecting to see the gates open and Vikings streaming into Warbreck. They were met with the sight of the guards on the walls looking back at them, shrugging their shoulders. That was strange, Agmunder couldn't shake the feeling that the attackers had missed a very obvious trick. There was nothing happening on the gate-side wall.

It was unlikely that there could be such a battle without casualties on both sides and Agmunder's men received their share of injuries, though minimal. Matthew caught an arrow in his left arm as he pointed out an exposed position to his archers and sat, looking sorry for himself, on the wall walkway. Edwald had thrown his last spear and lay in a pool of crimson with a spear embedded in his chest. Two others had received injuries severe enough to put them out of action, but in the main the men were in good health and exceptionally good spirits.

By the time the sun had fallen far enough below the horizon to bring on the dusk there were just a few of the attackers left, and those had no stomach for continuing the fight. Agmunder had to dissuade his men, exuberant as they were in victory, from leaving the safety of the fortress to chase them across the fields and back to their ship. They watched from the walls as maybe fifteen men, some of those injured, limping and nursing wounds, slowly made their way down the slope of Warbreck Hill, toward their camp on the shore.

The lookouts were posted and the men welcomed down from the walls by Svala and Erik who had quickly brought out a feast of pork, fish, chicken, bread and cheese. With plenty of ale to wash away the day's labours. The men were in good spirits and ate heartily. The injured were seen to and the dead wrapped for return to their families and burial later.

The beacon was restocked and lit again to show that they were still in control of the fortress. If the enemy had won, they wouldn't have lit the beacon. They might have torched the whole fort, but that would be a much bigger fire and the Fylde population would know what that meant too!

Toward midnight there was a single fire arrow that came flying like a shooting-star through the slowly turning constellations of the coal dark, night sky from the black land outside the fortress. It landed, harmlessly, in the earthen floor of the courtyard and burnt itself out after a few minutes. The lookouts thought it might be a preamble to another attack and prepared to sound the alarm at the next incident, but after another half hour, there was nothing else to remark on. The night, for all in Warbreck, passed peacefully.

The Thane emerged from his dwelling to take a deep breath in the frosty early morning twilight, before the sun brightened the sky to something resembling a new day. He looked around at the fortress that had done such a good job of protecting him, his men and his family from an attack force approaching a hundred crazed Vikings.

'Good morning, Agmunder,' said Henrik as he came down from the walls where he'd been in conversation with the lookouts.

'Anything to report?'

'One fire arrow, my lord, about midnight. Nothing else over night. A big fire and lots of smoke this morning from their coastal camp.'

'Viking burial. We will have to deal with the dead they left, out there, later. I can't have them rotting in the field next to my house, can I?'

'No, my lord. Do you expect an attack today? There was that rogue arrow in the night.'

'Probably an angry Viking getting some revenge for the loss of a brother, or a son. I expect they will leave today, they have burnt their dead. Shall we ride to see?'

'As you command,' said Henrik with a nod.

The horses were prepared and a party of six armed men left the fortress to ride the two and a half miles to where the Vikings had their camp. Agmunder and Henrik were among their number. Agmunder liked to lead by example. He would never ask anyone to do something he would not do himself. This was, after all, a dangerous mission. They did not know for sure if the Vikings had left, or even if they had indeed sent all their men to yesterday's attack. There could be another war-party on the way and they could be riding to meet it.

They rode for fifteen minutes to the coast. They came across a burnt out longship full of the charred and smoking bodies of those that had made it back to the camp, only to die before the longship was ready to leave. The blackened and still smoking remains floated a few yards off shore. Apparently it had run aground shortly after being set adrift and the Vikings, who had obviously already been on their way, taking advantage of the ebbing tide, hadn't turned back. Looking out to sea, Agmunder and his search party could not see any sign of the departed longship. What was left of the Viking revenge party were long gone.

Henrik asked, 'Do you think they will be back, Thane?'

'I'm not sure. The fortress certainly did the trick for us, I don't mind admitting that this revenge had me worried for many days. It turned out that we built the fortress at exactly the right time and it protected us admirably. I expect that those returning home, if indeed they dare, won't want to come back to try again. They may paint an even blacker picture of their failure than was the case. Strangely, *they* may be our best hope of not hearing from Jorgen's father again.'

CHAPTER 19
June 783

The months passed by after the departure of Jorgen's avengers with nothing remarkable to alter the day to day lives of those making a living on Agmunder's Ness.

The crops grew in proportion to their tending. The days were warm and dry. Enough rain fell to bring on good growth in their fields. Michael's pigs would have enough to eat in the autumn. There would be beanstalks a plenty and turnip tops as well as a steady flow of fish heads and fins to keep their bellies growing. One would be chosen for the winter celebration, but Michael hadn't decided which to keep for Agmunder's table yet.

Now the threat of attack seemed to have abated, Agmunder, Svala and Erik, travelled to the farms by the Skiff Pool every two or three days to help out with the work, go fishing and help bake bread. They were always welcome, particularly now that Anne and Eleanor were so far along in their pregnancies. Michael was distracted from his pigs, even though he had a few litters to keep an eye on. Svala was at their farmhouse more than anywhere else. Anne, being in her thirties was having a particularly bad time of it, and Michael was glad of Svala's help.

Agmunder had taken to sailing the larger boat, Signy, out into the bay with Erik as crew. He looked toward the eastern shore as they emerged from the river Wyre estuary and said, 'Shall we try for Glasson today, son?'

'Have we got time, father? The sun is approaching mid morning. Don't we need a full day?'

'With this warm south wind we can sail quickly both east and west. If we get to it now we can be there before they close the market and get something to eat in an inn. We can be home before sundown tonight.'

Erik looked dubious, 'Sailing up the estuary won't be easy against the wind.'

'The wind might alter farther west in the evening cool, besides, if it doesn't, we can always row!'

'That's nearly three miles.'

'Don't worry, son. We'll be alright.'

With that he pointed the bow at the eastern shore and sheeted in the sail to make better use of the breeze. He could hear the sound of the bows breaking the waves as they took on more speed. He saw the monk on the beach, picking up driftwood, and waved.

The monk waved back and carried his load up and over the dunes as Agmunder watched from the bobbing, heeling vessel.

'Matthew should have come with us today. He would have liked seeing Glasson again, I'm sure,' said Erik.

Agmunder thought of Matthew back at the farm under the care of Henrik and Eleanor. He had been brought back from Warbreck after the battle with the arrow removed from his arm and a tight bandage stopping the bleeding. They had bathed it in river water and kept the wound as clean as they could. They had sent Erik to the beach on the west coast to dig up some Lugworm. They had been assured that the yellow secretion they exuded would help the wound heal cleanly. Despite this, or maybe it saved his life, Matthew had deteriorated and lay for nearly a week without opening his eyes at all. He hadn't died. The wound had gone slightly purple below the yellow stained skin and had swollen for that first week. Luckily, though, it hadn't gone green. They had given him sips of nettle tea and chicken broth, which was all he would take. After another week he was slightly better and ate bread, but he was, and remained, very weak. His muscles were shrivelling and his wound looked like it might never properly heal. Just this morning Agmunder had looked in on him and found him asleep at ten in the morning. This was going to be a long recovery from a simple arrow to the arm. He looked at Erik, with sympathy,

'Matthew is too ill, as yet, to make such a journey. He would certainly like to come, but he is too weak to travel. If luck be with us and Grim's prayers do their work, he will be well before harvest.'

'It's been nearly three months, father.'

'Yes, and yet he lives. We must hope that he continues to improve, however slowly. Another month and he should be well on the mend. '

Erik looked at the pennant on top of the mast, it was veering slightly west of north, nothing to worry about, it would help on the way back, if anything. He roped in yet further the sheet on the left yardarm and the boat continued without losing speed.

Agmunder was pleased with Erik's understanding of sailing. When he decided to bring his family to the Fylde he had one troubling thought. That was the worry that Erik wouldn't grow up with the instinctive feel for sailing that Vikings gain as they travel the seas. He was pleased that he had taken so well to fishing and had, apparently, picked up sailing skills with Waverider. Signy, was significantly larger than Waverider, ideally she needed a crew of two men, but Erik, even at just nine summers, knew what he was doing and handled her very well, even in this stiff breeze. It was chilly out on the water, exposed as they were, but Erik didn't moan as some children might. He accepted the conditions as they were and went about the business of keeping the keel above the mud banks that dogged the northern Fylde coastline. He kept a careful watch on the sea ahead for brown up-stirrings from the sea bed and skilfully navigated to avoid them. At least it was a sunny day, and that helped Erik to see the brown water ahead.

It took less than two hours to enter the river Lune estuary, where the water became instantly smoother and the wind, surprisingly and suddenly, warmer. Another half hour of dodging reed beds and they were putting in to the harbour at Glasson. Agmunder lowered the sail as Erik handled the tiller to steer the boat alongside the jetty. A pale looking man with a white beard and dusty smock shirt, who was stacking flour sacks when they arrived, walked down the jetty from his work to catch the rope thrown by the Thane. They made a perfect berth, without bumping Signy, and were soon tied up safely alongside the quay.

'Thank you,' shouted Erik, to the flour covered man, who waved as he returned to his own chores.

'Lunch time,' said Agmunder to Erik, with a smile.

They disembarked and walked the hundred feet along the jetty, passing the pile of sacks where the man had left them. They climbed three steps and were on the busy wharf. There were larger vessels, some of which Agmunder saw on a daily basis, from Warbreck, as they passed down the coast bound for Preston and beyond. Moored at the quay, there was a dark grey boat of about fifty feet length. It had two tall masts and two triangular sails, of quite a pretty bluey green colour, that had been reefed to their huge sloping booms. There was no-one aboard but somehow the ship looked threatening just the same. There was also another large trading vessel, also with two masts, that had five square-rigged sails. The Thane and Erik stood a while in contemplation, looking at the complicated rigging and the many cross-trees and yardarms, and marvelling at the size of the hold.

'She's a beauty,' Agmunder said to a sailor coiling rope on its deck.

'She's hard work, mate!'

'I can imagine,' said Agmunder.

They carried on the short walk to a large building at the end of a row of stores and shops, the Sun Inn.

It was obvious, even from the river, that this building was an inn. There were seats and tables outside the front and the gleam off the four foot diameter metal 'sun' was seen for many miles, like a day-time lighthouse, when the sun was in the right position. Today, the metal disk shone bright in the summer afternoon.

Agmunder and Erik entered the cooler gloom from the fresh sea air. Their noses were assaulted with the aroma of roast chicken. There were a number of people eating and drinking while a serving maid trotted about between the tables, refilling and clearing, as befit her duties.

'Welcome, friend,' said the tall man behind the serving table.

'Thank you. We are in need of a meal,' said Agmunder sorting through the coins in his purse, 'Here's two pennies for some fare and two ales.'

'My pleasure,' said the man, taking the money.

They took a seat by the one window in the front wall and looked out at the hubbub of the seaport's industry. There were people everywhere with sacks, boxes and livestock. They were going to and from various warehouses and vessels.

'We'll have lunch and see the market. Maybe get something for your mum and some supplies. We'll be on the water again before the sun is more than half way down...'

'That's my seat,' came a rough voice from behind them. Erik turned to see who it was, but Agmunder continued to look out of the window.

'I don't see a name!' said the Viking.

'I said...'

'I heard what you said. I answered you.'

'If I were you I'd get out of my seat before I make you,' said the rough looking sailor.

'And if I were you, George Ashenwhite, I would go and find another seat rather than disturbing the Thane!' said the barman as he brought the ales.

'Thane or not, that's my seat. I always sit there. He's got no right!' protested the sailor.

'Look, when you're off at sea, other people sit on that bench without your complaints ringing throughout the inn, disturbing my other patrons. So, why don't you accept that this gentleman, Agmunder, Thane of the Fylde, was here before you this once. I'm sure, after he's eaten, he will take his crew and leave,' he winked at Erik, 'and you can sit looking out of the window as usual.'

The man's face wrinkled up as he thought about it.

'It's my seat...' was all he said as he walked to the door and left the inn.

Erik said, 'He wasn't a very nice man, father.'

'No, son. Not everyone in this world is as nice as the people on the ness.'

When the barman's serving girl brought over the plates of food, Agmunder asked her, 'Who was that lout?'

'He's the captain of the grey ship out there,' she nodded to the window.

'He's a regular?'

'Oh, he's here one week in five or six through the summer. He brings a real mix of things,' she lowered her voice and leaned closer, 'People suspect he's a pirate. All the other ships have one or two different things on board when they arrive, but not Captain Ashenwhite, his hold is always crammed with a jumble of five or six different things.'

'I see,' said Agmunder picking up a chicken leg, 'that is suspicious. What can be done?'

'I'm not sure they want to do anything, Thane. The authorities turn a blind eye. His crew rent a stall at the market. He sells his things very cheaply. The locals love it!'

After the meal Agmunder took Erik to look at the Market and they bought some beef to take back to the ness. It would make a nice change to the plentiful pork, chicken and rabbit they constantly ate.

By four o'clock they had a few provisions and were heading back to Signy under their weight. They passed the flour-covered man wheeling one of his sacks along the lane.

'It's a busy place this!' said Agmunder in response to the man's raised eyebrows.

'It never stops, sir.'

The man set down the handles of his barrow and continued.

'A word of warning, Thane. George has rounded up his crew and set sail about half an hour ago. If you're sailing this afternoon I would watch out. He's not a man to be crossing. He spent a good few minutes looking over your boat. '

Agmunder thanked him and the flour-merchant went on his way, the wheel squeaking as he pushed the barrow up the slight incline to the warehouse.

'Every one seems to know who we are, Erik.'

'Is that good?'

'It depends on who *they* are, I suppose. The barman might not have sorted out the disagreement if I had just been a stranger, but Captain George Ashenwhite, if he *is* a pirate, will not only have taken offence, but will have made a note of my name and assume that we have riches aplenty. He may, as the flour merchant implied, be waiting for us to put to sea.'

'What are we going to do? Will we stay the night?'

'Erik! I am surprised at you. I am the Thane of the Fylde and a Viking. I have run down the outlaw, Knut. I have thwarted the hundred strong attacking force of Jorgen's father at Warbreck. I have the skill to out-sail him or out fight him. I will not be seen to be scared of bullies and braggarts,' he patted Erik's head, 'We sail as planned. Your mum is waiting. Come on, son.'

It didn't take them long to have to have Signy ready to cast off, and as the sun made its way into the lower half of the sky the ropes were gathered in and the sail unfurled. A heave on the tiller and she moved away from the jetty and made a skilful turn out into the river heading south west and homeward.

Erik trimmed the sail expertly as they made the transition into the sea. Agmunder scoured the horizon for the grey ship. There was a vessel, but it appeared to be larger than Captain Ashenwhite's and moving north on the far horizon.

'He can't have put to sea if we can't see him, there's nowhere to hide.'

Erik said, 'Maybe he went up the river, not down?'

'Maybe. The flour merchant didn't say anything beyond George setting sail. I suppose he could have gone upstream,' answered Agmunder, still scouring the sea ahead.

They continued to make good time along the coast, the southerly wind continuing to blow steadily slightly from the south east. Clouds started to form in the west and it looked like there would be rain in the morning. Agmunder felt the air turning colder, even as the sun disappeared behind the clouds. The reduced light made spotting the muddy upwellings from the shallows more difficult to see, and so Erik sailed farther from the coast, to give the mud-banks a wide berth.

'There!' said Agmunder, pointing towards the northern coast of the bay.

Erik looked. At first he could see nothing but the sea and the sky, but he persevered and eventually saw what his father had seen. The colour of the sails, a sort of duck egg blue, blended with the horizon and sky well. Once he could see the ship he could find it, but the sails made it unlikely that it would be seen on the casual glance. It was surprisingly close, maybe only three miles away. Up close Captain Ashenwhite's ship had seemed fancy with its bright sails, but on the sea, the ship was camouflaged as well as a grasshopper in the august wheat.

Erik studied the angle of the sails. Because they were triangular it was difficult to make out which way the ship was sailing, but after a few minutes puzzling, it became obvious that it was coming their way, and fast!

'They must have hugged the northern coast of the bay for an hour then come south looking for us,' said Agmunder, thinking aloud.

'Shall I turn south, Father?'

'Only slightly, son. We have to stay off the mud-banks and turning too far south would reduce our speed too much. See the monk's cooking smoke? Head directly for that.'

Erik adjusted the heading of the ship until the smoke was dead ahead, it was only a small correction to their heading, but it delayed the arrival of the grey ship and kept their speed up. Erik watched his father collect and inspect the weapons that were stowed in the foredeck. There was a shield, three spears, two war axes a sword and a bow with about half a dozen arrows. A good selection to chose from, but with only one man to wield them, not a lot of defence capability. Erik's brow became furrowed.

Agmunder seemed to be thinking along similar lines to the boy, 'How good are you with this bow?'

'I'm a fair shot. I can hit a turnip at a hundred paces if there's not much wind.'

'Well, it looks like you'll get about six shots at their crew before they arrive. I'll man the tiller until they get within boarding distance.'

Erik stepped aside from the rudder and let Agmunder take control. He looked at the approaching ship to the north east. It seemed to be falling behind them. They had steered too close to the wind and lost some speed, was Erik's assumption. Maybe they could make the Wyre estuary before the grey ship caught up with them. He trimmed the sails again to get every last bit of speed out of the boat as Agmunder edged the bow further south towards the break in the land that indicated the estuary's mouth.

Erik checked the following pirate ship again. It was holding its distance but not gaining. They might make it. Erik knew that they had a better chance on land, if they could get ashore by the monk's residence, they could attack the grey ship as it came to shore. He was sure that Agmunder had the same plan. He seemed to be steering very close to the wind in an attempt to get to shore. Erik hoped he hadn't forgotten about the mud-banks. He hadn't.

'Erik, get up into the bows, watch for the mud! Point directions to me.'

Erik rushed to the front of the ship and stood on the rail holding on to the bow-post. He knew that to see the mud he had to be as high as he could get. On a larger ship he could have climbed up the mast, but Signy wasn't quite large enough for that. Empty of Vikings as she was, the extra weight at the top of the mast might even unsteady her so much she would almost topple, and that wouldn't be good for speed.

Erik could no longer see the grey ship, it was hidden behind his father at the tiller. They were almost directly behind them. Erik knew that Captain Ashenwhite's ship would be faster with a side wind and hoped that his father had a plan.

Agmunder did have a plan. He had steered closer in to the shore, knowing that the pursuing vessel drew more water. That meant that Signy could sail in shallower water than the larger ship and could escape Captain Ashenwhite as long as they stayed off the mud-banks themselves. It was a dangerous game. He watched Erik and the pirate ship equally.

Erik indicated to turn right a little, Agmunder made the adjustment. The grey ship closed on them, they were less than three hundred paces apart now. Agmunder was convinced that he could hear the crew shouting on the grey ship behind.

Erik pointed left, left, left! He was desperate to turn. Agmunder threw the tiller full left. He knew that they would lose a little speed, but anything was better than running aground. There was a slight shooshing sound as Signy's keel slid along the edge of a sand-bar below. Agmunder looked behind to see if the grey ship was still following them and straightened up onto the original heading. He called to Erik, 'Come back here. Send a few arrows to distract them, son!'

Erik had the bow with its arrows nearby him, in the front, and knew he could hit them, with a following wind, from where he stood. He grabbed the bow and nocked an arrow. He took careful aim in the slight swell and let the first arrow fly.

Agmunder hoped that the following ship wouldn't be put off following, but would have their attention taken away from the treacherous shallows. As he watched they continued to follow. Erik loosed another three arrows. One of the arrows struck one of the crew in the chest and Agmunder clearly heard the shout from just a hundred feet away. He prayed quickly to Odin and saw another crew member go down with an arrow sticking out of his thigh. Erik was doing a great job. Their crew was two men down. Only three more including the captain, but only one more arrow.

In a very mature move, Erik shot the arrow high into the sky toward the ship. At this crucial moment the crew needed to be watching out for the sand-banks and not looking upwards. But, upwards they looked, even the look-out in the bows. Before the arrow fell to the deck the grey ship lurched and toppled sideways as she drove onto the submerged slope of the mud-bank. The speed that she had been going had momentum enough to slide her to a point where she was stuck.

Agmunder swung the tiller and headed north, running with the wind and putting a few hundred paces between the two boats, as he kept a keen eye on developments.

Erik cheered in the foredeck and started making his way back along the deck. He knew that the tide was going out at the moment, there was a line of wet sand along the beach waterline, so the grey ship was stuck for at least six hours. He said as much to Agmunder.

'Don't assume anything, Erik. They could throw an anchor out of the back and, who knows, three men might be enough to haul them back afloat.'

The wind had started shifting round to the west as the clouds continued to grow thicker. This would make their journey down the river easier.

'I have found another arrow,' said Erik, 'Shall I try for the captain?'

'No, son. Shooting someone when they're closing in and intent on murder is one thing, but shooting them when they're stuck, like a rabbit in a trap, is something else. We outwitted them and out-sailed them. That should be enough. We shall sail home now, and keep an eye out for the next few days. I doubt that they will bother us now we have bested them in their own element.'

Without provoking the grey ship with shots or by waving goodbye, they turned south and entered the Wyre estuary. Within half an hour they had lost sight of the grey ship and were sailing pleasantly upstream with banks of bulrushes and reeds at each side closing in to the point, after another hour, where they could turn sharp right into the Skiff Pool, to home, and safety. They ran the bow of Signy into the shore, just below the big farm house, next to Waverider. The daylight, accelerated by the gathering cloud, had dropped rapidly to twilight as two pairs of feet landed on the riverbank.

'See,' said Agmunder, 'I said we'd be home before it was night.'

CHAPTER 20

Third Summer Harvest

Two months passed by after the adventure at sea and harvest fortnight approached. The farms had three horses between them to help, and there were an average of two and a half people per farm to bring in the crops. Michael would help in the fields, though Anne could not. Lars was busy with his beans and his first crop of turnips would be ready in a couple more months. On the big farm at Agmunder's Ness, Henrik was busy coordinating the harvest and trying to look after Eleanor as well. So, he was relieved when Agmunder brought his family down from the fortress house to help.

Svala, naturally, helped Eleanor with her rest and cooked for them all in the big house.

Agmunder helped Henrik and Thomas with the three fields. Michael helped Will Tanner with his crops. The work was suited to the older man as the bulk of Will's crop was turnip, and wouldn't need harvesting until October. Erik carried on his usual duties of fishing and milking the goat. Each farm had staff and each crop was expected in before the end of the two weeks.

On the morning of the first day of harvest work, Erik set off in Waverider with his fishing lines and Fjord in the bow. The two were a common sight on the water in the mornings. The sun was shining and the men were in the fields tending to last minute preparations before harvest started.

Agmunder looked around. This was all his doing. He had a feeling of great pride in the hamlet of farms that nestles on the ness by the Skiff Pool. He could see his fortress on the hill some two miles away and thought how lucky he was to have had such success in such a short time. If the weather had been bad the first year he could have had very little money, hardly any time for friends as he struggled to try to regain the lost crop. As it was, he had been successful in that first harvest, enough to build a big house. He had been made Thane when he had rid the land of a violent criminal and expanded his farm. He had had enough forethought to install a manager and welcome new tenants to the area to build a community. He had built a fort that had repelled this enemy. And, somehow, he had defeated a sly pirate on the open sea. This was turning out to be a great life he'd started.

'Michael,' he shouted, 'One of your pigs has escaped!'

Michael turned to see that one of his gates was open and the big sow had pushed her way through and was making a bid for freedom. Michael looked horrified. How would a man of his age catch up to a pig with a quarter mile head start?

'Don't worry,' added Agmunder, 'I'll sort it in no time.'

He ran to Alsvior and mounted him quickly. The pig was making her way toward the hawthorn stand to the south but Agmunder headed for Michael's farm enclosure. The pig could be rounded up later. The important thing was to stop any more of Michael's livestock escaping. He reached the gate as a smaller, but no less inquisitive animal, was eyeing the gap in the fence.

Agmunder threw his leg over Alsvior's neck and slid onto the ground. The pig was startled and ran back into the enclosure, with a squeak. Agmunder closed and roped the gate shut. Now for the escapee.

The pig had made it to the hawthorn stand before Agmunder made it there. *This is going to be fun!,* thought Agmunder sarcastically.

Agmunder got down from Alsvior very slowly and quietly, the pig was busy rooting about under one of the prickly bushes. He unslung a length of rope from his shoulder. He walked around the other side of the bush. The snorting and sniffing noise stopped. The pig had noticed. It looked through the bush for a second before turning and heading off to another bush a good few yards away. Agmunder had to come out from behind the bush and start again. He felt a little silly that a pig had seen through his plan, and even though Alsvior was the only witness, he actually blushed slightly.

The pig became engrossed in another patch of shaded ground under another bush and Agmunder, once again, started to approach from the other side. This one was in thicker leaf than the first, and the pig did not see him. He crept ever closer until he was close enough to reach through the bush and grab the pig. He readied himself to lunge. He took a long slow, deep breath. The pig decided there were better places to explore and trotted off again in search of fresh pasture.

Agmunder cursed beneath his breath. *'Fun,'* he thought, *'is not the word for this! I should have sent Erik, with his bow.'*

He quietly made his way toward where the pig had started and made a loop in the rope that would close when the long end was pulled. He laid the rope out in a circle close to the foot of the bush and led the length of the rope through the bush and laid it out on the other side.

He sneaked around behind the pig and approached carefully. The pig noticed, of course. He quietly got closer until the pig had seen enough and walked on, back to the first bush it had tried. There was unfinished business under that bush, obviously.

Agmunder skirted wide around behind the bush and made his way, silently, until he was looking at the pig through the bush again. The pig was engrossed once again in the roots of the hawthorn. Agmunder waited until, as it moved around, one of its feet stood within the loop of the rope. He hauled as hard as he could on the rope and ran backwards, looping the rope round his fist to make sure the pig didn't run off now it was snared.

The pig let out an unholy squeal and stood its ground for a few seconds before Agmunder's inertia and the effect of surprise upended the animal. Agmunder looped the rope around a sturdy trunk and held on. The more the pig struggled, the harder the rope held.

Eventually, the pig lay panting with exhaustion. Agmunder released the rope from the tree and approached the wheezing sow. He made another slipknot noose on the other end of the rope and passed it over the pig's head. He released the rope on the foot and tied that end to the tree.

'You've been a bad girl!' he said gently.

He went and brought his horse and then tied the rope around Alsvior's neck, but not with a slipknot, just a loop.

The pig was getting its breath back now and stood up. It looked a little forlorn with the rope round its neck and its head drooped in defeat.

Agmunder mounted Alsvior and the three of them returned along the frequently travelled track, to Michael's farm, where Michael had returned to inspect his stock in the meantime. Michael stood with a stick and the gate ajar as Agmunder guided the sow into the enclosure. Michael tapped the sow on the shoulder as she passed, but she just carried on walking toward the other pigs, without faltering, or even a grunt. The gate was shut and firmly secured.

'Right,' said Agmunder, as if nothing had happened, 'Shall we go back up to the farm?'

'Any particular reason, Thane?' asked Michael, with a wicked glint in his eye.

'I thought I'd check on the goat!'

Michael sniggered as they set off toward the big farmhouse on the ness.

When they arrived they found that work had progressed a pace without them. Erik was back from his fishing with mackerel a plenty and was talking animatedly about helping his friend, Henrik with the wheat. Agmunder could see that Will and Michael were busy in Will's fields with his small patch of rye, just enough for his needs. Svala was currently in the big farm house baking bread and preparing the lunchtime meal for everyone. Anne was at her own farm, resting. The baby wasn't due for another few weeks, so there was no need for constant attention. The crops had to be in for sale at the market before the autumnal equinox to bring in the money to pay their taxes. They would have to be paid no matter what by the first of October. Agmunder looked around. There was enough labour and the crops didn't look troublesome. After lunch they all set about the first afternoon's harvesting of the wheat on the farms of the ness. Each farm had a horse and a team to do the work. By the end of the first day there was a considerable amount of produce gathered in and under cover for the night.

The next morning, the land was bathed in the honey of glorious sunshine. Not a cloud marred the crystal clear, blue sky which stretched from sea to fells in an azure arch of perfection. Agmunder saw Erik already out on the water in Waverider. Presumably off to fish, nice and early, to get back before the main work started.

'What a morning!' exclaimed Henrik, as he emerged from the farm house.

'A good day to harvest,' said Agmunder in agreement.

'Another two days and we'll have it all in,' mused Henrik.

'Good morning, gentlemen,' said Thomas, coming up the track from Henrik's old farm.

'A very good morning,' answered the Thane. 'We are ready for the full day's work,' said Agmunder and strode off toward the stable to get Alsvior.

Henrik went over to the tools and selected a blade that would cut the wheat-stalks with ease. The two men met at the side of the field of summer wheat and looked it over.

'Let's to it!' said the Viking.

They toiled all morning in the field, cutting, stacking, baling and covering. By the time it was lunch, which was brought out to them on harvest day, they had half the first field's crop in. Erik had made it back before ten with yet more mackerel filling his small boat and had joined Henrik in the field, helping to stack the cut wheat.

The afternoon saw the rest of the field cut and stored and the three of them returned to the farmhouse for a rest as the sun met the sea. Agmunder got up after a few minutes, keen to see how the other farms had managed on the first day, before it got too dark. He walked over to Will's to speak with Michael and Will about how their day had gone, though he could already see that the field was nearly empty of rye. Will was talking to Michael about how easy it would be for him to have a small plot of turnips, just for the pigs to eat, on his own farm. Agmunder thought this would be a good idea.

'In the two years I have been on the ness,' he started, 'I must say that the harvests have all been strong crops and easy!'

'Easy! You call this easy,' exclaimed Michael, rubbing the small of his back.

'It could be worse,' said Agmunder.

'It could rain,' said Will, 'or there could be a blight.'

'There could be Vikings!' said the Thane.

'Or pirates!' said Will, which earned him a glance from Agmunder.

Michael stood up straight and dropped his hands from his back, 'Or pigs in the hawthorn!'

The three laughed and surveyed the field at Will's farm. Agmunder looked at the farm building. The peculiar look of the cob walls reminded him of a loaf he'd seen in Garstang once. But the building had stood through the winter and, Will said, now it had had a full hot summer to thoroughly dry out, it would stand for many years against the worst weather that the Fylde had to offer. It certainly looked strong with the roof beams coming through the very walls, and the low slope of the reeds on top. It was a low building, capable of withstanding a gale without much effect.

'How are you getting on in your house, Will?' asked Agmunder as he admired its construction.

'It's warm enough and there's room for everything I need. I live a simple life and I'm pleased not to overindulge. I'm no monk, Agmunder, but I have no interest in marriage. My house is all I need. That, and my land.'

'Well, I'm pleased that you are happy, Will.'

'I am, Thane, I am. You have created a fine hamlet here.'

Agmunder left the two discussing the ease of turnip farming and returned to Svala and Erik at the big farm.

The next day dawned slightly overcast and nothing like the glory of the first day of harvest. But, despite the slight cloud cover, the sun was making a show, and they were in for another fine day for their second day of this year's summer harvest. Erik was out on the Skiff Pool with Waverider, and Fjord, as usual, was with him. There was an urgency about his manner, he was rowing desperately from the north end of the pool. As Agmunder watched, intrigue turned to horror as Captain Ashenwhite's grey ship came round the bend into the pool under sail and fast. Agmunder sprung into action and ran to get his axe and his spears. He called to Henrik to do likewise. Henrik was slow to comprehend, but when he looked out on the water, he dropped the tools he was carrying and ran towards his farm.

Out on the pool, Erik was being quickly caught by the grey ship. There was a wind directly from the west and it was allowing the triangular sailed ship to take good advantage of the southerly direction of their travel. Waverider's square rigged sail could get little energy out of a side wind. Erik was forced to row, but his young arms weren't up to powering such a vessel at speed for long. Agmunder willed him to carry on rowing, but could see the strokes slowing with each dip into the water. Fjord sensed something was wrong and was pacing about in the front of the little boat. Henrik arrived back from his farm, armed with axe and three spears, as his Thane was.

They ran further up the pool, toward Erik and the grey ship that closed on his position with every second. Someone on the grey ship loosed an arrow and it struck the back of Waverider. They weren't having fun with Erik. They meant harm. The others on the farms had noticed the commotion and Will and Thomas too were preparing for the skirmish that would follow. Agmunder, although hastening toward Erik had managed to count the people he could see on the grey ship: ten. That was twice the fighting men he had at the ness. He had to figure a way to get Erik out of harm's way. But, looking at the closing speed of the grey ship it was hopeless. His only hope was that Erik hadn't stopped thinking, in his hurried desperation. It was obvious what he should do, and Agmunder prayed to anyone that might listen to allow Erik to see it.

Erik suddenly shipped the oars, as the grey ship was closing within fifteen yards. He crossed to the other side of the little boat and moved quickly to the back. He sheeted in the sail and pulled it square, then leaned on the tiller to swing the boat out of the wind. A quick turn left that gave the little boat the advantage of running before the wind. The fastest Erik could manage. The grey ship, however, couldn't turn so quickly, and although they initially started to make a turn, realised that they would be losing speed and closing on the shore at the same time. They corrected course and continued on their original heading, ignoring Erik, as he sailed toward the eastern shore of the pool. The grey ship ploughed on through the water, nearing the landing point for the ness farms.

Agmunder and Henrik were waiting, maybe the captain had made an error. While he was chasing Erik Agmunder's thoughts were distracted, his planning paralysed. Now, though, with Erik safe, for now, he could see that the ship had to turn shortly or run aground. When they did they would lose speed and wallow in the crosswind as they altered their sails. He and Henrik stopped running north along the shore and moved as close as they could to the approaching ship. Henrik threw a spear, letting out a yell of exertion as he did so. It flew well and with the wind it went far, but fell short. This was not disheartening, though, the spear wasn't very far short and both men knew that before the ship could turn it would be within range.

Agmunder waited for what seemed like an age, but was actually only something in the region of half a minute, then he flung his first spear high into the sky. The grey ship began its turn, those on board working furiously at the ropes and sheets that controlled the sails. The spear passed through the main sail and hammered into the rail on the far side of the ship. Several of the sailors forgot themselves and momentarily stopped what they were doing, as they looked at the quivering spear. Henrik threw his second spear, he knew that the chances of actually hitting anyone was very slim, but he'd seen the disruptive effect that Agmunder's spear had had and hoped for something similar. His spear arced through the air and, with a thud, hit the near side of the ship as it turned slowly away from shore. Then, strangely there was the *whiz* of an arrow and someone on the ship cried out as he fell overboard. *Whiz*, another struck near the steerboard and the steersman let go in fright. The ship foundered for a few seconds before he grasped the steering tiller again and the ship resumed turning. Agmunder looked behind him at the source of the arrows. They had been joined by Will Tanner. Will quickly nocked another arrow and loosed it at the ship. It struck the main mast and gained the attention of the crew, again diverting them from their tasks. *Obviously, not full time sailors,* thought Agmunder. Henrik hurled his last spear and Will took advantage, as the crew stood watching the approaching weapon he shot one of the gawkers, who stood open mouthed waiting for the spear to fall. He didn't live to see it *thunk* into the deck.

'Where did you learn to shoot like that?' asked Agmunder.

'Erik taught me. He said my life might depend on it one day,' said Will.

'I'm glad he did such a good job!'

'We have been shooting rotten turnips at a hundred paces for the last month,' added Will with a grin, 'Erik still has a better aim than I, but I can beat him on distance. When he's older he will be formidable with a bow.'

Agmunder was reminded to see what had happened to Erik and searched the pool for his little boat. Sensibly, Erik had gone over the eastern shore and sailed south, toward Lars' farm. He wouldn't try to sail the rapids, but he could land and run on foot to the safety of his friend's farmstead in the woods. The grey ship wouldn't go down to the south end, they would find it harder to sail back out of the pool from there. Besides, they were far too interested in the arrows coming from shore. Michael arrived from his farm with two very old looking spears, 'Any help?' he asked.

Agmunder took the spears and looked at them, 'Anything will do at the moment, Michael. Thank you.'

Will sent another arrow scything through the air at the boat as it finally made its turn and headed north east, toward the exit from the pool.

'Henrik, follow them up the shore and make sure they see these,' he gave him the spears, 'Take Will with you.'

Michael said, 'What's the plan, Thane?'

'Just make sure they sail out of the pool and go back down the river. Keep reducing their numbers if you can.'

'Will do, Agmunder,' said Henrik, tapping Will on the shoulder, 'Come on,' he said.

The two started to make their way up the shore, trying to keep in touch with the grey ship as it headed for the narrow exit from the pool as fast as it could go. Luckily for the pursuers, the wind was calming down and the ship couldn't manage much more than a walking pace.

Agmunder turned to Michael, 'Well, we know they have designs on getting some sort of revenge. We're lucky we saw them in time today. We will have to see what we can recover of our harvest time. There's always tomorrow.'

'I will do what I can to help, Agmunder, you know that.'

'I know you will, Michael. Thank you again. You know, if anything should happen to me...'

'It will be an honour, sire.'

Henrik and Will returned from their task after about an hour. They reported following and harrying the vessel for two miles before it got too far away, hugging the eastern riverbank. They had killed one more of the crew. No, it wasn't Captain George Ashenwhite, they explained, sadly. There was a shout from the shore as Erik jumped onto the muddy beach of the landing ground. Fjord followed, happy to be on firmer ground again. Agmunder could see that Erik was very excited and felt proud as his son ran towards him up the slight incline from the shore. He was out of breath when he arrived, but wouldn't calm down.

'No, no, father...' was all he could say between gasps. He kept pointing up toward the house and shaking his head.

'What is it? Take your time.'

'Smoke,' he managed to say, 'Lots of smoke... Close!'

Agmunder ran up to the house on the slight ridge. He looked west and there was smoke. Three or four stacks of smoke rising less than a couple of miles distant. Five distinct columns of smoke!

Agmunder ran to get Alsvior.

He mounted quickly and shouted to Henrik, 'Alert Lars, ride! I'm going to light the beacon. We haven't got time to get us all to Warbreck, especially the ladies with child, but the beacon will summon the fyrd. We have no choice but to go to them, before they come here, if we can.

Henrik ran toward his farm to get Alfred, as Agmunder kicked Alsvior along the track toward Warbreck. If the raiders had a party already there, he was done for. Their only chance was to call the fyrd to battle before the raiders made it to the ness.

CHAPTER 21
The Marsh

Agmunder was pleased to discover that the fortress at Warbreck, luckily, had not been captured. He quickly opened the smaller side of the double gate and went inside. He rushed to scale the ladder and ascended to the wall walkway. He opened the box that contained the equipment used for lighting the beacon. This would be a daytime burn, so they would need smoke and lots of it. He took the dried leaves and wooden splinters and put them in a small metal tray. He positioned the ridged metal rod above them. He held the flint and ran the it along the rod's length, above of the tinder. Sparks fell onto the wooden chips and he repeated the action briskly and often until several sparks had hit the same place and a tiny flame burst into life on one of the shards of wood. The whole operation took about a minute, but seemed very much longer in the reeling mind of the Thane.

He cupped his hands around the pile of dry wood chips and blew. Each breath brought more redness to the glistening points of heat until another burst into spontaneous fire. It held and grew. Agmunder held another splinter of wood over the tiny flame and that too caught. He did this three more times until there was a strong fire in the tinder. He then held it up on its metal tray to where the goose-fat smeared twigs were hanging below the main wooden mass of the beacon's fuel. The twigs caught quickly, accelerated by the goose fat, and within another minute the fire was spreading rapidly upward through the twigs and small branches that made up the bulk of the flammable material within the metal hoops of the iron basket. Agmunder left the canvas cover on top, its waxy coating would add to the smoke. He climbed down the ladder and looked back at the beacon. The fire had really taken hold in the bright sunny day. The goose fat and canvas were starting to do their job and the billowing, dark grey smoke rose from the fortress corner beam, beckoning the fyrdmen, once again, to attend their Thane.

Agmunder closed and secured the gate, wishing that he could have brought everyone to Warbreck to weather the onslaught. Tomorrow, the fyrd would arrive and find it empty. Perhaps he should try to get the farms of the ness to come, even if it is harvest. He mounted Alsvior and made his way down the approach path. Once on the level he galloped north back toward the farms on the ness.

As he arrived he could see Matthew getting ready for battle with Henrik and Thomas. He slid off his mount and walked over to speak to Matthew.

'No-one expects you to fight, Matthew,' he said as he shook his hand.

'I know, Agmunder, but I will die at their hands in my bed if they win anyway. I have resolved, at least, to try to help.'

'I appreciate that. Your help is most welcome, Matthew.'

Agmunder looked him over as he spoke. He did look reasonably strong, his recuperation had done him good and that man before him no longer looked at death's door, as he had for the last couple of months. He turned to Henrik.

'Lars?'

'Lars was not at his farm, Thane.'

'He will see the smoke,' said Agmunder as he gave Alsvior's reins to Erik.

'What do you think, Agmunder?' asked Thomas.

'I think that the pirate ship worrying us this morning was possibly some sort of diversion. If not, an evil coincidence. Whatever forces have landed, and made their way inland a way, expected to make an easy crossing from the coast and attack at the same time, or maybe a little later. It turned out that we repulsed the grey ship and they have probably fallen foul of the marsh to the north west. Maybe we will have a chance if any of the fyrd arrive this afternoon, before dark, though, I would rather have faced them at Warbreck than in the field'

'I have been preparing the cache of weapons, Thane,' said Thomas, indicating a stack of spears and axes against the wall of the living quarters.

'Good. We will need them at the ready.'

A few of the fyrd arrived shortly afterwards. The brothers, Tom and Jack, from Garstang arrived first, then someone, who Agmunder didn't know the name of, but who he remembered from the fight at Warbreck. Another, luckily for Agmunder, arrived on a horse.

'You,' he said.

'Aethelbert, Thane.'

'Thank you, Aethelbert. Will you ride to Warbreck and direct any fyrdmen, that arrive directly there, over to this farm?'

'It will be my honour to assist, Thane.'

He remounted his horse immediately and set off along the track to the fortress at a canter. Agmunder looked out to the west for signs of the approaching foe. Apart from the smoke, that continued to rise just a mile away, there was no sign that anyone was approaching at all. A movement out of the corner of his eye made Agmunder start. He looked again. There was someone approaching at a gallop. He strained to recognise the rider. It was Gothman, a fine soldier of the Fylde.

'Ho!' shouted Agmunder, waving.

Gothman slowed his horse as he approached the farm. He raised his hand in salute and slid from the horse, expertly catching the reins as he landed on the ground, leading the beast the last few steps to stand in front of the Thane.

'Agmunder, help I have come to give.'

'Thank you, Gothman. Your help is most welcome.'

Erik took the reins from the Dalmatian man and led his horse to the barn. The evening light was fading and Agmunder doubted if any more of the fyrd would arrive that evening. He thought that if there were no more in the next half hour, there would probably be no more tonight. He was partly right. The only other event was that Aethelbert arrived back from Warbreck with news and two more fighting men on horseback.

'Thane, we have restocked the beacon with dry clean wood to burn brightly through the night. We collected as much as we could, I left young James Fleet there to keep it stocked and redirect the fyrd. He is only twelve, but answered the call of the beacon nonetheless. I thought he would be best employed in a non-combative task tonight. I ordered him to remain there keeping the beacon alight and to send new arrivals over here as they arrive,' said Aethelbert.

'Good thinking. Let's hope they don't attack the fortress over night!' said Agmunder, as Aethelbert gulped, realising the danger James may be in at his command.

Everyone at the farmhouse was readying the weapons, cleaning, oiling, mending, stacking. They knew that the attack could come at any moment, though they hoped it wouldn't come at night. Erik prepared his bow and saw to it that his arrows were in good shape.

'Erik,' said Agmunder, 'I don't want you following us tomorrow morning. Stay here and make sure your mum can care for Anne and Eleanor in peace. They're very close to giving birth now, and need rest and quiet. We will take the battle to the attackers tomorrow morning and try to keep them away from here.'

Erik didn't look happy to remain, but nodded his agreement to his father.

'Henrik, are we low on spears? We lost a good few repelling the grey ship this morning.'

'Yes, Thane. We only have ten left. I didn't like throwing them, seemed a waste. But, at least all but one hit the ship.'

'Fine. Make the most of what weapons we have. How are the axes?'

'Fifteen axes, sharp and gleaming with fresh oil, Thane.'

'Good. Distribute them to the men after we've eaten. Everyone, get something to eat. They could be here soon if we are unlucky.'

The fyrdmen took their weapons to the table and continued to prepare between bites of the meal that Svala had provided.

The attack did not come that night. A sleepless one it was, with much more preparation taking place, men grabbing an hour's nap here and there, but mainly bustling about with weapons and equipment. On the escarpment, the beacon burned all night, visible through the hawthorn line to the west of the farm. Agmunder wondered if young James was frightened up there, and whether he was alone, or whether any more of the fyrd had arrived, since Aethelbert gave his orders.

Riders, three of them, arrived at first light from Warbreck. They told of the excellent work James was doing and could not praise his actions high enough. He had refused any help in tending the beacon and had no sleep, preferring to spend the night following his orders. One of the men had gone to keep watch, but James had insisted they all needed their sleep for the battle today, and kept the lookout himself whilst tending the fire. Agmunder decided that after the battle, he would reward James' hard work and professionalism.

He looked around the farm. He could count sixteen people in sight and maybe there were another five, dotted about inside the buildings. Twenty one soldiers wasn't a lot to stage a battle against an unknown number of foes. He had to hope that another twenty or so arrived soon, summoned by the beacon. He despatched a rider to view the enemy forces. He warned them that although the ground of the marsh looked firm, with the recent hot weather, they should avoid straying from the ancient path that wound its way through the boggy ground. He warned them against heroics, he needed every man, and he needed that intelligence bringing back.

Tom, Jack's brother, offered to ride out to see how their enemy was preparing and their location. Jack immediately offered to go with him. Agmunder considered this. If one of them got injured or captured, the other might still make it back.

'Very well. Don't take any chances, and ride apart.'

'Yes, Thane,' they chorused.

When the two had ridden off, Agmunder turned toward the skiff pool, looking for any sign that Captain Ashenwhite was making another return. He couldn't see any sign of motion down river. He looked carefully for a mast top among the reeds. Nothing.

He had thought that the attackers would have arrived at dawn, but it seemed that was not their plan. By mid morning men had arrived from Warbreck and from the direction of Lars' farmstead. Lars himself, though, was not one of them.

'*I wonder where he's got to?*' wondered Agmunder, hoping that nothing untoward had happened to his oldest friend.

There were now thirty men at arms and their three commanders, Agmunder, Henrik and Thomas, at the farm. The men were armed and ready for the march. Agmunder worried about Lars. The lookout shouted that news of the return of the scouting party, Tom and Jack. Shortly afterwards, they rode into the farm enclosure and went straight to Agmunder, who was standing in conference with Henrik and Thomas.

'They are just the other side of the marsh. Less than a fifteen minute walk on firm ground, but they're bogged down in the soft earth beyond the old track. If we could close to within two hundred paces we could start to attack with the bowmen.'

'If we could stay on firm ground and let them come to us through the bog, we might increase our effectiveness. What have they been doing? Why didn't they attack at dawn?'

Jack answered, 'It looks like they have been cutting reeds and straw, Thane.'

'To what end?'

'They have a huge stockpile of it on their side of the marsh. My guess is, they plan to lay a road through the marsh with the reeds spreading the weight of their feet,' said Jack.

Tom added, 'They have no horses, Thane. None that we saw, at any rate.'

'Good. I don't think we will be able to make use of our horses on the soft ground. It is good to know they are having trouble crossing the boggy ground. The thorns to the south have put them off trying that way. But, worrying it is, that they knew where we were and didn't go to Warbreck,' said Agmunder, with a knitted brow. It makes me wonder if they were indeed working with Ashenwhite.'

At that point, Lars rode into the farm enclosure. Agmunder, smiled broadly as his friend dismounted and shook his hand.

'Preston,' was his explanation as he continued to pump the Viking's hand.

'Well met, old friend,' said Agmunder. 'Now we are ready.'

He appraised Lars of the news that the scouts had brought back from their ride to view the enemy's battle. The big Dane liked the idea of the attackers struggling with the boggy ground. He also liked the plan to stay on the firmer land to launch an arrow attack.

Lars was already attired for the fight, Agmunder less so. He quickly put on his helmet and slung his axe over his shoulder. He hefted the shield that Erik had brought from Grim's as a present from the churchman. He thought it might provide some extra protection, or luck, and held it close to see the fit of it. It felt good. They were mounted and ready for the march in just a few minutes, the horses loaded down with sheaves of arrows and pointed staffs. They set off before the sun had reached half way up the sky and hoped to be in sight of the enemy in time to slow their progress through the marsh.

CHAPTER 22

The Battle on the Marsh

The fyrdmen could see the enemy making slow but steady progress across the soft ground, as they approached the edge of the firm ground on the eastern side of the marsh.

'Deploy here,' commanded Agmunder as he brought his horse to a halt. The raiders were still out of arrow range, but he liked to have time to plan. He surveyed the enemy's line from horseback as the men readied their arrows and drove the wooden stakes into the ground at a rakish angle pointing attack-wards, in front of where the archers would stand. They unloaded spears and axes from the horses and made ready. They had been spotted by the raiders, who, it seemed, redoubled their efforts to lay a dry path through the squelching ground.

As soon as their battle was in place and the enemy was within arrow range the first volley of arrows left the bows. Men on both sides watched their path through the sky. At the limit of range, the aim wasn't perfect and the raiders had plenty of time to anticipate the target area and move. This, Agmunder thought, was just a warning. Though, there was little doubt what they were here to do, with their helmets and breastplates shining in the afternoon sunshine and the edges of their weapons glinting.

'Hold for a few more minutes, men,' ordered Thomas.

'Hold,' agreed Agmunder, 'They aren't going anywhere, and if they continue to come on at this snail's pace speed, we will have time enough!'

There was a murmur of agreement, which ran through the assembled members of the fyrd, standing on the slightly higher ground on the eastern side of the marsh.

Lars hefted his spear and felt the weight of his axe. He was ready. These raiders had come to bring fear to the Fylde and to attack his friend. They would pay for their insolence.

'Shall we send six archers ten yards into the bog, Agmunder? Maybe they can strike all the sooner and we can get back to the harvest,' asked Thomas.

'I would rather wait for them to come closer, Thomas. We don't need to risk our few fyrdmen in the unstable ground of the marsh. Patience, my dear friend, these fools will be with us soon enough and the crops will still be there tomorrow.'

'As you command,' answered Thomas, placated.

The raiders continued to move inexorably closer, laying bundles of reeds, despite the obvious onslaught they would soon be under. Agmunder thought about the situation before him.

'Either their commander has some very compelling reason why they should proceed to get themselves killed, or there is something that we're all missing!'

He looked over to where his scouts were standing by the largest phalanx of archers, ten men all together, directly in front of the slowly advancing raiders, 'Jack and Tom, to me, now!,' he shouted.

The two brothers immediately came over from their position on the right.

'Thane?'

'How many smoke columns were there this morning?'

'Five, Thane.'

'How many men would that normally signify?'

'About seventy five, sire,' answered Tom, the older of the two.

'I thought so. How many are in the field before us? I make it only forty.'

'Agreed, sire.'

'Then where are the other thirty five?'

Jack spoke, 'They might need some men to cut and transport more reeds, sire.'

'I think they took all day yesterday to cut the reeds and gather the straw. I don't think they are doing that now. I think...'

He tailed off his sentence as his thought was interrupted by the sound of many hooves. They all turned to look in the direction of the sound and saw the missing raiders. They were mounted and galloping up the track from the rear. Agmunder and the fyrd were trapped between the bog and the charging raiders.

'Behind!' shouted Thomas to the assembled men. They immediately came under fire from the field, as the attacker's bowmen took advantage of the disruption to loose off a volley. Several of Agmunder's best archers fell, clutching arrows that stuck gruesomely out of them.

The horsemen approached the standing fyrd without slowing. The Vikings and Saxons alike tended to ride to battle then dismount to fight, but the attackers were employing a tactic from further afield. They held long spears at head height as they charged the line of militia. At the last second they lowered the lances and ploughed into the line of soldiers. The noise was phenomenal. An almighty crash of metal on metal, horses whinnying, and men crying out. The horses pulled up before they entered the bog and then wheeled round to attack again.

Agmunder staggered as his shield took the brunt of the force from a lance, and swung his axe at the passing horse. He did no more than open a small cut on its flank. The rider was unharmed.

Lars threw his spear at an approaching raider and narrowly missed his shoulder, the spear found its mark in another raider's chest as they pressed in closed ranks.

Lars unslung his war axe and stood to receive the next wave. The horses came at them from both sides and Thomas was cut down by a huge blow from a war hammer. He crumpled onto the floor with his breath coming out as a high pitched wheeze. He wouldn't last, even if he survived the charge, but Agmunder saw him trampled and he lay, unmoving, on the ground looking for all the world like a discarded pile of old clothes.

Tom was the next one to strike a blow for the Fyrd as he removed the axe arm from a charging raider with his sword. The raider looked surprised as the adrenalin in his veins suppressed the immediate pain. As Jack ran up to the startled horse, who's rider had lost control of the reins, another raider speared him before he could finish off the one armed horseman. He fell to the floor and as Tom looked on, he was speared a second time. Tom raised his axe and ran at the spear-man, only to be cut down by a second volley of arrows from the field archers.

Agmunder looked around for some way for him to lead his men in escape of the situation and for a way to gain the upper hand in this battle, there was none apparent. The marsh, quickly becoming stained red with the blood of Fylde fyrdmen, was blocking their escape to the west. Some of the raiders were holding back to the east, even as their comrades attacked. There was no way out from between the two groups. The raiders made another charge and cut down another five men, only losing one rider to Henrik's spear thrust. Then, the noise of battle seemed to diminish and there was nearly silence on the marsh edge. The raiders had pulled their horses back to the track they had ridden in on and were lined up across the firm ground of the eastern side.

One of their number had his sword raised high and as he slowly brought it down the whole line of mounted raiders began to move forwards at a walk. Agmunder looked about. Behind them the raiders in the field were making steady headway across the unstable ground and would also be with them very shortly.

Agmunder knew that his time was close and he would have just a few moments to think about the things he had put in place for his family. His mind raced, and time slowed. Svala would be protected, as long as the raiders didn't go to the farm. She would take care of Erik and in a few years, Erik would look after her, he was a good boy. Max had pointed out that Erik would not be Thane, just a land owner, and landlord when old enough. The title was not hereditary. Agmunder had to concede. Svala knew where the Norse gold was hidden in Warbreck. Agmunder had made Thomas, Henrik or Michael his estate manager, Svala's choice, until Erik was old enough. To whom the post fell, would look after their interests in Garstang. He remembered the moment on the first full day, when he and his family stood and viewed their canvas dwelling. '*All shall be forgotten,*' he thought.

Agmunder wondered, for a split second, if Anne's and Eleanor's babies would survive and grow up knowing no other home but the ness.

There was a clash of steel. The raider's advance had arrived amongst them. Shouts went up as metal pierced and hacked the bodies that stood before them. Horses whinnied as stray blows and cuts met with their thick hides. Agmunder had a strange feeling that it had begun to rain, and worried, abstractly about the harvest, still waiting in the field. He looked to wipe the rain off his arm and saw it was bright red. Like the marsh around him, the world seemed to be tinted red everywhere he looked. Then he felt a searing pain through his thigh and sank to the floor.

He looked around at the men he had brought here to die in his company. They would not be bringing in their crops either, this year, or any other. They would not see their families again, as he wouldn't. An arrow struck him in the front of the shoulder, just above the edge of the shield and he looked at it quizzically. He toppled backwards and hit his head on the hard ground. He raised his ringing, swimming head to see across the field to where Lars could be seen on the edge of battle, still swinging the war axe to good effect. Another wave of arrows came in from the boggy field, and the cries of the wounded increased again. Agmunder strained to see the state of the fight and was dismayed to see just a handful of his brave fyrdmen still standing, still resisting the irresistible greater force of mounted men.

Momentarily, Lars looked straight into Agmunder's eyes. Agmunder could see his distress and managed to wave his friend away. Clearly, this battle was a lost cause. Lars slashed the raider he was engaged with, who collapsed where he stood, and ran to a horse. Agmunder's last sight of his friend before his eyes closed, was of the big Dane, galloping away down the track to protect the farms at Agmunder's Ness waving his right arm high overhead.

Agmunder slowly turned onto his back expecting it to be somehow more comfortable, the goose-feather arrow flights casting a shadow across his blood spattered face. The shield slipped, unnoticed, from his grip and settled on the floor, it's white-painted boss shining like a beacon in the sunshine. He released his helmet strap with his usable hand, and the heavy, horned helm fell off beside his weak and pain racked body. His eyes closed as his vision became dull and narrow in the summer sun. They flicked open once more, to look fleetingly at the golden orb of Sunne, as Alsvior and Arvakr, the horses that pulled his chariot across the sky, did their job. He eyes closed again.

Strange thoughts flitted through his brain as he slowly drifted into half-consciousness. How he'd hoped he would have lived long enough to see the new century: 801 a.d. That would have been amazing. Who would sail Signy? Who were these raiders that got the better of his fyrdmen, in ambush? Would they go, once he was dead, or did they plan to indulge in a reign of terror on the ness?

The sounds that filled the air around him were amplified as his senses compensated for the lack of vision. Smells became more pronounced, the metallic stench of blood, the most overpowering. The pitiful sounds of wounded and dying men, and animals, almost unbearably loud. A skylark. He waited, with a strange calm, for his body to give up the ghost and for his new life in Asgard to begin. He wondered if his father would be proud of his achievements. He wondered, how it felt to walk the Bifrost and, just for a second, before he blacked out completely, he wondered if anyone would remember him...

EPILOGUE

Agmunder had a strange entry into the afterlife. He did not remember crossing the Bifrost bridge, but had strange experiences involving people he had known. He had a conversation with fiery Jack Smith about Thor's hammer and Henrik was there, somewhere, arguing that he could sleep anywhere. He couldn't see Henrik anywhere, but his voice was clearly heard. Grim appeared as a ghostly silhouette and said a prayer, glimpsed through sweat-drenched hair as Agmunder endured roasting in an oven with the rising loaves of a Garstang baker, who twinkled strangely in the dawn light. He saw his father, Jinny Greenteeth, a monk on a windswept coastline and Knut, risen from the dead.

Agmunder looked around and hoped he wouldn't see Lars in this place. Not because he didn't want to see him again, but because that would mean he too was dead, although Agmunder thought he must be. There were more strange sights and noises. Like the sound of many people laughing and sharing a meal in another room, muffled but close by. As time passed, voices from the living became more noticeable, louder and more distinct. The vision of Asgard faded and a version of his familiar bedroom ceiling replaced it. As he opened his stinging eyes and focussed, he turned his head a little, and there was the face of Henrik.

'Svala! Erik!', Henrik shouted.

Agmunder wondered why Henrik would be shouting the names of his family at him. His mind still reeling, the blurry brightness before him steadying. There was the sound of rushing feet and the door opened. There, before him, as his vision became sharper and the fuzzy colours faded, was his wife and son. Agmunder was caught between deep sorrow and an overwhelming love. They must have died too, but they were here with him.

'You're awake!' said Svala, through her tears.

'Father, you gave us a fright. This last three weeks has been a horrible experience!'

Agmunder tried to speak but his dry throat gave out just a squeak.

'Rest!', said Henrik.

'You're exhausted, husband,' Svala said, 'Henrik has been here by your side for twenty days. He slept on the floor. No-one could shift him!'

Henrik helped Agmunder take a long draught a horn of ale.

Finally, he was able to speak, 'What happened?'

Erik was quick to take up the tale and did so with great enthusiasm, even though Svala had advised rest for his father.

'As Lars saw you shot he ran to a horse and left the battlefield waving madly to a huge force of our friends and allies from Garstang who were approaching. Although you had a small contingent from the people of the town with you on the field, Gothman had arranged for the rest to follow him. They arrived, fresh and fully armed, just as the advantage was swinging toward the Vikings. The attackers were greatly outnumbered and were slaughtered to a man. They couldn't fight effectively as they were trapped by the same patch of boggy ground they trapped you with. Sensing victory, they had foolishly dismounted and advanced on foot to finish off your war-band.'

Erik took a breath and had a little ale himself before continuing.

'The people of Garstang hold you in such high regard, Thane Agmunder, my father. They came in the hundreds to assist you in resisting this foe! There were women, even children and the old and infirm. They all came to help you, as you had helped rid them of Knut and provided homes and employment. They respect you and welcome you as one of their own, father.'

This brought a tear to Agmunder's eye. It had always been a worry to him that, despite what people say, they secretly regarded him as nothing more than a meddling foreigner, and a Viking dog at that! As he often said to Erik, 'Deeds not words, are the measure of a man.'

The door opened again and there stood Lars.

'I knew it,' said the big Dane, 'No Viking arrow can slay the mighty Agmunder!'

Agmunder smiled and asked, 'What of the harvest?'

Lars replied, 'The townspeople of Garstang gave us aid. After the battle some of them, maybe ten, stayed on to help bring in your crops. Some went home but then returned with carts to transport your produce to market, where, I believe you were given a preferential rate, set by old Weasel-face himself!'

Svala said, 'These last three weeks, while you were just lying in bed, have been very fruitful for the rest of us!' She said it with a sincere smile of affection. She wanted to play down how ill Agmunder had been, but he could see in her eyes that it had been a close thing.

He held out a hand to Henrik, who's voice had wafted into his fitful dreams and shook it warmly. His eyes said, 'Thank you.'

'Welcome home, Thane,' said Henrik.

Over the next few weeks, Agmunder's health continued to improve and family life on the ness returned, more or less, to normal. The winter crop was doing well in the field and the late summer turned out to be long and dry. Some of the people who had helped with the summer harvest returned to the ness, with tenancies, and started building their own houses on the shore of the Skiff Pool. Agmunder's Ness settled down into prosperity and an assured future. Although they didn't know it, there would never be another Viking raid on the Fylde. Never again would there be a longship on the horizon bound for plunder.

Six weeks later: Agmunder returned home, following the sale of the winter harvest, and got into bed next to Svala as they prepared to sleep. Agmunder thought to himself, as he lay gazing out of the window, 'I *will* be remembered.' Beyond the window frame, the deep azure night was peaceful, still and soothing. Saturn was culminating in the south. Saturn, the bringer of old age, shone its light on the Viking. Agmunder slept soundly on his ness, and peaceful dreams filled his rest.

THE END.

If you would like to see more of my stories,

please visit my website:

https://barrycooperstories.jimdofree.com

AFTERWORD by the Author.

I've been interested in how people and places got their names since I was very small. My grandad used to take me fishing to **Skippool Creek** on the **River Wyre**, when I was between six and ten years old. We used to catch Grayling. 'Fiery Jack' was one of my great grandads! It was my grandad who told me that the name **Skippool** came from a corruption of Skiff Pool, named for the small boats that plied their trade there in antiquity. Many people's names come from their trade, origin, or physical attributes. I have tried to demonstrate this throughout the story. A bit of fun, throughout.

I constructed this story to illustrate how people and places get their names from the strangest of incidences and occurrences. The place names in this story are largely correct, but their origins have been largely fabricated for the sake of the tale.

The Black Pool: Of course is where the town, **Blackpool** (My home town), gets its name. The **Marton Mere**, as "the Black Pool" is now known, still is linked with the Arthurian legend.

'breck': A breck is a way through a wall or barrier: The break in the hawthorns just south of Agmunder's farm is around the area of **Breck Road**, near Poulton-le-Fylde (which is a Norman name – Nothing to do with us Vikings!) There are many 'brecks' in this story and in this area.

Eauxton: The modern village of Euxton (Pronounced Ex-ton) near Chorley.

Garstang: Current town and a historic town of the ancient Britons.

Glasson: Glasson Dock. A current town on the river Lune, close to Lancaster.

Isle of Man: Seen by Agmunder on the western horizon. The tops of the five highest peaks can be seen in favourable conditions from the Fylde coast. Chapter 6

Kilgrimal: Old English "Keel Grim Haugh". Church built of a Keel, Grim (The Reverend) and his Burial place. A church/village that is fabled to lie under the waves, off shore, at Lytham St. Anne's. Another tale first heard from my grandfather and commemorated in the song 'Kilgrimol', by The Blue Pig Orchestra. Some historians now believe that the village became derelict and fell into nothing somewhere around Royal Lytham St. Anne's Golf Course!

Kirkham: Current town, on the Fylde in Lancashire. Village of ancient Britain (Name meaning: Church Hamlet).

Knut's End: Of course, the people of **Knott End** might recognise the description of their locality?

Lars' Breck: The locality of **Larbreck** today.

Pilling: An area along the north coast of the Fylde. Pilling sands are a well known shallow area of Morecambe bay.

Preston: Current City in Lancashire, Town of ancient Britain (Priest's Town).

Red Marsh: The site of the final battle. An area on today's maps near **Thornton**.

St. Anne's (a modern town) is close to where Grim built the keel-church of St. Anne's.

Shard: At the point where Michael and Anne Shard have their pig-farm, and planned a crossing of the Wyre, is where, today, you can find **Shard Bridge.**

Stanah: The exact area where Agmunder erected his first farm.

Thorn Town: 'Thornton' - Does exist — Exactly where Agmunder predicted it.

Warbreck: The hill that today is topped by the water tower that overshadows Warbreck Hill High School, a few hundred metres to its south. A place where there was a beacon in days of old — The high school badge features a beacon. A place I know well!

How did this story come about?

There is a road that connects Skippool to Fleetwood, called the '**Amounderness Way**'.

I wondered where the name came from and found sketchy details of a chap called Amounder (Or Agmundr) who settled in the area in Viking times. This story evolved as an explanation of how the settlement went. Indulging myself in the etymology of the place names of the Fylde, I enjoyed creating this tale for you.

My grandfather is also responsible for telling me about **Jinny Greenteeth**, when he used to take me pond fishing in Poulton-le-Fylde. He used to tell some dark tales to a seven year old! I sincerely hope you enjoyed this story.

Finally

There is a nod to Fleetwood – Not mentioned or existing in this story – On page 66. There is a mention of a 'Fisherman's Friend'. In the story this turns out to be Henrik – Nowadays, a 'Fisherman's Friend' is a warming lozenge produced in the town of Fleetwood, originally developed by pharmacist James Lofthouse in 1865.

Barry Cooper August 2018

If you would like to see more of my stories,

please visit my website:

https://barrycooperstories.jimdofree.com

Printed in Great
Britain
by Amazon